# Flight 103

Also available by Sam Green

*Max*

# Flight 103

## SAM GREEN

C

Century · London

Published by Century 2008

2 4 6 8 10 9 7 5 3

Copyright © Sam Green 2008

Sam Green has asserted his right under the Copyright, Designs
and Patents Act 1988 to be identified as the author of this work

This novel is a work of fiction. Names and characters are the product of the author's
imagination and any resemblance to actual persons, living or dead, is entirely
coincidental.

First published in Great Britain in 2008 by
Century
Random House, 20 Vauxhall Bridge Road,
London SW1V 2SA

www.rbooks.co.uk

Addresses for companies within The Random House Group Limited can be found at:
www.randomhouse.co.uk/offices.htm

The Random House Group Limited Reg. No. 954009

A CIP catalogue record for this book
is available from the British Library

ISBN HB 9781846053627
ISBN TPB 9781846052705

The Random House Group Limited makes every effort to ensure that the papers
used in its books are made from trees that have been legally sourced from well-
managed and credibly certified forests. Our paper procurement policy can be found
at: www.rbooks.co.uk/environment

**Mixed Sources**
Product group from well-managed
forests and other controlled sources
www.fsc.org  Cert no. TT-COC-2139
© 1996 Forest Stewardship Council
FSC

Typeset by SX Composing DTP, Rayleigh, Essex
Printed and bound in Great Britain by
Clays Ltd, St Ives PLC

While *Flight 103* was destroyed by a bomb, this novel deals with one theory of how it might have happened. All characters in the book are ficticious and are the product of the author's imagination. They are not in any way linked to any real person whether living or dead and, should there be any resemblence to actual persons, then it is entirely coincidental.

To Tsila, Atalyn, Don, Todd, Zoé and Lula for
their immeasurable love and support.

# ACKNOWLEDGEMENTS

I wish to acknowledge the steadfast guidance of my publisher and editor, Mark Booth, whose patience and words of wisdom helped bring this book to fruition. Also, I would like to thank Matthew Lynn for his invaluable contribution.

Many thanks to Daniel Aharoni, Esq., my lawyer and best friend, for always keeping me out of harm's way.

I am indebted to my staff at Interfor Inc. for their endless support.

# Part One

# The Crash

# ONE

## London, 10 November

Sam Woolfman put down the card. He'd recognised the handwriting at once: his daughter Samantha, now almost seven. The slope of the letters was the same as his, and so was the slight wobble in the crossing of the T. Funny how our children inherit random part of ourselves, he reflected. Even when we aren't there to teach them anything.

He glanced through the window, tracking the swift movements of the workman who was hanging the elegant white candle lights that ran down the street in the run up to Christmas. It had been more than six months since he'd seen her, and that was only for a few days when he had been passing through Tel Aviv, attempting to track down a valuable Guillaume Grohe desk that he believed had been taken there by a Russian collector. She'd been lively, healthy, and overjoyed to see him, just the same as her brother, Luke. The same was hardly true of their mother. Elena hardly seemed to be missing him at all. When Sam had quit the Mossad, and decided to try and make a go of the antiques business he'd first set up as a cover, she'd spent a few months trying to adjust to life in London, but she found it impossible. Their marriage had disintegrated into a series of petty rows. In truth, they'd never been married at all: he'd spent so long undercover for the Mossad, it had robbed them of their formative years together.

She married an Israeli warrior, a man fighting for his country, Sam could recall thinking to himself as he rode back towards the airport after seeing her for the last time. And what she got was a not very successful antiques dealer in London, still trying to break free of his past. It wasn't surprising that she ended up feeling cheated.

Sam settled into the back of the shop. It wasn't a big operation, never had been. The Mossad had given him the funds to get the place going because 'antiques dealer' made a perfect cover for an assassin: you travelled a lot, you dealt in cash, and kept strange hours. In total, the shop measured fifty feet by twenty, and was filled with the items Sam had acquired over the past year. Traffic was sparse, but then in the antiques trade that didn't matter very much: it wasn't who came into your shop that was important: it was what they were looking for.

He smiled to himself. As often as not they were looking for the former Mossad man, not the antiques trader.

But that wasn't what this shop was selling anymore.

There were a couple of pieces at the front of the shop he'd acquired recently: a fine writing table made in Paul Sormani's Paris workshop in the mid 1850s, and a side table made by Alphonse Tahan, a furniture maker who supplied Napoleon III with many of his finest pieces. As the Soviet Union slowly came apart at the seams, Sam had used some of his contacts in that country to buy up some fine antiques on the cheap: many of the most exquisite works of art in Western Europe had been looted by the Nazis, then looted again by the Communists, and were only now slowly coming back into circulation. There was money to be made in that trade, so long as you knew how to tap into the right circles.

And a Mossad contacts book certainly gave you the right introductions.

There were plenty of spies in that country trying to quickly reinvent themselves.

Just as I am.

*Maybe that's why we can do business together.*

A woman was standing next to the antiques, examining the exquisitely detailed surface of the wood on the Sormani desk. Sam had noticed her the moment she came in, but then he'd been distracted by the arrival of another woman, a tall, fiftysomething brunette who had been dithering over a mirror for the past few days. She'd been in to see it three times already, taken its measurements, but Sam was starting to lose faith in her actually buying it: lots of people bought on the second visit, but very few on the third. Still, he needed to find out. Business had been slow for the past three weeks. He'd sold a few items at the start of November, but after that, the trade just knelt down and died. For the British economy, 1992 had been a tough year: and when times were hard, nobody wasted money on antiques. They were luxuries, made in luxurious time, and right now there weren't many buyers out there. 'Have you made up your mind yet, Mrs Beasanti?'

She took off her glasses, and looked again at the mirror, noticing Sam standing right behind her. There were traces of a smile on her lips. She was a handsome rather than beautiful woman, with immaculately cut, jet-black hair, and pale green eyes that curled into the rest of her face. 'I think . . .'

Sam already knew what was coming. He'd owned the shop for almost four years now, although less than two as a real business, but he'd learned plenty about when people bought things and when they didn't. And the hesitation told him the mirror would still be on the shop wall come New Year's Day.

'If there's something else?'

'Maybe,' she replied, turning away. 'If I could find a . . .' She hesitated, as if she were trying to learn how to pronounce an unfamiliar name. 'A piece by Albert-Ernest Carrier de Belleuse.'

5

Sam nodded. 'And the budget?'

'I couldn't go to more than $100,000.' She laughed lightly. 'Of course, it's ridiculous.'

'I'll see . . .'

'Don't even worry about it,' she persisted. 'It wouldn't be possible.'

Sam allowed her a few minutes to examine the rest of the items. His eyes turned to the girl who'd stepped into the shop a few seconds before. She was far from the average antiques lover, although Sam had long since learned there were no stereotypes in this trade. They came in as many strange shapes and sizes as the stuff you were selling. But she was too young, for starters: no more than twenty-three, or twenty-four. She had short black hair, cut in a bob, and eyes that sloped away from the sides of her beautifully sculpted nose. She was wearing tight jeans, and a baggy grey sweater that didn't so much disguise her figure as drown it.

'You like the desk?' said Sam to the girl.

Sam was never sure whether to talk to the customers. Some people liked to contemplate a piece in solitude, others wanted to discuss its origins, its history, and its likely value. On balance, he kept away: most genuine antique lovers were introverts, and they went about their business in silence. Maybe that was why he liked them.

This was an exception. She'd been looking at the desk for so long, it was possible she might actually buy it. 'Sormani?' she said.

Sam nodded. 'You're familiar with him?'

The girl raised her chin just a fraction. Her eyes flashed up to meet Sam's, and for a second Sam wondered if he'd seen her before somewhere. He had a fine memory for faces: that and the ability to shoot straight was what had made him a capable hit man for the Mossad. He flicked through his mental filing cabinet, trying to locate her: there were literally thousands of names stored away there, many of

6

them now dead, but he couldn't place her. 'Not really,' she said casually.

'But enough to recognise one of his pieces?'

'Well, I don't know if it is a Sormani . . .'

'How would you tell?'

The girl paused for a second, flicking away a lock of hair from her fringe. 'He usually engraved his works on the inside of the lock-plates,' she replied. 'Of course, it depends on the period. Paul Sormani started his cabinet making firm in Paris at 10 rue Charlot in 1847, making mainly repro-ductions of Louis XV and Louis XVI stuff. Quite nice, if you like that sort of thing.'

'Would you like to buy it?'

The girl laughed, and it was only then that Sam detected the Irish accent: there was a throaty, cough-like quality to her giggle that you only found in Dublin. 'Me, no.'

Sam nodded, but remained silent.

She looked up at him directly. 'It's you I'm looking for.'

'What for?'

The girl turned around. Her eyes were tracking Mrs Beasanti, watching her as she finished examining a couple of pieces, then waiting for her to leave the shop. 'I need some help,' she said.

'In finding an antique?'

The girl's mouth turned down. 'Not that. I don't have any money, and even if I did, I wouldn't be spending it on this stuff. I like new things. I want . . . your help.'

'I'm an—'

'We need to speak in private,' she continued. 'I have a letter of introduction.'

Sam glanced down at it: the letter was from a firm called Falcon and Arcelia, legal advisers, based in Boston. Sam had never heard of them, but then he'd never heard of many people. He knew he should throw her out. Conversations that started like this never went well. What she was looking for, he couldn't tell, but he could be certain it was his old skills as an agent for the Mossad she was interested in, not his new life as an antiques trader.

And that life was behind him now. *Forever.*

There was something about her eyes, however. He could see something there: something between a mystery and a chase.

It wouldn't do any harm to listen.

*Unless I'm just kidding myself.*

'Okay,' he said.

The shop was empty anyway, and he'd hear the moment a customer stepped inside. Sam led her into the back office: a simple room, with a desk, an electric heater, and piles and piles of reference books and trade magazines. The girl accepted the cup of tea Sam made for her, stirred in two sugars, then sat down opposite him. 'Orla Sheehy,' she said, looking bashfully up at him. 'Thanks for taking the time to talk with me.'

'And what is it you want?' asked Sam.

'I need to find some money.'

Sam laughed. 'We'd all like to do that,' he replied. 'Try a bank.'

'I'd have tried that already if I thought it would do any good,' she replied.

Her face creased up into a smile, and for the first time Sam noticed how pretty she was. Her skin was pure white, like cream, and her lips were full and angry, like splashes of fierce red streaked across a blank canvas. Her eyes were the deepest blue, and her hair jet black, turning her face into a riot of colours that only just managed to pull themselves together at the last moment. Does she know how beautiful she is, Sam found himself wondering. She wears shapeless clothes, and not much make-up, as if she was a woman who cared nothing for her appearance, but perhaps that was just a mask, a game of sexual double bluff: maybe she knows just exactly how beautiful she is, but disguises it so that men would think they were discovering something hidden. Forget it, he told himself sharply. You've spent too long walking through the mirrors and shadows of the spying game. She's just a young girl who needs some help.

'What I want to do,' said Orla, the smile disappearing from her face as fast as it had flashed up there, 'is tell you a story.'

# TWO

**USS Madison, Persian Gulf, 10 November**

Second Petty Officer Jim Mullery put his coffee cup down on the side of the desk. He'd been on duty for eight hours now, and he was starting to feel the strain. There were five men in total in the Combat Information Center of the battleship, but he was the only man trained to detect incoming attacks.

If anything happens to this ship, he reflected to himself, it is going to be my fault.

*Mine alone.*

He looked down at the screen in front of him. The AN/SPY-1 radar system was the most sophisticated available to the US Navy: most of the sailors knew it by its nickname 'The Shield of the Fleet'. Unlike a conventional, mechanically controlled radar that would 'see' a target just once during a 360-degree turn, the SPY-1 sent out a continuous beam of electromagnetic energy, allowing it to monitor the space above, below and parallel to the battleship. It could quite literally see everything. As soon as it located a target, the system would lock on to it, providing not just warning of an attack, but the means to retaliate as well.

Like a hunting dog, the SPY-1 could find you anywhere, Jim could recall his instructors telling him. And then it would destroy you.

So long, that is, as the man in charge of the system was up to the job.

Jim tapped his fingers against the desk, and finished off the coffee. He could feel the caffeine hitting his bloodstream, but the shot of energy was short-lived. The tiredness kicked straight back in. He'd only just returned from two weeks' leave, and his wife Jodie had just given birth to their second child, Darren. He'd hardly slept for the two weeks: Jodie was worn out from looking after the house and the kids by herself all day, and he'd spent the two weeks trying to let her get as much rest as possible.

Exhausting.

It made a battleship seem peaceful by comparison.

It will be better when they get older, Jim told himself. And when I get the next promotion, and kick myself up to the next pay grade.

He could see something on the screen. He looked closer. A flock of birds? No, he told himself. Too big, and moving in too straight a line. This thing was travelling at 500, maybe 600 miles an hour.

And it was coming straight at them.

Like . . . what? Mullery asked himself.

Just like an Iranian Air Force F1-14A Tomcat fighter jet. That's what.

It had been an exhausting twenty-four hours. The *Madison* had been dispatched to the Gulf after the Iranians had started laying down mines along sea lanes used by other American ships. It was part of a small group of US battleships struggling to keep sea lanes open as the Iran-Iraq war raged around them. It had already crossed into Omani waters, been challenged by that government's gunboats, and had been forced to change course. Since then, it had crossed into Iranian territorial waters, and had already been ordered back by the Iranian Navy. Everyone on board knew that Iran had just purchased a consignment of Chinese Silkworm missiles.

11

The *Madison* was one of the few ships in the American fleet that could handle that threat. But the crew was on edge, well aware that even though the US was not at war with Iran, they could be at any moment.

And if they were, this ship would be in the thick of it.

Mullery looked closer at the screen.

It sure looked like a Tomcat.

And we should recognise the bastards.

*After all, we built them.*

As he tracked the rapid movement across the screen, it struck Mullery as ironic that an American warship was following the movements of an American-built warplane. The Tomcat had gone into service in 1970, and a batch of eighty of them had been sold soon afterwards by Richard Nixon to the Imperial Iranian Air Force, as it was known before the shah was overthrown. The fighter had long since been retired out of the US forces, but the Iranians were still flying them. It was old, and technologically outdated. But that didn't mean it couldn't pack a hell of a punch, noted Mullery grimly.

Enough to take out this ship with a single missile.

'What the hell's happening?'

Captain Steven Roberts was standing right behind him. He was a tall man, six foot three, with grey-blue eyes and a hard, coppery complexion. His mouth was set firm, and on his forehead he wore a permanent frown. He was standing just inches from Mullery's back: so close you could smell the sweat on his skin.

Mullery put his finger down on the screen. 'Incoming.'

'Tomcat?'

Mullery nodded. 'Could be.'

He was sure he could see a bead of perspiration on Roberts' forehead.

Leaning over, he looked into the screen. For all its sophistication, the SPY-1 was a radar. All you saw was a tiny dot of light advancing towards you. Fast.

You didn't see a plane.

Or anything that looked like a plane.

*Just this dot.*

'Commercial?'

Mullery shook his head. The system was designed to lock into the flight controls of a commercial aircraft. If any civilian aircraft were in the vicinity, SPY-1's computers should know about it and alert them. The machines talked to one another: one of the key safety mechanisms built into the system to try and make sure it never attacked a civil aircraft.

And, so far, it never had.

'Nothing that we know of,' he said. 'Anyway, it's too small for a commercial craft.'

With a shake of his head, Roberts stepped back from the screen.

'Make contact,' he said.

His voice was tense and drawn.

The voice of a man who knew he had just made a big decision.

Two feet away, Communications Officer Matt Burrell slipped his headphones into position and tapped a rapid series of commands into the keyboard on his desk. Standard operating procedure said you should try to contact any unidentified aircraft before engaging with it. You gave the pilot a chance to respond, to say who he was and what he was doing. If necessary, you gave him a chance to turn back.

If he didn't respond, there was only one assumption you could make.

He was an enemy.

And if you didn't kill him, he was about to kill you.

'No response,' said Burrell, looking back towards the captain.

'Then try again,' snapped Roberts.

Burrell ran his fingers across the keyboard. Mullery was keeping a close watch on his face as he did so, his eyes darting between the captain and the radio operator. In his three years in charge of the *Madison,* Roberts had carved out a reputation as a maverick: he was a tough, disciplined officer, who had little sympathy for his men, and swore violently at every command that came down from the admirals. But this time he was playing it by the book, noted Mullery. They were inches away from a shooting war, and even Roberts wasn't taking any chances. Not with 1,000 tons of warship and 300 men under his command.

Not to mention the possibility of a war with Iran.

'Nothing,' said Burrell again.

'Check the flight schedules,' said Roberts, the tension threading through each vowel in the sentence.

Burrell went back to his keyboard. Every commercial flight was logged into an air traffic control system, and the SPY-1 computer could check those records. It didn't matter where the flight was going, the system should have it logged. If it changed direction, then the pilot should let someone on the ground know so the system could be updated.

'Nothing on the logbook, sir.'

Mullery was looking closely at his radar screen. He could feel the captain standing behind him. He could feel his heart thumping inside of his chest. A lot of the men he had trained with joked about how they'd like to take part in a real shooting war one day. It was a long time since the US Navy had seen any real action: not since Vietnam: and nothing serious since they'd made peace with Japan.

Perhaps that was about to change.

The plane was advancing towards them.

Fast.

Sure as hell looks like a Tomcat, Mullery told himself.

And within a few minutes, we could all be swimming for the Iranian coast.

If we're lucky.

'Then bring it down,' said Roberts.

# THREE

**Beirut, 10 November**

Mark Slota checked his watch. It was just after ten in the morning, and he didn't have much time to waste. There were twenty minutes until his next meeting, and he still had a couple of papers to read. He glanced up and down Riad El Solh Street. Known locally as banking street, with its imposing stone-clad facades, its heavy citrus trees, and men in light-cut blue suits, it was thick with people at this time of the morning.

He ducked into a café, and ordered himself a coffee. He'd been four days in Beirut now, and he couldn't say the place was growing on him. I can't imagine it grows on anyone, he reflected to himself. He glanced around the room. There were about a dozen people in there in total, all men, most of them smoking. If you can't sell insurance around here, then where can you sell it, he thought to himself with a grim smile.

If the civil war doesn't get you, then the way these people smoke, they'll sure all die of cancer before they hit fifty.

Slota looked down at the papers. They appeared to be in order. Harrison Interstate Insurance had sent him out to the Middle East three times now, each time lining up reinsurance contracts with local underwriters. He hadn't wanted to come, not on this trip: his wife Sarah had gone sulky when he told her, complaining that she didn't know how she was expected to get everything ready for Christmas with three kids running around her feet, her family coming over to stay, and her husband away for three weeks.

*What did she know?*

There was good money to be made in this country, Slota reflected, as he studied the papers. Even with the war raging around them, there was still some business running through Beirut. Oil and construction and shipping for the whole region been based here for decades, and not all of it had fled. Not yet anyway. They needed the insurance more than ever. You could do well so long as you didn't mind the risks. And there wasn't much point in being in the insurance business if you were scared of risk.

*Women just don't understand that kind of stuff.*

Slota drained the last of his coffee, folded up his papers back into his bag, and stepped back onto the street. It was only 200 yards up the street to his next meeting.

He hardly even noticed the man walking alongside him, his eyes shaded by a thick pair of dark glasses.

He didn't even notice the Steyr M1 pistol jabbing into his ribcage.

And by the time he did, it was already too late.

He'd already been bundled into the car.

And driven at high speed out of the city.

Marie Holt checked out of the hospital. Walking across the busy road, she ducked into one of the cafés just across the square. She knew she should probably go straight back to the two-bedroomed apartment she shared with one of the other nurses who worked in the Red Cross hospital but she didn't feel like it this morning.

Sleep could wait.

If she could get to sleep, that is.

It had been a long, twelve-hour shift, starting at ten o'clock last night, and only finishing at ten this morning. A car bomb had exploded on a residential square yesterday evening: a common enough event in Beirut right now, noted Marie to herself, but no less horrific for the men, women and children caught up in it. Two dozen wounded had been rushed into the hospital through the night, and the surgeons had done their best to get through them all, but it had still been a punishing, exhausting shift. The hospital didn't begin to have the capacity to deal with those kinds of emergencies: half the patients just had to be put under anaesthetic and stacked up in the corridors until the doctors had time to treat them.

Marie glanced up from the stainless steel counter of the café. She'd had to help one of the surgeons amputate a badly wounded leg off a six-year-old girl: she'd been holding her hand as well when the little girl woke up confused and scared with no idea what had just happened to her. Even for a hardened nurse there were some sights that were hard to take. There was a row of spirits lined up against the back wall, and for a moment a rum or a vodka seemed tempting. No, she told herself. Not at this time of day.

She ordered herself a coffee and sat close to the window. Even though it was nearly Christmas, the weather was mild. Back in Chicago where she had grown up it would be minus ten by now, and would get colder still through January and February. Marie sipped on the coffee, letting the caffeine revive her. Right across the road was a place where you could make cheap international phone calls. In a minute, she'd ring her boyfriend Jim. Another two months, and her one-year posting to the Red Cross in Beirut would be finished. She and Jim were planning to get married in the spring. There was still so much to do.

A honeymoon to plan. A house to buy.

Marie finished the coffee in one gulp. She didn't feel like sitting around in a café anymore. She wanted to talk to someone from home. Checking the road, she walked swiftly over the street swerving out of the way of a motorbike that was riding close to the pavement. It was just a few yards to the phone shop. A man was standing, blocking her path. He was tall and thin, with a stubby beard dragged across his face, and small brown eyes like dried dates.

'Excuse me,' she said.

He remained silent.

Still blocking her path.

Marie felt a shudder of fear.

She glanced nervously down the street.

'I need to get—'

But before she could finish the sentence, a hand had already clamped itself across her face.

Ed Ryan walked through the swinging doors of the hotel. He walked swiftly down the street, giving himself ten minutes to stretch his legs before hailing a taxi. He had only just finished breakfast, and had already put a couple of phone calls in to his office back in New York. Some fresh air would do him good before the working day began.

The project was going okay, he told himself as he twisted through the office workers making their way to work. A new office and shopping complex on Kaslik Street, right at the centre of Beirut's commercial district, he'd been delighted when the firm had been given the contract to design and build the centre. It was Ed's first proper contract since he'd been appointed to develop an overseas arm for the company, and in any job, he'd discovered, there was nothing to beat a few early home runs. First impressions counted, and if the board decided you were a winner in the first few months it was unlikely they'd reverse that opinion later on.

Get the first month sorted, and you could write your own contract.

Which is exactly what I plan to do.

It had gone better than he expected. Plenty of people had warned him about trying to finish any construction project in the Middle East. Even worse than New York, they told him. The builders have no idea what they are doing, they'll cheat you blind, and if you think our mafia is bad, wait until you meet theirs. Nobody makes any money. They're just giving the job to some Americans because none of the local firms want to touch it.

Well, they can talk that way if they want to, Ed told himself. But the way we've been running the site, the building might even get finished ahead of schedule. That way, the developer would have to pay them a bonus for getting it done on time. And there were a couple of big road-building projects coming up for tender from the government shortly. With this under our belts, I reckon we'd have a good shot at getting them.

Life didn't often go as well as this.

And you needed to savour it when it did.

Ed stopped at the taxi rank he usually used. It was empty, but no sooner had he glanced along the street than a car pulled up. He climbed inside.

'Kaslik Street,' he said to the driver.

The car pulled away from the kerb, the driver slamming his fist on the horn to muscle his way through the morning traffic. Ed sat back in the seat. The driver had put all his windows up, and switched the air conditioning on. Some Arabic music was playing on the radio. They swerved left, then left again, running through one red light as the car sped towards the docks. It took only a few seconds for Ed to realise they were going in completely the wrong direction. The taxi drivers were terrible in Beirut, he was used to that. Even worse than New York. But this guy was driving like a madman.

No, he corrected himself. Make that a madman on speed.

'Hey,' snapped Ed, looking towards the back of the driver's neck. 'This isn't the way.'

The driver ignored him.

He tapped his foot on the accelerator, taking the taxi up past fifty miles an hour. He swerved viciously, avoiding a truck that was unloading some fruit for a shop. Ed was thrown sideways. 'What the fuck . . .' he shouted.

The driver honked again, pushing through the lights, and speeding up again as they hit an open stretch of road that led past the docks, and out into the open coastal road to the east of the city. The buildings were flashing by faster and faster. Ed gripped hold of the front seat, and leaned forwards. 'Where the fuck are you going?' he shouted, his voice turning hoarse with rage.

Remaining silent, the driver picked up a Steyr M1 pistol from a box next to the gearstick. He kept his left hand on the steering wheel, and glanced around only briefly as he jabbed the gun straight into Ed's face. His eyes were dark brown, with a shrouded, menacing appearance, and there was a trickle of sweat running down his face. 'Shut the fuck up,' he said, his voice so quiet that Ed could hardly hear it above the screeching of the tyres against the tarmac.

Ed leaned back in the seat of the taxi.

He could feel a trickle of sweat falling across his face.

*Just when my life was going so well.*

Alicia Pisani sipped on the coffee and looked again at the guidebook. The Robert Mouawad Private Museum was only a few blocks away from the hotel where she had stayed the night, and it was the one thing that she really wanted to see during her three days in the city.

The museum had one of the finest collections of traditional Arabic pottery in the world, and even as a civil war raged around it, neither side had wanted to destroy any of the artefacts stored inside. Like most Arab fighters, reflected Alicia, they were brutal, savage, and relentless. But they weren't philistines.

They cared about their history.

You could even argue that was what they were fighting for.

She was now into her second year of her History of Art course at Berkeley. She had been doing a course on pottery through the ages, and some instinct that she couldn't quite figure out herself had told her that she should specialise in Arabic pottery. There was something about the delicacy of the designs that she felt certain would resonate with modern audiences if she could find a way to resurrect them.

Alicia drained the coffee, paid for it, and bought a postcard from the counter at the same time. She quickly scribbled a note addressed to Stephen Pisani. 'Doing fine,' it said simply. 'Spending the day sightseeing, then heading off for Jordan. Love Alicia.'

Her father had been horrified at the thought of her travelling through the Lebanon, Syria and Jordan by herself: he'd forced her to agree to send him a postcard every day before he gave her the money for the flight. It was a decade now since her mother had died, and dad had never remarried. Between his software company, and Alicia, he used to joke that he didn't have time for any other women in his life. Sometimes she wished that he would, Alicia reminded herself. When she was a little girl, she loved having her dad all to herself, didn't want to share him with anybody. But she was growing up now: she was starting to become aware of just how much her father depended on her for emotional support and companionship. Soon she wasn't going to be there for him anymore, not if she was to start carving out her own life, and someone was going to have to fill that space.

Someone will have to take my place, she reflected as she put an extra x on the bottom of the card. Just so long as it isn't one of those blonde trophy babes that manned the reception desks of just about every software company and venture capital house in California. Dad's company had struggled for years, but it was making plenty of money now, and Alicia was damned if she was going to let some money honey with nothing but air between her ears sweep in and take the lot.

Any woman who took Mom's place would have to be very special.

As she stepped out into the street, Alicia dropped the card into the postbox, then started walking towards the museum.

'Hey,' shouted a guy.

She glanced around. He was five nine, or ten, with dark brown eyes, a slender build, and a crooked smile that creased up over the rough features of his face. Jesus, thought Alicia. It's still hours to lunchtime, and these Arab dudes are already out hitting on girls. Worse than campus . . .

'Hey, honey,' he called, louder this time.

Alicia turned a cold eye on him. With long dark hair, bright blue eyes, and hips that were just the right side of full, she knew she was attractive to men, but usually the feeling was far from mutual, and walking around campus for a couple of years had taught her everything she needed to know about getting rid of them. Usually anyway.

'Just one minute . . .' he cried.

'Get lost,' she said, missing only a single step as she glanced backwards.

In the same instant, she felt a man bump into her. 'I'm sorry . . .' she started, blurting out an apology.

Then she realised.

No apology was necessary.

Not from her anyway.

The man had already encircled his arms around her. His hand, thick, rough, and brutal, had clamped itself around her mouth. She was frozen, immobile: a fear so complete, and so cold, it had gripped hold of her, and she no longer felt able to move. The second man, the guy who'd been

23

shouting at her, was running towards them, closing down the few yards that separated them in a fraction of a second. On the street, she could see a blue Honda screech up towards the curve. The men were pushing her towards it, shoving her the five yards towards the open door. It was impossible to resist: she could feel the strength of the muscles slamming into her like slabs of rock. She was tossed across the back seat, a man clambering across her, and slamming the door behind her.

Oh Christ, she thought to herself. Tears were already starting to form in her eyes.

He was lying on top of her, his breath hot and sweaty, making it impossible for her to cry out, or to look out of the window.

The Honda was screeching away from the kerb, its horn blasting, pushing its way through the morning traffic.

It was pushing hard up towards its top speed, the gearbox crunching as it did so. She could feel herself being rocked to the side as the car swerved to avoid a truck.

What the hell are they going to do to me? she asked herself.

# FOUR

**London, 10 November**

Her eyes barely moved as she spoke.

Whether she'd learned that somewhere, or it was natural to her, Sam couldn't tell. Either way, it was effective. She looked straight into him, as if she was probing the impact of every word, assessing its weight and effect before moving on to the next.

And as it went on, Sam couldn't help but be drawn in.

'I grew up in Carlow. That's in Ireland, do you know it?'

Sam shook his head. For the Mossad, he'd tracked down Palestinian terrorists to the four corners of the earth, but somehow that hadn't included the Irish countryside. It wasn't the kind of place that appealed to Hamas and the rest of that mob: they didn't like golf, and they didn't care for Guinness either.

'Lovely countryside. Green as your eyes are blue. You should come sometime. Anyway, my parents died when I was just ten . . .'

'I'm sorry.'

'There's no need, you didn't kill them.'

She looked sharply at Sam.

Does she know I used to kill people for a living? he wondered to himself.

True, none of them were Irish.

But they were all somebody's children or parents or brothers. And maybe that makes me guilty in her eyes.

'And so I was taken into the orphanage,' she continued, after missing just a fraction of a beat. 'The Order of St Luke's it was called, in a village called Leighlinbridge. Me and my brother Rory. He was five at the time. He hardly even knew what had happened. The priests fed him some line about how our parents were visiting God, and we'd all be back together in heaven one day soon, but I wasn't listening to any of that. It was all bollocks to me, and still is. It was a gloomy place, dark all the time. About ten nuns lived there, and six monks, and three priests who ran the place. In total there must have been thirty kids there, but they came and went. It was 1978, and Ireland was just about edging its way into the twentieth century. There weren't quite so many children being taken away from their mothers and handed over to the Church just because they didn't happen to have a wedding ring on their finger as there used to be, but it was still happening, no matter what anyone says.'

'And you were happy there?'

Orla shrugged. 'Happy enough, I suppose,' she said, 'There were some other little girls there, and three or four boys for my brother to play with. Kids get on with stuff. They cope much better than grown-ups think they will. Of course, it wasn't exactly fun. We slept in a dorm, we didn't have much food, and what we did have was terrible. And we prayed. Jesus, did we pray. And when we weren't praying we read the Bible. If there ever happens to be a quote you need to know, just ask me. I think I know the whole book backwards . . .'

'"No man, having put his hand to the plough, and looking back, is fit for the kingdom of God."'

'Luke, chapter nine, verse sixty-two.'

She didn't even pause before replying, Sam noted.

'And where did it go wrong?'

'Around the time Rory was seven.'

Her eyes flicked upwards so they met Sam's. 'That was when the abuse started,' she continued. Her tone was soft, controlled, but you could still hear the thread of anger within it, Sam reckoned: it was there, strong and immovable, like a strip of iron running through a seam in a mine. 'There was a priest called Father Robertson. Not Irish, not native anyway, not with a name like that. Might have been from Scotland originally. He was very close to all the boys in his care. Too close. I didn't know what it was at the time. I wouldn't have understood it, even if somebody had told me. But Rory was being abused.'

She hesitated, taking a sharp intake of breath. There was something about her manner that made Sam think of a witness in a courtroom. She was controlled and precise, laying out the evidence as if she was seeking a conviction. 'It started with just Father Robertson,' she continued. 'But then it got worse. There was a circle of priests, about a dozen of them, all living in different monasteries and orphanages. They'd find boys they liked, and then they'd parcel them out, sending them from priest to priest like some kind of piece of meat. I guess it was pretty good for them. Like some kind of personal harem, a different boy to bugger every few days.'

'And Rory told you?'

'Not until he was ten, and I was fifteen. I think he was just getting to an age where he was wondering if this was normal, whether there was something wrong with what they were doing. I went to see Father McCormack, the priest in charge of the orphanage. He told me I was wicked, that such things couldn't happen, wouldn't happen. He said the devil himself must have told me to attack the Church, that I had to exorcise the demons within myself. Then to help me along, he started beating me. He had this paddle, a wooden thing with splinters fraying off the edge, and he'd slice it into my flesh, stinging me, until I cried that I had been wrong.'

'And then?'

'There was nothing I could do. I had no power, I was just a girl, and they were hurting me. The beating stopped when I stopped complaining, but they were keeping a close eye on me all the time, and I knew they'd never forgive me. They talk about forgiveness all the time, but of course there's no forgiveness where the Church is concerned. Once you cross the line, they mark you down as an enemy, and after that there is no going back.'

She coughed, then went on with her story. 'Rory felt bad that I was getting hurt as a result of trying to help him, so he submitted. Every weekend, he'd be sent off to another priest. On Sunday nights, he'd come home looking sad and tired and then he'd just go to his bunk in the boys' dormitory and cry until he went to sleep.'

'But you're not there anymore,' said Sam. 'What happened?'

'I managed to get out seven years ago,' Orla answered. 'Without telling anyone I managed to get Rory and myself transferred to a seminary in Boston. I'd applied directly, and they accepted us, and so Father McCormack didn't have any choice but to let us go. I was seventeen, and Rory was twelve then. My plan was to get out as soon as I could, and settle in America, and to keep an eye on Rory at the same time. A year after we got there, I got myself a job at the library at Boston University. I would have liked to have enrolled as a student, but I didn't have the money for that. The library had all the books I wanted, though, and nobody minded if I sat in on a few of the lectures. It was fun, the first time in my life I'd seen any of that. Rory was still being looked after by the Church, but so far as I knew he was okay. Better than back in Ireland anyway.'

She paused, as if she was composing herself for the next

sentence. 'Three years ago, he hanged himself.'

For a second Sam wanted to reach out and comfort her, but he held himself back. The statement was delivered bluntly, with little emotional content: she'd learned to disguise the grief, but it was still there somewhere, Sam felt certain of it, if only you could find a way to cut through the protective layers she'd wrapped around it.

'And let me guess,' he said. 'They never admitted any connection.'

Orla laughed, but there was no humour in it: it was a harsh, mocking sound, the chill laughter of the gallows. 'They'd rather own up to faking the crucifixion,' she said.

Sam smiled.

'Of course they didn't. The official verdict was that he had been suffering from emotional and psychological problems for years, that the Church had been trying to treat them, but that unfortunately they hadn't been able to prevent this tragic accident.'

Her eyes flashed up into Sam's, like a pair of headlamps suddenly switched onto full beam. 'Of course, I knew that was just lies,' she said. 'It was the abuse that killed him. The Church killed him as surely as if they'd tied the rope around his neck with their own hands. And they didn't even have the strength or the guts to own up to it afterwards.'

'But they got away with it . . .'

'Not this time,' said Orla firmly. 'I was working in the library at Boston University, and I was familiarising myself with the law. If Rory had hanged himself in Ireland, there'd have been nothing I could do. The Church owns that country, every last rotten blade of grass of it. But not the United States. They don't own that country. I couldn't prosecute them, not for the suicide. Rory did that himself, or so they said, although for all I know, they could have tied the rope to him and made him do it. I could sue them, however. I could take a civil action for damages.'

'They'll fight . . .'

Orla shook her head, and Sam noted the way her nostrils flared angrily. 'They already have done,' she said. 'I put the case together myself at first, gathering all the necessary evidence, reading up on the law, getting the witness statements, getting it all to the stage where the action could be filed. Then I took it to a Boston law firm who agreed to take the case in return for a twenty per cent cut of the damages. We filed a complaint against the Boston diocese six months ago, for a total of $500 million dollars.'

'Then you'll soon be a wealthy young woman,' said Sam. 'Maybe I could help you furnish your mansion.'

Orla shook her head. There's a catch, thought Sam. There's always a catch. That kind of money doesn't walk through the door without some strings on it.

'They say they don't have any money.'

Sam leant forwards in his chair. It was just a fraction of an inch, but enough to show he was interested. You heard plenty of lies when you worked for the Mossad: they came in as many shapes and sizes as there animals in a zoo. But he had seldom heard a lie so cold, calculating and deceitful as that.

'The Catholic Church? Broke?'

'We're suing the Boston diocese,' said Orla. 'And that's what they say. They are broke.'

'Then they're lying.'

'I know they are lying,' said Orla. 'The question is, how do I *prove* it?'

That's always the question, reflected Sam. You could know all sorts of things. Proving them was something else entirely.

'There's money there somewhere. I feel certain of it.'

'Almost certainly . . .'

'And I'd like *you* to find it for me.'

She looked at him seriously for a fraction of a second, then

30

turned her lips up into a winning smile.

She didn't need to say anything. Sam already knew that was why she was here.

'Me? Why me? It's not the most preposterous request I've heard, I'll admit that. But it's top five. Maybe even top three now I come to think of it.'

'I was told you could do the impossible.'

Sam spread his hands out. 'Maybe once, not anymore.'

'You owe me,' said Orla.

'No I don't.'

She shrugged, flicking a lock of hair away from her pale eyes. 'Okay, maybe not,' she said softly. 'But you soon will.'

# FIVE

**Presidential Palace, Tehran, 11 November**

Fathali Saeedi looked down at the pictures on the table. He studied them the way a butcher might study a side of beef: as if he was deciding where to put his cleaver into the carcass.

He was standing in his office on the second floor of Tehran's Presidential Palace, a compound of densely guarded buildings that housed not just the President of the republic but all his most senior officials as well. The compound was directly opposite the original Sadabad Palace, built by the Qajar royal family that ruled the country in the nineteenth century. It had been occupied by Iran's rulers up until the fall of the Shah: after that, it had been turned into a museum, while the Islamic government built itself a new complex of offices in the districts surrounding the old palace.

He stood perfectly still. The pictures on the desk showed the wreckage of an Airbus A300.

All that remained of Flight IR 655.

As the Defence Minister, it was Saeedi's job to ensure the safety and integrity of the Iranian regime. After a decade working underground, in London and Paris and Tehran within the revolutionary movement, his career in government had started as soon as the Shah had been overthrown. The regime knew from the start it was besieged by enemies. There was no more important portfolio than Defence. And there was nobody who took the protection of the Islamic Revolution more seriously than Saeedi.

And yet in the three years since he'd held the post, this was the most direct challenge Saeedi had yet faced.

One that couldn't be shirked.

To let this lie would be a sign of weakness. And, as Lenin once observed, once a revolutionary regime appeared weak it was already as good as dead.

'How did this happen?' he asked.

He was looking straight at two men. Ali Hatami was the head of the Revolutionary Guards, the inner circle of the Iranian Army, and Mohsen Farhadi was the head of the VEVAK, the Vezarat-e Ettelaat va Amniat-e Keshvar, the feared Iranian secret service, which crushed dissent with a ruthlessness of which even the KGB would have been proud.

Within the whole of Iran, no two individuals inspired more fear. Not even the president himself.

But today both men were silent.

'I said, how did this happen?' growled Saeedi.

The pictures were taken from the air. Within minutes of the IranAir Airbus losing contact with ground control, helicopters had been scrambled and flown out to sea. The plane wasn't responding to radio signals, and although it hadn't sent out any kind of Mayday alert, it was soon clear why. It had been shot clean out of the sky. The fuselage of the A300 had broken into three clean pieces as it plunged 40,000 feet on its way down to the sea. The wings had broken off and shattered into hundreds of pieces as they twisted through the air. How long it had taken the 113 people on board to die, it was impossible to say. Most of them probably died the instant the missile struck the plane. Still more would have been killed as the engines and fuel tanks exploded. Certainly none of them were left alive by the time they hit the water.

You could see parts of the plane spread out across a huge radius. The pictures were incredibly detailed. You could make out seats, suitcases, even body parts. But there was no point in looking for any survivors. They weren't any.

'A missile,' answered Farhadi.

'From where?'

'The USS *Madison*.'

There was a pause. Farhadi could see the anger burning in the Defence minister's eyes. 'You are saying the Americans deliberately shot down an Iranian plane . . . Why?'

'They are terrorist scum,' said Hatami.

Saeedi ignored the remark. The Revolutionary Guards were, in his opinion, a rabble: a formidable fighting force, admittedly, but you would no more ask their opinion than you would seek out the views of a guard dog. They could snarl, bark and sometimes bite, but they weren't much use at thinking.

'I asked why?' he said looking back at Farhadi.

'We believe it was an accident,' said the intelligence officer. 'The *Madison* was sailing close to our waters. It had already received warnings to back off. So far as we can tell, its missile system locked onto the plane, and a missile was fired. Our best intelligence suggests that they thought they were under attack.'

Saeedi slammed his fist on the table. 'An accident must still be avenged.'

He walked towards the window. Down below, he could see tourists starting to line up towards the entrance to the Sadabad Palace. 'We need an American plane to be brought down.'

'A . . . civilian plane?'

'Of course,' snapped Saeedi. 'Does the Koran not say a life for a life, an eye for an eye, a nose for a nose, an ear for an ear, a tooth for a tooth, and a wound for a wound?'

Farhadi nodded. 'The Table, chapter five, verse forty-four,' he replied. Like everyone within the regime, he knew every word in the Koran, and could recite it backwards if he had to. 'But to bring down an American airliner may take months of preparation. The security surrounding their airports is intense.'

'The president wants it,' said Saeedi coldly. 'He wants it done before the end of the year. And there can be no argument with the president.'

# SIX

**Beirut, Lebanon, 11 November**

The back of the van was hot and uncomfortable.

Hussein Lahham checked the four people strapped inside it. Mark Slota, Marie Holt, Ed Ryan and Alicia Pisani were all bound and gagged. Ropes had been put around their legs, plasti-cuffs had been snapped onto their hands, and their mouths had been filled with rags, then taped up. None of them could move.

Or, more importantly, scream.

One guard, a young Hamas warrior called Nizir Sultani, was sitting next to them. He had an AK-47 strapped to his chest, and the barrel of the gun was pointing menacingly at the four hostages. Should any of them create any kind of disturbance, then they would be dead within an instant. Lahham was quite clear on those orders. There were plenty more American tourists or businessmen that could be picked up on the streets of Beirut. There was no point in running any risks with any particular hostage when another one could be acquired so cheaply.

Lahham turned the key in the ignition, and started to drive. It was twenty-four hours now since the four hostages had been captured, and so far the operation was going like clockwork. The four victims had been taken to a safe house close to the waterfront, then sedated to stop them from causing too much trouble. It was standard operating procedure within Hamas to drug hostages, usually with heavy doses of valium: it was ground up, and slipped into the one bottle of water they were allowed each day.

Overnight, they had been fed, then sedated again, and hauled into the back of this van. It was another ten miles drive up the coast to the second safe house. The hostages would be moved every twenty-four hours, again in accordance with standard Hamas operating procedure. Keep them in one place for too long, and there was always the possibility that you could be betrayed. It only took one person to notice something unusual, and they could pass on a tip to the Americans. No doubt there would be a rich bounty on the heads of the four hostages, and Beirut was full of men who'd sell you out for a few dollars. The only way to survive, to keep the location of the hostages absolutely secret, was to keep moving. Once a day, at least. Twice a day if necessary. Too much was at stake for any risks to be run.

The drive took twenty-five minutes. Lahham pulled the van up outside a plain, whitewashed house, one mile back from the coastline. It was a quiet, suburban district: years of experience had taught Hamas that the suburbs were the best place to keep hostages, for the simple reason that they were quiet, discreet, and nobody asked too many questions. A thick pair of metal gates swung open, and Lahham reversed the van into the courtyard. Two armed men were waiting inside, their faces masked. The four hostages were dragged out onto the dusty ground. There was sweat pouring from their faces, and there were tears in the eyes of both the women, but Lahham just ignored them. He had already watched plenty of hostages die, and felt not so much as a flicker of sympathy. 'Move it,' he snapped.

His accomplice, Nizir Sultani, led them down into a darkened basement. There was straw on the floor, and a bucket in the corner if any of them needed to empty their bowels: the bucket had been washed, but that was the only thing in the cellar that was clean. In a few minutes, one of the guards would bring them down some food, and cut loose their plasti-cuffs long enough for them to get something to eat.

Lahham remained upstairs. There were two other men in the main room of the house, both senior figures on the Hamas 'state bureau', the committee that directed the terrorist organisation. Mahmoud al-Zahar was the taller of the two men: rakishly thin, with jet-black hair and eyes like nuggets of coal. Khaled Khouri was shorter, with rolls of fat around his face and eyes, but with a hard, stony edge to his jaw line that spoke of the toughness within. Although Lahham was junior to both of them in terms of his place in the hierarchy, in terms of his experience of inflicting terror upon the world, he outranked just about anyone in the Middle East. Born into a dirt-poor family, Lahham's father had been shot by the Israeli Army when he went to fight alongside the Palestinians, and the rest of his family had been torn apart in the civil war that followed the Israeli invasion of the Lebanon. He had grown up on the streets, scavenging and scrounging his way through life, until he got taken in by Hamas. Its ideal of an Islamic Republic in the Lebanon, of driving the Israelis out of the Middle East, became Lahham's ideal. It was his vision, and his life. There was nothing he wouldn't do to achieve it: no lives, including his own, that would not be gladly sacrificed to the cause. There had been hostage-takers before, plenty of them. But the ruthless manipulation of hostages as a political tool, that was Lahham's creation, and it was one he took a quiet, professional pride in. He was the undertaker of global politics, he sometimes told himself. Nobody knew how to trade human bodies like he did.

'The hostages are safe?' asked al-Zahar.

'Like lambs,' said Lahham.

'Have they been reported missing yet?' asked Khouri.

Lahham shrugged. 'How should I know?' he said, his tone rough. 'We chose all four of them because they were Americans, and not just any Americans either. They are all photogenic, young, and with families that will no doubt miss them. Each one of them is perfect for the media. Their stories will get huge coverage – and that is what will put the maximum pressure on the American government. Only once the media are screaming about this will they start to realise the power we have over them. And then they will bend to our will.'

'We have formulated our demands?' said al-Zahar.

'There are thirty prisoners in Israel that we want released,' said Khouri. 'We have drawn up the list of names. It can be published immediately. In addition, we want $30 million to be deposited in a Lebanese bank account. Then, and only then, will we consider releasing the four men and women.'

'The Americans will insist that they can't control who is in and who is out of an Israeli prison camp,' said Lahhman.

'But they'll be lying, and their public will know it,' said Khouri. 'The Zionists have always worked together.'

'Then we should make our demands known immediately,' said Lahhman.

'And if the Americans won't agree?' asked al-Zahar.

'Then the hostages will die, one by one,' said Lahhman. 'We'll start with the men.'

# SEVEN

**Tehran, 11 November**

The agent was known only as Mehrak.

He had dark, pale eyes, like a snake's, darting from side to side, constantly assessing his prey, deciding when to pounce. Even Mohsen Farhadi didn't like him much, and as head of the VEVAK, he was the man who controlled his every breath and thought. He had the impatience of a wasp, and the cunning of a rat, Farhadi reflected. An ugly combination that made just about anyone who came into contact with him wish he'd never been born.

But Mehrak was good, Farhadi told himself. More than good. He was the best, and that was why the VEVAK held him tight to the centre of the organisation. The word 'impossible' had never been coined, not as far as Mehrak was concerned. He took to every challenge with relish, and always rose to it. No task was too difficult, nor was any act too cruel. If it needed to be done, it was done. That was how he justified his existence.

'We need an American plane brought down,' said Farhadi. 'Before the year closes.'

Even as he delivered the sentence, Farhadi glanced anxiously in the direction of Saeedi. When you ran the intelligence operation for the whole of Iran, then you grew used to be being feared. People stopped talking as you walked down a corridor. You could sense them backing away from you even when you couldn't see it. But in the last few hours he had learned what it was like to be afraid himself, and, if he was being honest with himself, it wasn't an experience he'd care to repeat. The president had been driven to a state of cold fury by the downing of the A300. He was swearing that the Iranian people would be avenged.

And if they couldn't deliver what he wanted? Then the vengeance would fall upon the men who failed to deliver the retribution he demanded. Of that there could be no question.

If this didn't get done, then they were all as good as dead.

'An American plane?'

Mehrak wheezed, blowing air through his gappy, nicotine-stained teeth, making a sound like the air coming out of a punctured tyre. He reached into his pocket, fished out some cigarettes, and flipped one into his mouth before lighting it up. A small, angry cloud of smoke started to swirl around his face.

'That's what I said,' snapped Farhadi.

'Okay, okay, I hear you,' said Mehrak.

'Can it be done?' asked Saeedi.

Mehrak started to chew at the fingernails of his left hand. There wasn't much left: just scabby, gnawed pieces of skin topped out by flakes of nail. 'There's one man . . .'

'You can't do it yourself?' asked Saeedi.

'It's a science,' said Mehrak. 'Planes don't come down out of the air by themselves, you know. This will take preparation. It will take planning, lots of it. Most of all it will take expertise. But there is a man . . .'

'Who?'

'A man called Ahmed Shabaan,' said Mehrak.

A slow smile started to spread across Farhadi's lips. 'The Falcon . . .'

'That's the guy,' said Mehrak.

'Tell me about him,' said Saeedi.

41

They were sitting in a small room, in a large private house, just off the Vozara, a smart suburb of northern Tehran, which, before the revolution, had been home to many of the ministers in the shah's government. Its opulent, leafy villas were starting to fade, but behind the ornate flowers that covered their facades you could still catch glimpses of the wealth that was once contained within. The VEVAK maintained a villa here: not so much a safe house as a resting place. Agents were parked here when the agency didn't want to put them in a hotel. Diplomats would sometimes be allowed to stay overnight. And senior officials of the VEVAK would come here when they wanted to make certain that no one was listening to anything they said.

'The Falcon?' said Mehrak.

From the expression on his face, it looked as if he was wondering where you would possibly start.

'He was born in a town called Arcelia, about a hundred miles south-east of Mexico City, but he's actually Jordanian, at least he's believed to be. Some people say that he rose up from the sewers fully formed. Nobody knows too much about his parents. His father was some kind of engineer, working on bridges or something, and his mother was nothing. He was an only kid, and he's still like that. He works alone. He left university, and joined the Mexican Communist Party when he was nineteen. The Mexican Commies are a vicious bunch of bandits, little more than criminals. Even Moscow didn't want much to do with them, even though they would have loved nothing more than to bring Mexico under Communist control.'

He stubbed out his cigarette, then quickly lit another one. 'Then he came to Europe, and drifted into some of the radical Communist groups that dominated the mid 1970s. The Red Brigades in Italy, all that crowd. They were just middle-class students, of course, at least most of them. But there were a few who were the real business, particularly in

Baader-Meinhof. For a while there, they were right out there on the cutting edge, developing the techniques of modern terrorism, and the Falcon was right there alongside them.'

'Did he help out on some of their jobs?'

Mehrak shrugged, jabbing his cigarette into the air like a gun. 'Probably. That's the myth anyway. He honed his techniques in Europe, then moved across to the Palestinians. Some people reckon he was working for the KGB by this stage, that they'd tapped him up, given him some more training, then pushed him into the PLO to edge that organisation further towards terrorism. Maybe it's true. Or maybe the Falcon went of his own accord. He was never a man for following orders. Either way, he soon became the key architect of the PLO's terror strategy. He led the executions of two senior Mossad officials, one in Paris, and one in Strasbourg, and as we know, not many people manage to outsmart the Mossad. They sent everything they had to try and get him, but they failed. The Falcon was too smart for them. Over the next ten years, he bombed and killed and tortured his way around the world. The Falcon was the brains behind at least three PLO-directed hijackings of planes, maybe more. He was the man who let off at least eight major bomb explosions in cities around the world, killing more than 200 people. And he performed countless hits, striking fear into the hearts of the Israelis. The Mossad aren't afraid of very many people, and neither are the CIA. But they learned to fear the Falcon, and with good reason.'

'And then?' said Saeedi.

'He retired.'

'So he's no use to us. We're not looking for retired assassins . . .'

'Not quite retired,' said Mehrak.

'More like a vacation,' said Farhadi.

'He became disillusioned, so the story goes,' said Mehrak.

'I've never met the man, so I only have this second or third hand. About five years ago, he lost faith in the Palestinian cause. Not in its people, but its leadership. You have to remember that the Falcon was first and foremost a Marxist. He believed in a worker's state, and he thought destroying Israel was one step towards that. Then, he started to have his doubts. Maybe he'd been to the Soviet Union once too often. That's usually enough to cure most people of any faith in Communism. Anyway, he quietly withdrew from the Palestinian cause.'

'But he still works,' interrupted Farhadi. 'As a freelancer, and as a criminal. And probably one of the best in the world.'

'So if we could contact him, and if we could persuade him, then he would be the man,' said Mehrak. 'Because if anyone can bring down an American plane then it is, without question, the Falcon.' He glanced towards the window, tossing the remains of his cigarette into the dirt and scrub beneath it. 'And only the Falcon.'

'But can we trust him?' asked Saeedi.

'He's a terrorist,' said Mehrak.

'And a Marxist,' said Farhadi.

Saeedi nodded. He walked towards the window. It was late in the day and the sun was starting to set in the distance. Before the day finished, he would have to talk to the president. And the first question he would ask – probably the only question he would ask – would be when the American plane was to be brought crashing to the ground.

'Do we have any alternative?'

Mehrak shook his head. 'If we want the job done, and we want it done quickly, then no.'

44

# EIGHT

**London, 12 November**

She moves through the shop as if she works here, Sam noticed.

Orla paused over a desk, then glanced up to look at Sam. She looked slightly different today, he decided. Her skin was fresher, her lips were redder, and her cheeks were smoother, although he felt certain she wasn't wearing any make-up. And there was a sparkle to her eyes, as if she was trying to hold on to a secret.

'I don't owe you anything yet,' said Sam.

'But you're about to,' Orla replied.

Sam walked out from behind his desk. It was just after eleven on a cold, damp November morning. Some light drizzle was spitting out onto the street outside, and some workmen were splitting open the pavement twenty yards away with their jackhammers and drills. It wasn't the best of mornings to be running any kind of shop: but in the antiques business, this was about as dead as it would ever get.

'One of your customers was looking for a piece by Anne Seymour Damer,' said Orla. 'I overheard him discussing it with you. A rich City guy, so he probably pays pretty well.' She paused, her eyes rolling up towards Sam. 'I can get one for you.'

Sam paused. There had been a man coming into the shop just as Orla had been leaving last time. A guy called Richard

45

Best, he'd made a packet of money when all the City stockbrokers were sold to the Americans after Big Bang. He kept a place in Chelsea, and another one in the country, and they both required a lot of furnishing. He was slow, and pedantic as well, Sam had discovered: he kept on searching for the right thing, for years if necessary, mainly because it filled up his days, but if you did find something he liked then he didn't mind spending good money on it.

'I wouldn't have thought you'd have heard of Damer,' said Sam.

'She lived in Sundridge in Kent, and she was the daughter of Henry Seymour Conway, the field marshal, who was briefly also the commander-in-chief of the British Army. In Lord Rockingham's government, if I remember correctly.'

'Which was . . .'

'July 1765 to July 1766, then again for three months in 1782,' said Orla. She spoke quickly, with the manner of someone who didn't like being bothered by details. 'Not one of the more distinguished holders of the post. Anyway, Damer turned to sculpture after her husband committed suicide, even though it was rare for women to become artists in those days, and ever rarer for aristocratic women. But she made a great success of it. Probably her best-known works are the heads of the river gods Isis and Thame, which you'll find on the bridge at Henley-on-Thames. But she also produced an over-life-size marble statue of George III, as well as loads of classical portrait busts of all the greats of the time. Caroline, the Princess of Wales, and Nelson, of course. For a decade or so every merchant on the make in London wanted a Damer bust done of themselves, their wife, and probably one of their mistress as well. It was a bit like having a top of the range Mercedes.'

'How much time did you spend in that library?'

'Not enough.'

'And you reckon you can find one?'

46

'I already have.'

Sam couldn't help himself from smiling. In the couple of days since Best had been into the shop, he'd thought a few times about where he might be able to find him an original Damer sculpture, but he hadn't got any further than checking her out in the reference books. He certainly hadn't gone as far as picking up the phone yet.

But Orla claimed to have already located one.

'Where?'

Orla walked through to the back office. Sam started to follow her, noting again the ease with which she moved through what was after all his property. She perched herself on the edge of his desk, and folded her arms across her lap, ruffling her skirt back down to her knees as she did so. 'One sculpture she did was of the Earl of Tiverton,' she said. 'It's a minor piece of its kind. She did one of the earl, and one of his daughter as well. Now, that's where it gets interesting. You see, she caused something of a stir by marrying a Polish nobleman and going to live in Krakow. Not the sort of thing that a nicely brought up girl was meant to do in those days. Anyway, my guess was that she took the statue with her. A girl wouldn't want to leave that behind. In which case it might be knocking around the area still.'

'And is it?'

'It's in the foyer of the Polish Engineering Society's clubhouse, which happens to be in Krakow. Just an ornament really. I spoke to the guy there, great bloke, and he said they didn't really know what it was, except that it was English in origin, and pretty old. All the armies they've had trudging their way through that country in the last two hundred years, it's a miracle it's survived at all, but the thing about a Damer is it's nothing that special, it's only a real collector that would value it, so I guess people just thought it was an ordinary bust and left it alone. It was donated to the society in the 1890s apparently, and has been there ever since.'

'I wonder if they'd be willing to sell it.'

A glimmer of a smile started to crease up Orla's face. 'Of course they would,' she said. 'A society like that is always short of funds.'

'Yes, but for how much, that would be the issue.'

'$80,0000.'

'You already asked?'

'Well, without a price, it's just some mouldy old piece of plaster sitting in a dusty corridor in Poland, isn't it?' said Orla.

She walked across to the corner of the office where Sam kept a kettle, a coffee jug, and some cups. 'You want some?' she said, glancing back at Sam as she did so.

'Make it a strong one,' answered Sam.

'I mean, I don't even like her stuff very much,' said Orla. 'A lot of it looks like the kind of tack you'd buy out of a catalogue to smarten up a suburban garden in Cheshire. And I reckon the Polish engineers aren't that into it either. A few beers and some sausage, that's the kind of thing they want.'

She put three heaped spoons of ground Colombian coffee into the pot, stirred in the water, and handed the steaming cup across to Sam. She added one sugar to her own, taking a sip reflectively. 'So why don't you call him, and see how much he wants to pay for it?'

Sam walked across to the desk. He kept all the numbers of his best customers in a black directory, in the second left-hand drawer. Richard Best answered the phone on the third ring. The conversation only lasted a couple of minutes. Some moaning about the rain, some pleasantries about the state of the stock market, then straight down to business. That was what Sam liked about men such as Best. They knew precisely what they wanted and what they were willing to pay for it. In the markets, they lived by their ability to price things accurately and instantly: once learned, that was a skill that never abandoned you. 'He says he'll pay

$120,000 for it,' said Sam. 'Assuming it's in decent condition, of course.'

The gleam in Orla's eyes was growing brighter. Sam was already running the mental calculations through his head. If they paid $80,000 for the bust, that still left them a clean profit of $40,000. It was more money than the shop had taken in the past six months, and more profit than it had made in the past year. And it was all sitting right in front of him, tastefully decorated on the plate.

*I just have to reach out and take it.*

'I still won't take your investigation,' he said, looking straight at Orla.

She shrugged. It was no more than a tiny flexing of the shoulder muscles, but it seemed to Sam she was tossing aside his remarks as an irrelevance. 'Then hire me,' she replied. 'You can see I'm good at this.'

'I can't afford staff,' growled Sam.

'Then I'll work on commission,' said Orla. 'I source a piece, we make a profit, and I get a cut.'

'How much?'

'Twenty-five per cent of everything I bring in,' said Orla. 'On the deal we just did, you'd owe me $10,000.'

'It's too little,' said Sam. 'You're doing all the hard work. You deserve much more.'

'I know,' replied Orla, a smile starting to flitter across her lips. 'But this way you *owe* me.'

# NINE

## CIA Headquarters, Langley, 12 November

Bill Horton looked down at the four photographs on his desk.

He examined the faces, peering into them, wondering what it was they might have in common. His knuckles tapped against the hard wood of his desk. Why them? he asked himself.

*Why the hell them?*

Slowly, he stood up and walked across to the window. His office was on the second floor of the complex of granite-grey buildings. When he became Operation Director of the agency a year ago, he'd been entitled to a bigger, grander office, up on the third floor, close to the suite for rooms occupied by the director himself. But Horton preferred to remain here. He'd occupied this office for five years now, directing the agency's Middle East operations, and although he was not a man who furnished places – even his own house still had the same rented furniture it had had when he moved in – there were enough mementos here to make it feel like somewhere he belonged.

There was a pair of horns from an Arabian oryx that had been given to him by one of the Gulf emirs. There was a map of the Euphrates that showed all the smuggling routes along that great river. And there was a finely polished Colt SSP stainless steel pistol that, he'd occasionally tell visitors to this room, told a long story, but one he'd vowed to take to the grave with him. Those were all reasons for staying in this office. But mainly he remained because this was where all the Middle East analysts had their desks. And it was where the field agents spent their time between missions.

Stay in the thick of the action, he told himself occasionally. Once you move upstairs, you become just another pen-pusher. And what's the use of that?

Horton was sixty-three now, and had spent his entire career in the service of the American state. After five years in the navy, he'd gone straight into the intelligence agency. After a couple of years of training, he'd gone into the Middle East service, spending several years in the field, with postings in Tehran, Damascus, and Tel Aviv. When he'd started, it had been something of a backwater. All the ambitious young men had wanted to clash swords with the KGB on the Russian desk. Or else work in Japan or Korea. But Horton had disagreed. He felt certain that the Middle East was where the real conflict for the United States was going to come. And when it happened, he wanted to be in the thick of it.

He'd remained unmarried, always living in a small, rented apartment close to the office. He had few friends outside work. The agency was his life, his entire purpose. He would do anything for it.

He looked back at the pictures. Four names were written alongside them, although they were already etched into the back of his mind. Mark Slota, Marie Holt, Ed Ryan, and Alicia Pisani. As he scanned their faces, he could see instantly what they had in common. It was completely obvious. They were all young, attractive, and presentable. A mixture of men and women. They all had families that cared for them, people they had to look after, people who would be waiting for them to return. It was simple really. They all had stories. And that was what would make them, in the right hands, such a potent weapon.

When the hell did our enemies become so smart? Horton asked himself.

Smarter than us, maybe.

Because they realise that against a well-spun narrative, all our weapons, our fleets and our armies, are completely useless.

The news had been broken late last night.

Released via one of the local Arab newswires – an outfit based in Damascus that the CIA already knew was in reality little more than a press office for Hamas – it stated simply that four American hostages had been captured in Beirut. They had been taken to a secret location. They had not been harmed. Not yet anyway. They would be released on two conditions. Thirty Palestinian prisoner held in Israeli jails had to be released immediately. And $30 million in gold, diamonds, and platinum had to be deposited in a bank in the Lebanon. 'They will share the suffering of the Arab people, held in captivity by the American-Zionist conspiracy,' it stated. 'And through them, all the American people will share the suffering of the Arab people.'

Naturally, it had caused a sensation in the American media.

It was the splash on the front pages of hundreds of news-papers across the country. They all had their own spin, but the spine of the story was the same in every case. Innocent Americans caught up in a brutal war, the victims of callous terrorists who cared nothing for their safety.

On the commentary pages, there were a dozen different analyses of the crisis. They could send in a hit squad to try and get the hostages out. They could pay the ransom demanded. They could lean on the Israelis to release the prisoners. If they wanted to, they could hang tough, leave the hostages right were they were, and let the terrorists decide on the next move.

Thanks guys, thought Horton as he read the pages and

pages of commentary. We already know all the damned options, thank you very much. We knew them as soon as the news had flashed up on the wire service.

It was just that we didn't really like any of the options very much.

In the end, the question posed was always the same: What is the government going to do about it?

Well, that's us, thought Bill.

And what are we going to do?

*I already know the answer to that question*

I just have to persuade the rest of the committee.

And send our recommendation up to the president.

The decision is his, of course, thought Horton.

But the truth is, he'll do what we tell him.

*Because he won't have any other options.*

# TEN

## Damascus, Syria, 12 November

Mehrak looked through the lobby of the hotel. Damascus claimed to be the oldest continuously inhabited city in the world, but there was nothing ancient about the Four Seasons. It was a brash, modern, chain hotel, its ceilings decorated with gaudy brass and crystal chandeliers and its floors covered in plush, thickly matted beige carpet. Mehrak didn't linger, walking swiftly through to the tea room. He never felt at home in places like this. It wasn't the travelling businessmen he minded, nor the diplomats, nor the queues of chauffeur-driven cars blocking up the driveway.

It was the spies.

He looked through the room, checking for anything suspicious. Even by Iranian standards, Syria had what Mehrak judged to be some of the most ruthless secret policemen in the world. Most countries had one intelligence agency. Some even had two. Syria, however, had four.

There was the Political Security Directorate, or the Idarat al-Amn al-Siyasi, charged with monitoring any sign of political activity, and also with keeping tabs on every foreigner who came into and out of the country. There was the General Security Directorate, or the Idarat al-Amn al-'Amm, charged with monitoring the Syrian population, as well as a separate division that kept an eye on all the Palestinian groups within Syria. Then there was the Military

Intelligence, or the Shu'bat al-Mukhabarat al-'Askariyya, charged with collecting files on all the senior military officers, and tasked with making sure the soldiers stayed loyal to the ruling Ba'ath Party: a subdivision was also charged with providing military assistance to Turkish, Lebanese, and Palestinian terrorist groups.

Then, lastly, there was the Air Force Intelligence, or the Idarat al-Mukhabarat al-Jawiyya. Despite its name, the Idarat didn't have much to do with the air force (it acquired the title because Syria's President Assad had been in the air force). But this was the most fearsome of all the four intelligence agencies, the one charged with spying on all the other spies. It was a country of mirrors, with every agency suspicious of every other agency. Mehrak sometimes wondered if Syria had more spies than it had people: maybe everyone was a double agent, spying on themselves. It certainly made it one of the countries in the world where you least wanted to be operating as an enemy agent. They kept tabs on everything. And nowhere was kept under tighter surveillance than the big international hotels.

It didn't matter whether you were a guest or not – and Mehrak was far too cautious to ever consider staying in a place like this – just the fact you could afford to buy a drink here meant at least one of the intelligence agencies wanted to know who you were and what your business was. Quite possibly all four of them.

It wouldn't take much to make him flee, decided Mehrak. Just a single glance from a man sitting by himself. A sudden quietening of the conversation between two businessmen as he walked past. Or a women bending down to pick up a fallen letter, then looking in his direction. Anything at all to suggest anyone at all was taking the slightest interest in him, and Mehrak would leave immediately. That was the only way to stay alive in Damascus. You didn't stop and think. On the slightest suspicion, you just ran.

Ibrahim Hueiji wasn't there yet. Mehrak checked his watch. It was just after three in the afternoon. The hotel's café overlooked a cool, shaded garden with a fountain at its centre. Mehrak carefully poured himself some tea, using the cup to partially shield his face. He'd worked with Ibrahim Hueiji before. A fat, sweaty man in his early fifties, he spent his whole life in the only career that, in Mehrak's opinion, Syrians were any good at: the noble profession of fixer and middleman. He made introductions and opened doors. What happened once the door had been squeezed ajar was no concern of his. If anyone knew where Shabaan could be contacted – whether indeed he was currently living in Damascus at all – then he would.

'You're looking well.'

Hueiji was standing next to him, extending a greasy palm. He was wearing a linen suit, and there was a bead of sweat rolling across his forehead, even through it was cool and autumnal outside. How the man managed to get through a Syrian summer without sweating off a single pound of weight, Mehrak couldn't imagine. He smiled briefly then offered him some tea, pausing while the man gulped it down, and reached for one of the several fruit and chocolate biscuits the waiter had placed on a tray.

'Since when were the VEVAK welcomed in Damascus?' said Hueiji.

His eyes had narrowed, and he was scrutinising Mehrak's face for some kind of reaction.

'I'm freelancing.'

Hueiji laughed. 'Even worse,' he said. 'Here in Syria we don't like foreigners meddling in our affairs, but at least with an intelligence agency you know what you are dealing with. Freelancers are just trouble.'

Mehrak shrugged. He knew Hueiji liked to pretend he had official connections. He had a desk at the Idarat, but whether he spied on spies, or spied on the spies who were

56

spying on the spies, it was impossible to tell. In reality, he was a freelancer as well. He brokered information to the highest bidder, and it didn't make much difference whether that was his own government or someone else's.

'I'll only be here a few days so long as I get what I want.'

'Which is . . .'

'Shabaan.'

'The Falcon?'

Mehrak nodded. 'He's here in Damascus. There a job . . . something that would be perfect for him.'

'We wouldn't tolerate a known terrorist like that, not in Damascus.'

Mehrak glanced around, double-checking that no one was watching them, then dropped his voice down to no more than a whisper. '$10,000 says he is.'

'In cash.'

Mehrak nodded.

He could see into the eyes of the man opposite him. In the flesh around his squinting brow you could see the profits being calculated. Already a mental shopping list was being prepared: an air-conditioning unit, a second-hand Mercedes, a holiday in Europe, he was checking off all the things a few minutes of work might buy him. Things he wanted.

'For an introduction, that's all,' hissed Mehrak.

'Wait here.'

Mehrak refilled his cup, and raised the hot tea to his lips. Across the room, he could see a woman glance at him, then look away. A wide-brimmed black hat was covering much of her face. Attractive, he noticed. But maybe a spotter, wondered Mehrak. He knew the Idarat, as well as the other intelligence agencies, placed women in all the smart hotels. Men were always much more willing to catch their eye. The VEVAK did exactly the same thing, and it netted a fresh haul of plotters and conspirators for the nation's jails every week.

He looked away. I'll wait five seconds, he told himself. If she looks at me again, then I'm out of here.

He counted down the time. One, two, three . . . but the women had been joined by a friend, and was already looking away from him.

'Go to the Souk al-Hamidiyeh,' said Hueiji.

He was standing over Mehrak's left shoulder. Briefly, the Iranian was startled: distracted, he hadn't seen him coming, and he could feel his hands shaking. He steadied himself. Maybe my nerves are getting too frayed for this kind of work, he wondered to himself.

Maybe . . . but what else would I do?

'What will I look for?' he asked, glancing back at Hueiji.

He knew the Souk al-Hamidiyeh, one of the most famous street markets in the whole of the Middle East. A twisty maze of streets, it covered hundreds of square metres, and had literally hundreds of shops and stalls.

'A stall specialising in exotic birds, run by a man called Anwar,' said Hueiji. 'Macaws, cockatoos, Senegals, African Greys. Just about anything.'

'And sometimes a Falcon?'

'If you look carefully enough.'

Mehrak pulled out an envelope from his jacket pocket. He handed it across. '$5,000,' he said.

Hueiji was about to speak, but Mehrak raised a single finger to his lips.

'Tomorrow,' he said softly. 'You'll get the rest of the money tomorrow. So long as I find what I'm looking for.'

'Today,' snapped Hueiji.

'It's too difficult,' protested Mehrak.

'You've no idea how much danger we are in just acknowledging that the Falcon exists . . .'

But I do, thought Mehrak.

And that's why I'm not taking any chances.

*Or trusting anyone more than I have to.*

# ELEVEN

## CIA Headquarters, Langley, 12 November

Bill Horton paused for a moment before asking his secretary to send the three men into his office. He knew the weight of the decision he was taking: he could feel it pressing down on his shoulders, like a sack, making him feel tired and old. But what choice do we have? he asked himself. Either we let these scum break us. Or we break them.

Once you put the question like that, there was really only one answer.

'Send them through,' he snapped, aware of the irritation in his voice.

He reached for a bottle of still mineral water, hoping it would calm him down. He could use a proper drink, but it didn't look good to take any alcohol inside this building. The CIA respected men who could hold their nerve: alcohol was taken as a sign of weakness, and that was the one quality in a man the agency didn't tolerate.

Jim Prentiss, Scott Valentin, and Ben Hanold walked slowly into the room. You could tell something from the order in which they entered, decided Horton. Nominally all three men were completely equal to one another. But like any group, they quickly formed their own hierarchy. Prentiss was clearly the most senior of the three men, and he came in first, followed by Valentin and Hanold. He has established his own form of dominance, judged Horton,

59

although how he couldn't tell. To his eyes, all three of them looked about as alpha as the male species could get.

Prentiss, at thirty, was the oldest of them, but only by a year. A Navy Seal by training, he had joined the agency two years ago, assigned to special operations. Six foot tall, with tanned skin, and rugged good looks, his record was flawless: there had been operations in Colombia and the Philippines that had been executed perfectly. His parents had both been in the military, his father a pilot, and his mother a nurse, and so had his two older brothers. To Prentiss, a military career had always seemed the only option. He never even considered anything else.

Scott Valentin was darker, stronger looking, a man who'd joined the agency out of the air force, and still had some of the wild exuberance of a born pilot about him. Scott was an only child, who had grown up in Alaska: his father Chuck Valentin had been in the oil business, opening up the vast icy wilderness of the north to the drills and the rigs. Scott had grown up loving the outdoors, passing his days on long treks through the mountains and the snow. He'd joined the air force because he loved the sense of space and freedom a man got when he was up in the sky, by himself, locked up within his own aircraft.

Ben Hanold had joined from the marines. He was the shortest of the three men, only five foot ten inches tall, but his muscles were built like lumps of rock. Of the three of them, he was the quietest, but maybe also the smartest, judged Horton. He didn't talk very much, but he listened, and there were few more valuable skills than that. Of the three of them, he was the odd one out. His father Daniel had been a lawyer in Boston, and his mother taught at the university. His elder brother Tom worked in Dad's law firm, and his younger sister Emily was working for Lehman Brothers on Wall Street. None of them could understand his choice of career, and they treated it with open contempt during family gatherings. His parents had protested against the Vietnam War, and had zero respect for the military and everything it stood for.

But not Ben.

To him, if a country wasn't worth fighting for, it wasn't worth living in either.

And so he put up with his family's ridicule, knowing that the work he did made their days in soulless offices seem irrelevant.

To all three men, working for the agency was just an extension of their military careers.

They just didn't have to wear a uniform, that's all.

'These hostages in Beirut,' said Horton, looking straight into the eyes of the men opposite him. 'We are going to go in there and take them out.'

The decision had not been taken lightly. Horton had already made up his mind before he went into the meeting, but it didn't automatically follow that he could get everyone else to agree with him. The Director General was there, along with representatives from the State Department, and Defense. None of the president's pollsters or political operatives were there, Horton noted, but that didn't mean they wouldn't be getting a full briefing on every word they uttered. In the end, these hostages had been captured as a political act, and the response from the United States would have to be political as well. That was the way the world worked.

You fought politics with more politics.

He'd argued his case forcefully. They had, in reality, only three choices. They could negotiate with the hostage-takers. That didn't have to mean giving them precisely what they wanted. They could get a skilled mediator, preferably from one of the countries that maintained tolerable relations with Hamas: the Italians could find them the right person, or, failing that they could use the Egyptians. They could find

61

out more about what they wanted. They might be able to lean on the Israelis to offer them some concessions. If they needed to, they could even give them some money. That's what the French would do in the same position.

But no. That wasn't the way to handle this. Once you opened up that door, you could never shut it again.

If the Lebanese terrorists and the Palestinians and the rest of them thought they just needed to take a few American hostages and immediately start asking for whatever they wanted, then it would never end. There were millions of Americans travelling around the world every year. Even if you stopped them from going to Beirut, you couldn't keep them out of the rest of the world. This kidnapping would be followed by another . . . and another . . . and another.

It would never stop.

So talking to the terrorist wasn't a course of action any responsible government could contemplate.

Of course, you could just leave them where they were.

Tell the terrorists the United States government wasn't prepared to negotiate.

Horton couldn't help but wonder why they couldn't do that. After all, when the fate of nations were at stake, what did four lives matter? They weren't even people of any significance. Thousands of people were killed on the roads every week. Hundreds were shot dead in the ghettos. Shit happens, and sometimes it happens to you. Any of these individuals could have been run over in the street, or shot in a robbery, or killed by their lovers. If they died they died. If the United States just ignored the hostage-takers, told them they would be hunted down as murderers if they harmed them, but otherwise the government would make no response, then they would soon stop bothering. It wouldn't be worth the trouble if they were just ignored. The problem was, the media and the public would never stand for it. The hostages were already plastered over every newspaper. Their faces were filling up the airwaves. In some other country, maybe we could get away with that, reflected Horton. But not in this one. We're too sentimental . . . too soft.

And that left option three.

A rescue.

It had only taken a few minutes of discussion to arrive at that conclusion. After all, if you couldn't negotiate, and you couldn't leave them where they were, then there wasn't a whole lot else you could do except for go and get them out.

Except for the risks.

The agency didn't have a great record in breaking hostages out.

Slightly more than a decade ago, it had tried to break the hostages out of Iran. That mission – known as Desert One – had ended in disaster: one of the most embarrassing calamities in American military history.

Nobody wanted to repeat that.

Maybe they should talk to the Israelis. They were much better at this kind of gig, reflected Horton. Or even the British. The SAS might have the expertise to go over there, and bring the four of them out alive.

But no.

The risk of embarrassment was too great.

If the hostages got killed on an American-led rescue mission, the public could probably live with that. They'd respect the fact the government had done its best. But to contract the work out to the Israelis or the British . . . and then to screw it up?

Horton shook his head.

It didn't bear thinking about.

*That leaves us.*

And we'll just have to pray we get it right this time.

He looked across the desk. The three men sitting in front of him were solid, impassive, with the faces of poker players. 'And you're the guys who are going to do it.'

'Where are they, sir?' said Jim Prentiss.

Horton shrugged. 'Beirut.'

'Big place . . . sir.'

There was just a pause there, noted Horton. He skipped a beat before the sir.

'We don't know precisely where,' he said.

He spread a sheaf of papers on his desk.

'It's less than forty-eight hours since these people were picked up on the streets of Beirut. Our information is that they are being moved every twenty-four hours. So even if we do get a lead on where they are – and believe me, we are offering wads of dollars in every sewer in Beirut for anyone who wants to turn informant – the chances are they won't even be there anymore by the time we find out about it.'

'Who's telling us that, sir?' asked Ben.

The smart one, thought Horton to himself. The one who wants to know not just what the information is, but where it comes from. How do we know what we think we know, that's always the most lethal question. Because, more often than you'd care to admit, the answer is that you don't really know at all.

'The Israelis . . . the Mossad, mostly.'

'And they're telling us the truth?'

Horton paused before replying. 'You think they might not be?'

'It just seems to me the Israelis have plenty of motive for making Hamas as unpopular as possible with the American public,' said Ben. 'It makes them look like the good guys . . . for a change.'

Horton nodded, taking another sip of his mineral water.

'Which is why we should rely only on ourselves,' said Ben.

'Meaning?'

'I think we need to get on the ground, find out as much as possible about who's taken these people, and where they might be holding them,' said Ben. 'And then we can see how we're going to get them out of there.'

Horton smiled.

'Precisely,' he answered, his tone clipped and resolute. 'Which is why you three men are already booked onto the next flight to Beirut.'

# TWELVE

**London, 13 November**

Sam wasn't used to seeing the shop open so early.

He usually opened up around ten, ten fifteen in the morning. Ever since Elena and kids went back to Israel he'd been sleeping later: the children used to wake him around six thirty in the morning, but now he could sleep through to seven or seven thirty.

Breakfast, shower, and then a five-mile jog down the Pimlico Road, across Chelsea Bridge and around Battersea Park, before coming back to wake the shop up. Antiques traders, like poker players, weren't early morning people. They drank, they smoked, they cheated one another: those were all vices that took time to sleep off. Nobody in the business answered the phone until at least eleven, and by that time they were probably already halfway through their first drink of the day. The customers didn't bother touring any of the shops until lunchtime at the earliest. Antiques was a trade with its own clock, running from noon to midnight, and, the way Sam saw it, there wasn't much point in trying to change it now.

But when he came back this morning, the shop was already open.

There was even a customer.

The guy wasn't buying anything. Not yet anyway. But at least he looked interested . . .

'Top of the morning to you,' said Orla, breezily, slipping into an exaggerated Irish accent.

She looked different this morning, he noted. Make-up? he wondered. No. She hadn't gone that far. Sam allowed his eyes to linger on her for a fraction of a second before looking away. She'd changed shape, he decided. The baggy sweaters and shapeless jeans he'd seen her in so far had been replaced by a simple blue linen dress, with straps for shoulders, that stopped just a couple of centimetres below her knees. It tightened in at the waist, making the most of her slim, pert figure. The neckline was cut low, and her bra was pushing her breasts up, creating an inch of creamy white cleavage, decorated with a simple gold necklace with a cross on it.

Who's the dress for, wondered Sam. Me?

Or the guy looking at the antiques?

'A bit early for this business, isn't it?' said Sam.

He checked his watch. Nine thirty.

Usually he'd be having another cup of coffee up in the apartment he kept above the shop, reading the papers for half an hour, before coming downstairs to open up. Instead, the *International Herald Tribune* and the *FT* were already on his desk in the back room, alongside a fresh pot of Colombian coffee and a croissant from the café down the road.

'That's what everyone thinks.'

'Meaning?'

Orla gestured towards the street with a shrug of her shoulders. 'All the shops along this street are closed,' she said. 'None of them open up until ten thirty in the morning, and even then they look like they are still half shut.'

'There's a reason for that.'

'Which is?'

Sam poured two cups of coffee, stirring milk into his but leaving hers black. 'Same reason as you don't find any pubs in Mecca, or juice bars in Dublin, for that matter,' he replied. 'There aren't any customers.'

'What's that, then?' said Orla, her blue eyes darting towards the man who was standing in front of an ornate, gilt-edged chandelier hanging from the shop's ceiling.

'Some guy you lured in off the street by flashing him some cleavage,' said Sam. 'He's probably looking for a new light bulb.'

Orla took a sip of the scalding black coffee, grabbed half of the croissant she'd put out for Sam, and turned around. 'We'll see . . .'

Sam noticed the way she walked towards him. She approached the man slowly, almost casually, as if she was only walking towards the exit. She paused for a just a fraction, then glanced across at him, a half-smile playing across her lips. He looked about fifty, Sam judged. Tall, with sandy blond hair, he was wearing jeans and a blue blazer, and a decent pair of black half-brogue shoes. Maybe a City guy, judged Sam. Maybe one of the property developers who'd made a fortune in London all through the 1980s until the market suddenly crashed. Either way, he looked like he had some money. You could tell from the way people looked at antiques whether they could afford them or not: and this guy looked like he could pay for anything he wanted.

Sam looked down at the mail on his desk. There was a letter from Elena back in Tel Aviv. A short, curt note, he scanned it briefly. Both the kids were fine, it told him. There were settling into their new school. Both of them liked the new home. They'd made some friends in the apartment block they were living in. Then, she added, they needed some more money. The move had been expensive, and there were still loads of things to buy for the apartment. Sam sighed, reflecting that in the end marriages always ended up as a conversation about money. Still, he had the profits Orla had conjured up from brokering the deal for the Damer. The shipment had been arranged from Poland, and it should be in the hands of the client within the next few days. The end of the week at the latest. The profits on that should enable him to send a cheque for at least $5,000 across to Elena. Enough to keep her happy for a few more weeks. *Maybe she'll even start thinking about forgiving me.*

He glanced at the papers. The *Tribune*'s front page was dominated by the story of the four American hostages captured in Beirut. The photos showed them in their old lives: four average citizens with families, friends, and communities that worried about them. One of them was preparing to get married. Another was expecting a new baby.

Tragic, reflected Sam.

That's the trouble with that part of the world.

The violence just goes around and around, in an unending cycle.

The story detailed the demands that Hamas had made for their release: a swap for prisoners held in Israel, and a huge sum of money. The American government was quoted as saying every effort was being made to secure their safety, while condemning what it described as a 'brutal act of senseless terrorism'. Some pundits were reported as arguing that it represented a ratcheting up of tension in the Middle East that was already running high. Nobody thought the Israelis would agree to release their prisoners: the country had long since decided to resist terrorism, no matter what the price in blood, and it wasn't about to change that view now. Whether the United States would take the same view . . . well, nobody knew.

Sam folded the paper to the side of his desk. He could imagine his old colleagues back in the Mossad examining every detail of the story. The Americans would be leaning on them to use their contacts and sources in Beirut to find them some leads on where they might have to be taken, and the intelligence guys would be weighing up how much to tell them, how much to hold back.

Naturally, the Mossad had a network of sleepers and informers it had built up inside Hamas and the other radical groups operating out of Beirut. One of them might even know something about where the hostages were being held. But those contacts had been put there to defend the state of Israel. They existed for dire emergencies only. You could use them once, maybe twice, but no more than that. You certainly wouldn't want to waste them on saving the lives of four irrelevant Americans, regardless of how much coverage their plight might be getting in the media. The trick would be to persuade the Americans you were helping them. To feed them enough information to convince them you were straining every muscle to find their people. Maybe even setting up some fake leads, just so that it looked as if you were doing your best. While at the same time, keeping all the real information to yourself.

I'm glad to be out of that game. *Right out.*

He looked across the room, his attention captured by a fragment of conversation.

Orla was standing right next to the guy now. She was almost a foot smaller than he was, and couldn't have weighed more than 100 pounds compared with his 180, but she looked at least his equal. It wasn't an issue of size or weight, reflected Sam, as he watched the pair of them. It was an issue of presence. And she had more of that than a whole roomful of people.

'François Linke?' said Orla. 'Well, of course I've heard of him.'

'Then who was he?'

The man had already introduced himself as Brian Marchiony. Sam had a feeling he'd heard of him. He seen a piece in the *FT* about the new breed of hedge funds that had been set up to imitate the fortune that George Soros had made from breaking the pound as it struggled to stay inside the European Union's Exchange Rate Mechanism. They were starting to make some serious money, and Brian Marchiony controlled one of the fastest growing of the new funds. Get it right, and the business would mint money. No wonder he looked as if he could afford anything in the shop, decided Sam. You could always tell.

'Arguably, the greatest of all the French cabinet makers of the belle époque era,' said Orla. 'Born in Pankraz in northern Bohemia, I think, in what is now of course the Czech Republic. He moved to Paris in 1875, where he found work among the mostly German craftsmen who lined the rue du Faubourg Saint-Antoine. He got a big loan from his father-in-law, and set up his own shop at number 170. His pieces were big and gaudy, but the late Victorians loved them. Kaiser Wilhelm II bought one of his cabinets, and then after the First World War devastated the French economy, he was kept going by orders from King Fuad of Egypt among many others. Royalty always liked his stuff, mainly because it was so showy. It was a time when the phrase "nouveau riche" was coined, and Linke knew exactly what they wanted.'

She looked straight up at Marchiony. 'One of his pieces would look great in the foyer of your hedge fund,' she said sharply. 'Your clients would love it.'

'Because they're nouveau riche?'

'I didn't say that exactly.'

'But you meant it.'

Orla smiled, remaining silent.

'But where can I get one?' said Marchiony.

'Try Christie's, Sotheby's, the usual places,' said Orla. 'They'll be expensive, but if you have the money . . .'

'That wouldn't be a problem.'

'Then buy one.'

'There aren't any for sale. I've already asked.'

Orla folded her arms across her chest. 'If I could find one, what would you pay?'

'More than it's worth.'

'Why? You could just wait for one of the auction houses to put one in its catalogue, and then buy it for what it's worth, and no more.'

'I don't like waiting, Miss . . .' he paused. 'Miss . . .?'

'Sheehy. Orla Sheehy. You can call me Orla if you like . . .'

'Meaning "golden lady", unless I'm mistaken.'

Another flash of that brilliant smile, noted Sam.

'I already knew that.'

'Of course . . .'

Sam watched them talking, chewing on the rest of his croissant. They're flirting, he reflected sourly to himself.

'And anyway, Orla, by the time a Linke cabinet comes on to the open market, it might be worth a lot more than it is now. So if I could buy one now, I'd be saving money, wouldn't I? Even if I did have to pay more than it was worth now.'

'Then I'll find you one.'

'How?'

Orla laughed, throwing her head back.

'If I told you that, you wouldn't need me, now would you.'

Marchiony smiled, handing across a business card. 'Call me when you've found something.'

He had already left the shop by the time Orla turned around. She walked towards the back office, refilling her coffee cup. 'There, you see,' she said, a smile creasing up her lips. 'A customer, right? He didn't just come in here because he wanted to stare at my tits.'

'But he was . . .'

There was a slight reddening of her cheeks, Sam noted,

but it only took a fraction of a second for her face to turn normal again.

'You think there aren't any customers before ten because that's what all the antiques dealers think,' she said. 'None of the shops are open, so no one comes shopping. But the market is changing, the City is spreading west, and east down to Canary Wharf as well once they ever get around to finishing it. We need to be where there money is . . . and I just made a start.'

Sam shrugged. 'You got yourself an impossible commission.'

'Impossible?' said Orla.

The vowels in the word curled around her lips, Sam noted, as if they had a bad taste.

'A Linke's not like a Damer,' he said. 'She's minor, but he's big time. There aren't likely to be any hidden away, and, anyway, I can't afford to pay you to spend a few weeks wandering around the French countryside looking for one. If one comes on the market, then its owner is going to know it's valuable, and give it to one of the big auction houses.'

Orla looked dejected; her mouth curled down, and her eyes flicked across the floor. Sam wondered if he wasn't being too harsh on her. 'I'll find it,' she said. 'Just give me a few days.'

'So where are you going to start?'

It was impossible to hide the note of incredulity in his voice.

A Linke was so rare even Sotheby's would only get a couple every decade.

Orla was good.

*But not that good.*

'Same place I always start,' said Orla. 'With the facts.'

# THIRTEEN

**Damascus, Syria, 13 November**

The Souk al-Hamidiyeh twisted through a maze of streets. It was sited close to the Grand Umayyad Mosque, next to the southern walls of the old city. First built during the Ottoman era, in 1780, it had been doubled in size in the 1880s, and had been renovated and rebuilt several times since then. It was covered with a high iron vaulting that allowed only trickles of light to creep down into the stalls and alleyways below: enough so that you could just about see what you were buying, but not enough to be scalded by the fierce rays of the midday sun.

Mehrak liked souks, always had done. They were his kind of territory. They were marketplaces, and that was the environment he thrived in. You could buy and sell anything, negotiate and haggle your way through your entire life, and contemplate any act of betrayal or treachery. Sure, there were goods on sale here, but just like any marketplace, its real currency was information: an antiquity was only valuable if it was genuine, a gold bar if the metal was pure all the way through, and an animal if its health was perfect. You needed to know what you were buying and that took knowledge: and that was the commodity Mehrak had always been comfortable dealing with.

He twisted his way through the main entrance, walking quickly past the stalls selling cheap rugs, fake Arabic swords, and worthless collections of pewter cups. That was just rubbish for the tourists who wouldn't ever get more than a few yards into the interior of the souk. It was there, within the dark heart of the market, where only the occasional drop of sunshine managed to struggle its way through the thickets of metal and canvas, that you would find the items that really mattered.

The souk had its own hierarchy. The stalls near the entrance might look the most valuable – after all, only a few people would ever be willing to explore the entire marketplace – but there was always a limited amount of money to be made from ripping off the tourists. They never spent more than a few hundred dollars at most. It was inside that the real business got done. To the eastern side of the market, there were the antiquities dealers, trading in urns, manuscripts, statues, swords, manuscripts, and relics, some of them stretching back thousands of years. To the north, there were the traders in commodities: the gold, silver, and diamond merchants, men who could tell you the weight and value of a coin or a necklace just by looking at it and would pay you cash within an instant. Mehrak avoided both of them, heading south instead, into a narrow strip of shops, which could only be described as selling 'miscellaneous items': you could find everything here, from livestock, to herbal remedies, to machinery, weapons, and chemicals.

And, in this case, birds.

Anwar's stall wasn't hard to find. You could hear the birds singing from a hundred yards away: sweet, delicate shards of sound that sliced though the brawling racket of haggling, shouting, and complaining that filled up the souk like a sword slicing through rancid flesh. Mehrak was sure it was a macaw he heard first, chirping busily. Then a parrot, moaning like an old woman. He paused directly outside the stall. A grey-feathered Senegal was looking down at him with a beady red eye, appraising him as if he was a piece of food. He didn't mind that. All his life, Mehrak had liked birds. They were always cheerful, and if they didn't like a place, they just flew away. They were creatures after his own heart.

They owed nothing to anybody.

And they liked to keep moving.

'Are you looking for anything in particular?' said Anwar, after he'd finished dealing with a German man who was buying a parrot. The bird was already caged up, and the money exchanged, but the beast was squawking furiously as it left the premises, as if it already knew it was leaving its friends behind.

'A bird of prey,' said Mehrak.

He's already rehearsed the line. Hueiji had given him a precise set of instructions, detailing a conversation that had to be followed to the letter. The code was an elaborate one, but then the Falcon had evaded capture by the all the world's most accomplished intelligence agencies for more than a decade now, so it should be obvious he wasn't a man who took any chances. If he wanted to risk any lives, they were always other people's, not his own.

'An eagle maybe . . .'

'An osprey.'

'A Maynard, from the Caribbean, perhaps?'

'No, a Vieillot,' said Mehrak, 'from Tasmania.'

'Migratory, or non-migratory?'

Mehrak permitted himself a brief smile. It was a long, pre-scripted conversation, but you had to get it precisely right to prove that you were the man that was expected here. Get so much as a single word wrong, and you would be instantly turned away: indeed, the chances were, your throat would be cut before you even got out of the souk. The Falcon would not tolerate an impostor coming to look for him, not in this city of spies and traitors. Knowing that your existence hung on every word lent a charge to the conversation: Mehrak could feel his pulse quickening with every syllable that rolled by.

'Non-migratory, of course. The Vieillot doesn't migrate.'

'You are looking for me?'

The voice came from someone in the shadows, inside the interior of the stall. It was already dark here on the outside, with hardly any of the late afternoon sun successfully seeping down to this part of the souk, but as he stepped forwards Mehrak could feel the darkness fitting him like a glove. There were cages hanging everywhere, like the low-hanging fruit from a tree, and Mehrak had to brush them aside as he pushed forwards. It was the eyes he saw first. They were small and hard, peering out of the murky light like a pair of dimmed headlights.

The Falcon, he thought to himself.

*I've found you.*

'I believe so.'

He took another pace forward. Like every stall in the souk, Anwar's bird house was far larger than it appeared on the outside. A souk was always like that. They stretched back, sometimes for twenty-five yards or more. Sometimes the traders lived in the premises, sometimes there was a back room where they kept the items far too valuable to be put on public display.

And sometimes it was a hiding place for a man.

Ahmed Shabaan switched on a pale light. The room measured ten foot by seven: a cramped space even if it were empty, but this one was piled high with the paraphernalia of a bird trader: books detailing the plumage of the different breeds, cages, seeds, water filters, and a dozen different types of perch. Ahmed poured two cups of thick, sweet coffee from a pewter jug, handing one across to Mehrak, keeping the other tightly gripped in his right hand. He didn't drink it, noted Mehrak, but he seemed to enjoy holding the cup, as if he was drawing some strength from its warmth. 'You wanted to see me.'

Mehrak nodded. 'There's a job.'

There was a silence, interrupted only by the noise of an argument between two parrots.

'For the Iranians?'

Mehrak nodded.

'Organised by the VEVAK?'

Mehrak nodded again.

With a man like the Falcon, you didn't persuade or cajole, he told himself. There wasn't any point. You just told him what the job was, and then let him make up his own mind whether to take it or not.

Mehrak had followed his career for years now. It surfaced sometimes in the press, but mostly the legend of the Falcon was spread underground, passed by word of mouth among the aficionados of Middle Eastern terror politics. The stories of his stunts had been embellished over the years, Mehrak figured, but there were still more completed missions to his name than any other terror master in the region. He had been the Mossad's most wanted man for three years in a row, and not many men survived that particular accolade. But when he wanted to, he could slip right back into the darkness, disappearing from the surface of the planet, so no one was sure any longer whether he was alive or dead.

He'd read somewhere that when you met someone you'd admired for years, they were invariably disappointing: they were smaller, more ordinary, than you expected. That wasn't true of the Falcon, Mehrak decided. There was a flinty hardness to him, like rock, that spoke of his relentless determination. He was five foot ten high, and weighed 160 pounds: all of it so far as Mehrak could tell muscle, with no sign of an ounce of flab. His nose was long and straight, like a dagger, and his eyes close set, hooded by his brooding forehead. 'Let me guess,' said Ahmed, switching the coffee cup from one hand to the other, but still not drinking it. 'An airliner.'

It was the razor-sharpness of his mind that kept the Falcon in the game when so many other terror masters had been killed or captured over the years, reflected Mehrak.

He could see what other men couldn't.

'Why?'

Ahmed shrugged. 'You're the VEVAK, right?' he replied. 'The Americans have just brought down an Iranian Airbus carrying hundreds of innocent people. They say it was an accident. But they can't expect us to believe that any more than any of the other lies they peddle to our people. The Iranians can't stand by and allow that kind of incident to remain unpunished. What was it the prophet taught us? A life for a life, an eye for an eye, a nose for a nose, an ear for an ear, a tooth for a tooth . . .'

He paused, still toying with the coffee cup.

'Who are any of us to go against the words of the Koran? A eye for an eye, and an airliner for an airliner.'

'Quite so . . .'

'The issue is how you are going to do it,' persisted Ahmed. 'If the VEVAK felt it had the capacity for this operation, then surely the mission would already be under-way. If you had a sleeper somewhere in an airport who could smuggle a bomb onto a plane, then you would have already done so. But those things are not easy. So . . . you have come to me. Am I not right?'

Mehrak nodded. 'An American airliner, that's right,' he said. 'Anywhere in the world, it doesn't matter. But it must be a passenger plane, with plenty of people on board. That is what the president wants.'

'And you want me to do it for you.'

'There is nobody else.'

Ahmed considered the words, not as a compliment, but as a simple statement of fact.

'But I am retired.'

For a moment Mehrak was deflated. Maybe I've heard wrong, he wondered. Maybe the Falcon really had retreated into a life of peace and solitude. Perhaps he wasn't available for operations anymore. If so . . . his heart was pumping as he contemplated the possibility. To return to Tehran with nothing would be a humiliation. Maybe even something far worse.

A death sentence.

The president was determined that an airliner should be bought down.

And Mehrak was the man who was meant to deliver it.

'From terrorism,' continued Ahmed, a thin smile starting to crease up his face. 'But not from business.'

Mehrak smiled too. In the few seconds between the sentences, he'd been contemplating whether there was anyone else who could be assigned the task, whether he could even attempt it himself if he had to. But no. The Falcon was the only man who could deliver an American airliner. There might be someone else with the expertise. There might even be someone else with the cunning. But no one else had both.

'You'll do it.'

'For a fee.'

Mehrak paused. He was authorised to offer up to $300,000, but it would be a mistake to start at that figure. This was a souk after all. You were expected to haggle. 'The president will pay you $200,000,' he said. 'In cash, or delivered to a bank account of your choosing.'

Ahmed finally took the first sip of his coffee. 'I don't want to negotiate,' he said. 'Just give me your final offer, then I'll give you my answer.'

'$300,000.'

'How long will I have?'

'By Christmas.'

For the first time, Mehrak felt certain he saw a flicker of emotion on the Falcon's face: the granite shifted slightly as he digested the words. 'That doesn't give me much time.'

'To be effective, revenge must be swift.'

'But it makes it more difficult,' said Ahmed. 'A plane . . . it requires meticulous planning.'

'By Christmas,' said Mehrak. 'That is the president's demand.'

'Then $400,000,' said Ahmed. 'There will be more expenses. Everyone will have to work quickly.' He drained his coffee in one quick gulp. 'But it can be done.'

Mehrak permitted himself another smile. The Falcon was hooked, that was all that counted, he told himself. It might cost us $100,000 more than they initially estimated, but that mattered little. He could persuade his masters that the price was a reasonable one. So long as the plane came down, that was all that counted. 'I'll make sure the arrangements are made,' he said.

Ahmed reached for a piece of paper, handing it across to Mehrak. On it, there was the name of an engineering company based in Ghent, in Belgium. 'Place an order with this firm for twenty-eight precision lathes,' he said. 'The total cost will be $400,000, although needless to say the goods will never be delivered. The money will find its way back into my control, but it is better if you don't know the details of that. I work in total secrecy. The money should start being processed tomorrow as soon as the banks are open for business. You will not hear from me again, nor should you attempt to contact me for any reason. A plane will crash before Christmas, and that will be my side of the bargain.'

Mehrak stood up. 'May I ask . . . how?'

'There is always a way,' said Ahmed.

Mehrak was certain he could detect a hint of pleasure in the man's voice.

'They think their systems are perfect, but that is what they always think of their systems,' he continued. 'In truth, there are thousands of planes flying between hundreds of airports every day. In any network that wide, there is always an opening somewhere that a determined operator can slip through. I met an IRA man out in one of the training camps they use in Libya, and he put it this way: "They have to get lucky all the time, but we only have to get lucky once." And we will . . . but luck won't have anything to do with it.'

'And the Americans will know it was in retaliation for their attack on our plane.'

Ahmed nodded. 'We won't claim responsibility, but it will be revealed.'

'How?'

'Don't worry, I have already taken care of that. You see, I knew you'd ask me soon, and a plan has already been set in motion.'

# FOURTEEN

## CIA Headquarters, Langley, 13 November

Bill Horton looked down at the papers on his desk. There were three sets of them, divided into neat categories. One detailed the downing of the Iranian Airbus, and the furious reaction to it around the Middle East. Another updated him on the crisis surrounding the capture of four American hostages in Beirut. A third rounded up the rest of the developments in the Middle East: the usual collection of kidnappings, wars, coups, and revolutions that characterised daily life in that benighted region, he reflected sourly.

Horton sipped from a glass of water. He liked to read the briefing documents, often staying late into the evening, then taking another pile back to his apartment to scan over a microwaved pizza and a glass of brandy before he went to bed. There were plenty of executives within the agency who insisted that fieldwork was at the heart of its work: they argued, usually with pedantic insistence, that it was only out on the ground that you could make any realistic assessment of the challenges and opportunities that any situation presented. They spent their lives in aeroplanes, checking into and out of a dozen different Marriots every month, and clocked up more air miles than a United Airlines stewardess.

But Horton reckoned it was just because they wanted to get away from their wives and kids. The real work was done here in the head office, he always said. It was the men who read the papers — the desk cowboys as the field agents referred to them dismissively — who made the real break-throughs. Intelligence was about analysis, otherwise it was just data. It was only when you looked at all the different reports, coming in from all the different regions of the world, that you could start making the connections, putting together the telling details that allowed the wider story to emerge out of the shadows. A field agent could never do that. They were too close to the action. You needed to step backwards, to assess reports from a dozen different countries, to start unravelling a conspiracy, a trend, or a revolution.

And to do that, you had to read all the papers.

*It was the only way you could be certain that you hadn't missed anything.*

He'd scanned the papers on Beirut first.

His three agents had landed there already, but it was far too early to expect them to start producing any results. Although the government would never admit it to the media, the best response to any hostage crisis was always to delay. No news was always good news. From experience, Hamas would hold their prisoners for weeks, months, even a year if necessary: threats to kill them usually came and went without any action being taken. Over that time, the media would move on. The agency would start having space to move and breathe. Then they could strike.

Right now, the story was still hot. The papers were full of interviews and profiles from the hometowns of the hostages. On the ground, the CIA station in Beirut was getting dozens of reports of where they might be held. That was to be expected. Thousands of dollars were being offered to spies and informers, and that kind of money always attracted a swarm of entrepreneurs: the businessmen of terror that would crawl out of every café and souk in Beirut pretending that they knew something. All of them would be carefully checked out — when you did get a lead on a hostage it was invariably because one of the guards or drivers they were using decided they needed the cash they could make by turning informer – but at this stage it was unlikely they would lead to anything. It might be weeks, maybe months, before you make a breakthrough. *Until then, they would just have to wait.*

Horton was more worried about the reports coming out of Iran.

The story of the downing of the Airbus had been blown off the front pages. Maybe that was because the papers didn't want to linger for too long on what was clearly a terrible error of judgement by the US Navy. Damn them, thought Horton to himself, as he surveyed the latest briefings from Tehran. If you had to blow up a civilian airliner, couldn't you make it a British or German plane? Somewhere where they might understand that mistakes happen. If there was one country in the world you didn't want to give the impression of attacking it was Iran. *But it had to be one of their planes we took down.*

The embassy in Dubai – where the Iranian staff had relocated after the American Embassy in Tehran had been closed down – had sent through two briefing papers. The first detailed the demonstrations and protests that were growing in force in the Iranian capital against what they were describing as an unprovoked American attack. The usual militants were stirring up anti-American feeling, but, the paper warned, it seemed to have struck a popular chord. Ordinary Iranians felt themselves under siege, it said. They were at war with Iraq, and engaged in a stand-off with the US and all its allies around the world. They were ready to lash out, the way a cornered animal will. And that made them dangerous.

The second paper detailed the response from within the government. It admitted that its sources were patchy, and that it couldn't claim to be a cast-iron summary of sentiment within Tehran's ruling elite. But its analysis ran like this. The war with Iraq had reached a stalemate, it argued. The Iranians could hold their border, although at a terrible cost in young lives. They didn't have the strength to mount an overwhelming attack on Iraq. There was a chance the Iraqis would tire of the daily slaughter on the front lines but it was unlikely. The real worry was that the Iraqis would summon a regional alliance, maybe including the Syrians, the Jordanians, possibly even the Egyptians, into a wider war of Arabs against Persians. That would only happen, the Iranian leadership believed, with the support of the Americans. But they already regarded Saddam Hussein as an American puppet. And so there were some voices in the ruling clique arguing the shooting down of the Airbus was just a prelude to a wider American-inspired assault on Iran.

Dangerous times, reflected Horton to himself.

We need to convince the Iranians it was a mistake.

*But how do you have a conversation with a country that won't even talk to you?*

There was one paper from a man known only as the Persian Sleeper. It was tucked towards the bottom of the pile. The Sleeper was so secret, even Horton didn't know his real name. He was supposedly an official within the Iranian Defence Ministry. He'd been recruited in 1984 by Steven Berry, an agent who'd been stationed in Tehran before the shah was overthrown and maintained a network of contacts among the officials and diplomats who'd moved from one regime to the next with little change in their responsibilities. Maintaining any kind of mole within the Iranian regime was so dangerous only Berry had known the man's real name. His dispatches were contained in a regularly updated gardening bulletin sent to a horticultural society based in Basel in Switzerland, and decoded from there. But Berry had been killed trying to bring an East German defector through the border into West Germany in

1987 — as it happened, the last CIA man to die on that battlefront before that border vanished into history — and now no one knew anymore who the Sleeper was.

Or at least who he claimed to be.

Most people within the agency dismissed the Persian Sleeper as a fraud. The payments — $1,000 a month — were still made anonymously from a CIA front company to a cousin living in Santander in Spain, but most of the few people within the agency who knew about the Sleeper reckoned it was a scam set up by Berry to supplement his salary. His widow was still collecting the money, they argued. Plenty of the field agents pulled that trick, creating phoney sources, and routing their regular payments back to their own accounts. Berry was one of the wildest, most irresponsible field guys they had ever employed, that was why he had got himself killed: he was certainly capable of pulling a scam like that. Most people reckoned the bulletins were fakes written by someone in Spain in ten minutes to collect a useful pay cheque. If they had their way, the payments would have been stopped by now.

But not Horton.

He'd been reading his dispatches regularly over the years. And he'd always found then uncannily accurate.

They didn't predict events with precision. The Sleeper, he reckoned, was a mid-to-upper level official. He wasn't at the top of hierarchy, but he was close enough to pick up some of the whispers and gossip. There was plenty of dross in his reports. But if you sifted them carefully, there was sometimes a rough, unpolished diamond.

Like today.

'One rumoured response to the downing of the Airbus is for Iran to arrange for an American civilian aircraft to be destroyed, despite the inevitable loss of life,' it read. 'Plans are already being made.'

Horton paused, taking another sip of cold water.

An American airliner?

He wondered for a moment if that was possible.

Airline security had improved hugely in the past few years. Airports had been equipped with scanners and guards. Passenger ID was checked and double-checked before they boarded the plane. A plane was meant to be invulnerable.

But there was one lesson you learned early in the intelligence business.

Nothing was ever a hundred per cent safe,

Horton reached across for his notepad.

'Make sure our field agents around the world are put on high alert to watch for any possible attack on an American civil aircraft,' he scribbled.

After all, he reflected, the Sleeper had been right before. He might well be right this time as well.

# FIFTEEN

**London, 14 November**

To Sam, it didn't appear as if Michael Boaz had aged so much as a day.

It was a couple of years since he'd last seen him, but before that they spent five years together, part of the same hit squad that tracked down the most wanted Palestinian terrorists in the world. And eliminated them one by one.

Three of the men on that unit had died, Sam had quit the Mossad, and only Michael had stayed in the service. Until now.

'So listen to this one,' said Michael, looking across the desk at Sam. 'President Bush calls in the head of the CIA and asks, "How come the Jews know everything before we do?" The CIA chief says, "The Jews have this expression: '*Vus titzuch?*'". The president says, "Hell, what's that mean?" "Well, Mr President," replies the CIA chief, "it's a Yiddish expression which roughly translates to 'What's happening?' They just ask each other and they know everything." The president decides to personally go undercover to determine if this is true. He gets dressed up as an Orthodox Jew – black hat, beard, long black coat – and is secretly flown in an unmarked plane to New York, picked up in an unmarked car, and dropped off in Brooklyn's most Jewish neighbourhood. Soon a little old man comes shuffling along. The President stops him and whispers, "*Vus titzuch?*"'

Michael paused, the way he always did before delivering a punchline.

'The old guy whispers back: "Bush is in Brooklyn."'

Sam laughed.

We all had different ways of dealing with the pressure when we were working for the Mossad, he reflected. Some of us drank, some chased women, and I became obsessed with an antiques shop that was originally just set up as a cover and still struggled to make any money. It was all a way of hiding what we did for a living every day. But Michael told jokes, with the same resolute determination of a seven-year-old boy.

It worked for him, I suppose, decided Sam

'I quit,' said Michael suddenly.

Sam paused. The call had come out of the blue. Michael rang to say he was passing through London, suggesting he should drop round for a coffee. Of course, Sam told him. The same shop in the same place. Come as soon as you can.

'The Mossad?'

First this Orla girl turns up in my shop. Then Michael returns, like a ghost from the past. Could they be connected in some way? wondered Sam. Is there something I don't understand here?

He pushed the thought aside.

He had trained himself to be suspicious of everyone. But not Michael, surely. The man was the closest thing to a brother he'd ever had.

'Six months ago,' said Michael.

'Why?' asked Sam.

But as soon as he posed the question, he knew the answer. There is only so much meat any man can throw into the grinder. They kill us, we kill them, so we start killing them again. It just goes on and on, and nothing anybody does seems to change anything. Maybe killing one more terrorist will make a difference, but after a while, you just stop believing.

Even Michael . . .

'I'd had enough,' he said flatly. 'After we finished our mission, I think they didn't rate me anymore. The Mossad is like that. They reckon you have five or six good years in you, and once you've burned them up, they toss you aside. The jobs were getting smaller and smaller. If I'd stayed much longer, they'd have had me fixing the air conditioning.'

'So what are you doing now?'

'Same as the rest of us,' said Michael. 'Freelancing.'

Sam knew that well enough. He'd been down the same route himself, picking up the tough investigations that would sometimes be made available for the small numbers of former Mossad men who were available for private hire. That was how he'd been caught up in the Max Robertson mystery. There had been a couple of other investigations he'd taken on since then, although neither of them had had the same explosive impact. The truth was, he couldn't hope to make enough money from the antiques business to support himself and a family back in Israel. Not yet anyway. But he stayed away from that world as much as possible. It paid well, but there was a good reason for that. The customers expected you to put your life on the line. And if you got shot at too often, sooner or later one of the bullets was going to strike home.

'I need some help, Sam.'

'What's the job?'

Michael paused for a fraction of a second, and Sam could tell he was calculating how much he should reveal.

'We're scouring the Soviet Union, or what's left of it,' he said. 'There are assets that are coming up for sale, oil wells, gold mines, the rest of it. You wouldn't believe the scale of it.'

'But they're being sold to Russians, right?'

'Of course,' said Michael. 'But there are still some Jews left in Russia, even after everything the Soviet bastards threw at them. We're working with some investors in Tel Aviv. They put up the money, and we find the right men in Russia to buy up the oil wells and the gold mines. That way everyone is happy.'

'They can't be that happy . . .'

'Why?'

'If they were, they wouldn't be looking to put assassins on the payroll.'

Michael smiled. 'You were always the quickest of us, Sam, that's how you stayed alive so long. It's a rough trade, I won't deny that. The whole country has fallen apart, and the pieces are just lying around for anyone who wants to pick them up.'

'I'm not interested.'

'It's the chance of a lifetime.'

Sam grinned. 'If I had a pound for every one of those that had escaped me . . .'

Michael stood up. Sam could see the disappointment in his face. He didn't really need him on the team, he judged. If the money was as good as he was making out, then there would be dozens of guys willing to do the work. He was calling on Sam because he wanted an old face alongside him, someone he felt comfortable with. 'If you change your mind, call me,' he said, shaking Sam by the hand.

'I'm trying to stay out of that game.'

'It's in your blood, Sam,' said Michael. 'It never leaves you.'

As Sam watched him walk down the street he reflected on the truth of that. You missed the rush of adrenaline, that much was true. The mystery and the challenge as well. But you didn't miss the constant sense of mortality that stalked you like a shadow.

Antiques dealers may not make much money, decided Sam.

*But people hardly ever killed them.*

'I think I've found something,' said Orla.

'What?'

'A Linke,' said Orla. 'One of the originals.'

Sam nodded carefully. Maybe antiques wasn't so dull after all.

'Where?'

She paused before replying.

'That's the problem.'

# SIXTEEN

**Beirut, Lebanon, 14 November**

Dan Foley was a quietly spoken man. His hair was a light grey, but it didn't make him look old. His skin was relaxed and so was his smile. For a guy who's been running the CIA office in Beirut for three years he looks in good shape, reflected Jim Prentiss. Most men in that job would have chewed up their fingernails and torn up their scalps. But Foley had the look of a man who could absorb pressure the same way a sponge absorbs water.

Nothing gets to him.

*Not even this.*

Foley was a lifelong agency man. Some guys went into intelligence work after a spell in the military. Some guys after working in business. But Foley had joined straight out of Harvard. His father had been a diplomat, ending up as deputy ambassador to Spain, and it was either the agency or the State Department. He'd chosen the agency because you didn't have to wear a tie all the time. And you could choose your own hours.

'The point is, we don't have any idea where they are being held,' he said, his voice even and measured. 'We don't even have a clue leading to a clue.'

The unit – Jim Prentiss, Scott Valentin and Ben Hanold – had landed in Beirut's Rafic Hariri airport late last night, after a flight that took them first to Rome, then on to a connecting flight to the Lebanese capital. They had been met at the airport, and driven to an apartment the agency maintained in a block in the city's Baabda diplomatic quarter. This morning they had completed the ten-minute walk to the agency's Beirut bureau, located a discreet distance from the heavily guarded American Embassy. It was on the third floor of an ordinary office building, underneath a travel agency, and above a firm of structural engineers. They might all be fronts for foreign intelligence agencies, Jim had joked when they looked at the nameplates in the foyer. None of them seemed to be very busy.

Dan Foley had met them immediately, ushering them into a private room. Not pleased to see us, noted Jim, and he exchanged glances with Ben and Scott that confirmed that impression. They'd expected that. Everyone within the agency protected their turf as fiercely as any animal marks out its territory. No doubt so far as Foley was concerned, finding the hostages was his job. The last thing he needed was three guys from headquarters strolling in and telling him what he should be doing. They had to assume he wanted them to fail.

'I bet he'd rather the hostages were found dead in the harbour than allow us to rescue them,' Jim had joked as they rode up the lift together.

'No informants,' said Jim now.

'Hell, hundreds of then,' said Foley. 'This is Beirut. Even the sewer rats get fed up with the ethics of the locals sometimes. But nothing that has panned out yet.'

Ben leaned forward on the slim wooden table. 'Was it expected?' he asked. 'Any chatter leading up to the capture? Anything to make you suspect Hamas was about to pull a stunt like this?'

'Nothing that we picked up on.'

'So what's your assessment?' interrupted Scott.

Foley thought for a moment before replying.

'There are two possibilities,' he said eventually. 'They've made two demands, the prisoners and the money. It could be about either.'

'Hamas needs money?' asked Scott.

'Sure, the operation they are running in this country is expensive. Ever since the civil war started, the economy has been shot to pieces. Nobody is doing any business anymore, and so that means the protection rackets run by Hamas aren't yielding anything like the kind of cash they used to.'

'I thought the Iranians funded them,' said Ben.

'Up to a point,' replied Foley. 'But that isn't a bottom-less pit of money either. The Iranians have their own problems.'

'But it could be about the prisoners?' said Scott.

'Sure,' answered Foley. 'We've looked through the names they've issued of the guys they want released from Israel. Most of them are just low-level operators. Front line cannon fodder who have been picked up in the line of duty. It wouldn't have made much difference to anyone whether they were shot or captured. But there are a couple of names there, guys that are important.'

'Who are they?' demanded Ben.

He could see Foley hesitating, unsure how much information he wanted to release and how much to hold back. 'A guy called Maher Hussami is one of them. We weren't aware of his name before, but it turns out that he is one of the main guys involved in organising finance for Hamas. He knows where all the bank accounts are. The Israelis have squeezed some of the information out of him, but not all of it. Then there is a guy called Bani Ershaid. He's involved in arms shipments, liaising with the Russians, the Chinese, the Libyans, even the IRA over in Britain, bringing in all the weapons Hamas needs. He knows all the smuggling routes, and all the places you have to go to buy the latest hi-tech kit, and even how much you should be paying for it. I reckon they want to get both guys out of Israeli jails pretty badly.'

'Any ideas where they are being held?' asked Ben.

'Like I said, not even clues about clues.'

'But techniques . . .'

'The modus operandi for hostage-taking is pretty well established, as I'm sure you know,' said Foley. 'There's no real science to it. You have a network of friendly houses, and you move the hostages from place to place, usually on a twenty-four-hour cycle. You use anonymous addresses, and you keep the information limited to as small a group of people as possible.'

'Until someone squeals . . .'

'Right,' said Foley. 'But even if they do, it's probably going to be too late.'

'But no one's talked yet.'

'Lots of people are talking. But nothing substantial.'

'So how the hell can we get a lead?' demanded Jim.

'Bribery,' said Foley. 'We need to find someone who wants money badly, and is willing to talk. That person won't come to us. We have to go to them.'

'And . . .'

'And we're working on it,' said Foley, not bothering to disguise the irritation in his voice. 'You guys think you can do better, then you're welcome to try. Believe me, no one would be more pleased than I would to see the hostages come out alive.'

Jim stood up to leave, with Ben and Scott following on behind him.

'I'm sorry not to be more helpful,' said Foley.

Jim nodded and turned around. The three men took the stairs down to the foyer, then walked out to the street, turning left for the short walk back to their apartment. 'There's something he's not telling us,' said Jim.

'Nobody likes getting guys sent down from head office,' said Scott. 'We couldn't expect to be popular.'

'Not that,' said Jim, with a curt shake of his head. 'Something else.'

# SEVENTEEN

**Beirut, 14 November**

Ahmed didn't like Beirut, never had done.

He knew that it was referred to as the Paris of the Middle East, at least had been before the civil war started to scar and disfigure the face of the city.

But then, he reflected, as he walked down the main boulevard that led towards the diplomatic Baabda quarter of the city, he didn't much care for Paris either. There was something too smug, too chic, about that city as well. He preferred Germany or Britain, with their grittier streets, and straightforward people. Damascus and Amman and even Baghdad were the cities he felt most at home in.

They were places where a man could lose himself.

Forever, if necessary.

He was still thinking about the visit from Mehrak, only yesterday: he was turning it over in his mind, worrying away at the details, the way he always did when he started a new job. After the man had left, he'd arranged for a car and driver to bring him down to Beirut overnight. It was risky for him to fly more than he had to: most of the intelligence agencies might have started to downgrade him by now, but he knew he was still on the Mossad's most-wanted list, and they had agents who had infiltrated every airport in the Middle East, and kept a close eye on all the passengers. The buses between the two cities were safer, but they were also too uncomfortable, so Ahmed maintained an air-conditioned Mercedes, with enough space in the back to lie down and sleep, for when he had to move around the Middle East. The price of $400,000 was a good one, he told himself: and it would, anyway, be a pleasure to bring down an American jet. He would wait a couple of days to check that the money had been paid before he started any detailed work on the job. There was no way of knowing whether Mehrak was for real. Maybe he was just freelancing, maybe he didn't have the backing of the VEVAK the way he said he did. After all, the Iranian intelligence agency would be reluctant to admit that it couldn't do this job by itself. Hiring the Falcon was an admission of ineptitude. Only when the money came into his bank account could he be certain that the job was for real.

After all, he told himself with a thin smile, money never lies.

An American plane, Ahmed decided, was going to present a formidable challenge. True, there were plenty of them up in the skies. And simply destroying a plane was a lot easier than hijacking one. He sat down at a café, and started sketching his options on a pad of a paper, at the same time as ordering himself a cup of coffee. Maybe a ground-to-air missile could be used. There were plenty of them in Afghanistan, and there were men there who were skilled in their use. If you selected an airport with chaotic security – one of the African countries maybe – then you could station a man within a mile of the runway, and fire a missile when the plane was in the first minute of its ascent into the sky. He'd talked to his contacts in the IRA about such a mission, and he knew they'd studied the possibilities of a missile attack at Heathrow. In the end, they'd decided the risks were too great: the security cordon around the airport was tough, and there was no more than a one in three chance of the missile actually striking the plane and doing enough damage to bring it down. The missiles, in truth, were designed to bring down helicopters and attack jets in close-quarters combat, not Boeings that were already 10,000 feet into the sky. Still, in a city such as Freetown in Sierra Leone, or in Brazzavile in the Congo, then it might well be possible. If he could find the right man with the right equipment. And so long as he could find an American plane that was actually stupid enough to fly to one of those cities.

Ahmed took a sip of his coffee.

'Mechanical failure', he noted in his pad.

No plane was completely safe in the sky, no matter what the manufacturers tried to tell you. With thousands of moving parts there was always something that could go wrong. The engines were vulnerable to breakdown. If you took a twin-engined plane – a Boeing 737, say, or an Airbus A300 – you might be able to engineer a simultaneous failure of both engines. If it happened over rough seas, with no chance of an emergency landing, that might be enough to bring the plane down. Alternatively, you could tamper with the hydraulics. If you could find a way of weakening the wires that connected the cockpit to the wing flaps and the rudder, then perhaps you could engineer a catastrophic failure on take-off. It would just be a matter of finding the right person to talk to: someone with detailed knowledge of how each plane worked; and someone who could get you inside a maintenance shed so that you could make the necessary alterations. Ahmed kept scribbling. It would be better, he noted, if it was outside the United States. Maybe one of the places where American planes regularly refuelled, but also somewhere they trusted the local technicians enough to check and repair their aircraft. Maybe Cyprus, he wondered. Or Madrid. There were plenty of Arabs in Madrid, and if he could just find the right man, that was a possibility.

The trouble was, you couldn't be certain of success. The

pilot might well spot the mechanical problems before the plane got up into the sky. If he aborted the flight, then all your work would have been wasted. Even it wasn't spotted, there was always the possibility the 'failure' wouldn't happen as planned. Or the pilot would find some way of bringing the plane down safely.

And then, the crash might be written off as an accident.

And that wasn't what the Iranians wanted.

They didn't want Boeing or Airbus to get the blame.

They wanted the world to know this was retaliation: that was what they were paying for.

'A bomb', he scribbled in the notepad.

Ahmed smiled to himself.

A bomb was always the best way to bring down a plane.

The question was how you got it onto the aircraft. And how you detonated it once it was on board.

Some of the best minds in Middle Eastern terrorism had been working on getting bombs onto planes for years. Ahmed knew many of them personally. A few he had even taught himself. There was very little he didn't know about the construction and hiding of bombs.

Making the bomb was no problem. You needed to know the right men, but so long as you knew where to look, they could be found.

If not you could always do it yourself. A bomb consisted of Semtex and a detonator. There was nothing complicated about it.

Ahmed was intimately familiar with the history of blowing up aircraft. Indeed, he could fairly claim to be one of its authors. And, like just about everything in life, he knew that it was harder than it looked. People might imagine that you just had to detonate some kind of blast within a plane to bring it down. But a modern aircraft was built to exacting safety standards. It could survive a buffeting from thunderstorms and turbulence, it could survive extreme heat and cold, and it could shrug aside most mechanical failures.

Mentally, Ahmed was already reviewing the history, making notes as he went. In 1970, the Popular Front for the Liberation of Palestine made its debut in the big league of international terrorism when it planted bombs on board two European aircraft. The first was an Austrian Airlines flight from Vienna. A device stashed in the baggage hold exploded when the plane reached 10,000 feet. It blew a two-foot hole in the fuselage, but after a desperate struggle the pilot managed to regain control of the aircraft, and made an emergency landing back at Frankfurt airport. Nobody was injured. A Swissair flight from Frankfurt to Tel Aviv was not so lucky. Again, the bomb was hidden in the luggage compartment, but this one exploded when it reached 14,000 feet. Initially, the pilot seemed to stabilise the aircraft, but eventually it plunged to the ground, killing all forty-seven people on board.

Two years later, the same group targeted an El Al plane flying from Rome to Tel Aviv with 140 people on board. The device exploded at 15,000 feet. But again the pilot had turned the plane around, and despite the damage to the fuselage, managed to land it safely back in Rome. The later investigation found the bomb had been built into a record player carried by two young British women: it had been given to them by a pair of Arab guys in Rome after making friends with them in a bar, and, insofar as the police could tell, they knew nothing about the attack.

Another failure, reflected Ahmed.

That same year, a young, pregnant Irish woman called Anne-Marie Murphy had been stopped at Heathrow by security officials at the El Al check-in desk. She was found to have a bomb built into her suitcase. It turned out it had been given to her by the father of her unborn child, a Jordanian called Nezar Hindawi. He'd told her to fly to

Israel, where he would join her in a few days. Later it turned out that Hindawi had been working for Syrian intelligence all along, and had been scheduled to fly to Damascus at the same time as Anne-Marie's plane had been scheduled to explode somewhere over the northern French countryside.

But the plane didn't take off, and the bomb never exploded.

Yet another failure.

That made one successful bombing out of four attempts.

After that, most terror groups even in the Middle East had given up trying to bomb planes.

It was just too difficult.

'Ahmed.'

He glanced up. The man pulling up a chair next to him in the café was Hussein Gezairy. Ahmed didn't like him much more than he liked Beirut, but, like the city he lived in, Gezairy was a useful middleman. After the civil war had started, Beirut had become one of the main world centres for global drugs smuggling. It had always been the main financial centre for the region, but the capital markets had been blown to pieces. Bankers from Goldman Sachs and Deutsche Bank weren't willing to fly to a city where the sound of gunfire lasted through the night.

And that meant the finance business had just about collapsed.

But the drugs trade used most of the same skills, reflected Ahmed: buying and selling, arranging shipments, predicting crops, prices, and demand, and most of all keeping secrets. It was no great surprise that the Lebanese had moved so swiftly from trading shares and bonds to trading narcotics: many of them hadn't even bothered to change their business cards. After all, 'broker' covered both trades equally well.

Ahmed had been arranging for shipments of heroin harvested from the Afghan poppy fields to be taken overland through Iraq, then down into Syria and on to the Lebanon.

He sold them to a range of middlemen: in the drugs trade it didn't pay to rely on any one individual. Business had been booming: the Americans, the British, and Germans had an insatiable appetite for high-grade heroin. The only issue was how fast you could grow it, process it, then ship it to its final destination. And making sure you didn't get caught along the way.

Since giving up terrorism, drug dealing had been his main business.

'You are well?' said Ahmed, ordering a coffee for Gezairy.

The man shrugged. He had sad-looking brown eyes, and a mouth that appeared to be set in a permanent scowl. Every time he saw him, Ahmed felt sorry for the man's wife and children. He had the look of a man with a quick and furious temper: obsequious with those he believed important, brutal to anyone he considered beneath him. Ahmed would no more trust him than he would trust a dumb animal. But so far he had proved useful. He could take three kilos of pure heroin a day and ensure it reached its destination. He paid the money into an offshore account either in Deutschmarks or Swiss francs, and he never skipped a payment.

I might not like him, but as a business partner he can't be faulted.

*And if I only did business with people I liked, I wouldn't have very much work.*

'Since the war started, life is tough.'

'Even for men like you?'

Gezairy shrugged, taking a hit on the coffee and asking the waitress for a glass of water. There was a bead of sweat on his forehead, even though the day was cloudy, and there was hardly any heat in the air.

'We survive.'

Ahmed didn't traffic the drugs himself. It was too risky, and he was a man who wouldn't lightly surrender life's comforts and spend time in jail. Transporting drugs was a high-risk trade. There were soldiers and policemen every-where. There were other drug dealers. Anyone with a kilo of heroin on him was a target: whether it was the govern-ment or a rival that was after you didn't make much difference when the bullet sliced into your flesh.

So Ahmed used mules from Damascus as his transporters: young guys mostly, half of them travelled by bike, using the back roads, and slipping through the borders quietly at night, the other half using fishing boats then a dinghy to travel discreetly by sea. So far, none of them had been captured. Two of them had run off with the stash: one of those had since been tracked down and killed. Otherwise, the route was reliable. The drugs arrived on time: a daily delivery, and a weekly payment.

'Can you take more?' asked Ahmed.

That was the purpose of the meeting. Three kilos was a useful amount, and the dollars were piling up in an offshore account Ahmed maintained in Cyprus to launder the profits from the trade. But production was booming. With the Soviets pulling out of Afghanistan, more and more fields were being planted with poppies: heroin was the country's only significant cash crop. And with the war between Iran and Iraq still fierce, the routes through those two countries were becoming easier. Right now, Ahmed knew he could supply five or six kilos a day without any problem. The only issue was whether he could sell it.

'It's hard . . .'

'But surely the demand is there. Prices are still rising.'

'But it is too hard to ship west,' said Gezairy.

'What interests me is how you're getting the drugs into the West.'

Gezairy paused.

He looked nervously around the café, and then his voice dropped to a whisper.

'The CIA.'

Ahmed was rarely surprised by anything. It was one of the characteristics, he'd sometimes reflect to himself, that allowed him to stay alive for so long in such a dangerous line of work. He took everything in his stride, dealing with it calmly, and getting its measure before responding. He would never panic, never act on impulse, and never take any more chances than he absolutely had to.

Yet this . . . this surprised him.

'The CIA?'

'Through the diplomatic bag,' said Gezairy.

Like many men, noted Ahmed, Gezairy was undone by his desire to prove his cleverness to others. The only way to keep a secret was to tell absolutely no one. But very few men had the self-discipline that rule imposes, and Gezairy clearly wasn't one of them. He knew who Ahmed was, he'd heard all the stories and the legends, and he wanted to impress him.

'That's how the stuff is getting to the West?' said Ahmed.

Gezairy nodded. 'A diplomatic bag travels from Beirut to Washington every evening. It is flown via Frankfurt and London. But because it contains sensitive diplomatic papers, it isn't checked by anyone en route.'

'Shit,' muttered Ahmed. 'How . . .'

'The initial contact was made by one of our associates. The CIA bureau in Beirut needs money, just like we all do. It isn't getting the funding it needs from Washington. So . . .'

'So they are smuggling drugs to make up the difference.'

Gezairy nodded.

'They are skimming the money for themselves? Or they are using it to fund undercover operations?'

This time Gezairy just shrugged.

'How should I know?'

'You just sell them the gear?'

'We put it in the bag for them.'

'You personally?'

Gezairy shook his head. 'It comes out of the embassy every night,' he replied. 'On the way to the airport, it stops at a building maintained by one of our associates. It is a different building every night to ensure security, but the driver always knows what address to go to. The gear is put into the bag, it is resealed, and then it goes on to the airport to be put on the plane to Frankfurt.'

'And nobody touches it again until it arrives in Washington?'

'Like I said, it goes clear through all the customs checks.'

Ahmed whistled under his breath.

'So you see, if we were to take more, it might create problems,' continued Gezairy. 'There is only so much space inside a diplomatic bag.' He chuckled out loud. 'They even put some papers and reports in there as well sometimes, I suppose.'

'Don't even think about increasing it,' said Ahmed. 'It's too good a deal to disrupt it by putting more stuff through the system.'

He put some coins down to pay for the coffee, stood up and started to walk away from the café.

If you just keep asking questions, he reflected to himself, then it is amazing what you sometimes discover.

# EIGHTEEN

**London, 14 November**

'So where is this Linke?' asked Sam.

Orla smiled. She glanced up towards the clock. It was close to six. The shop usually closed at six thirty, although Sam never shut up if there was still a customer on the premises, or if there was even someone walking down the street browsing in the windows of the antique shops. If he had some work to do at his desk, he left the lights on, and the door open, just in case somebody happened to be passing. But not tonight. It was raining heavily and from the look of the black clouds sweeping down the Thames the weather wasn't about to break any time soon. 'I'll tell you over a beer,' she said.

Sam nodded. 'Give me five minutes,' he replied.

The Orange Brewery was right over the road from the shop. A traditional London pub with panelled walls, a decent selection of beers, and some food that was edible. Sam had been there lots of time in the years he'd been living in the Pimlico Road. There weren't many old-style pubs this close to Chelsea, he'd remind himself. Most of them had been turned into cocktail bars and restaurants. We need to support the few that are left.

By the time he'd closed up the shop, Orla was already sitting in a quiet corner, two pints of Guinness in front of her.

'Those both for you?'

She shook her head, pushing one pint across the table.

Sam didn't much care for Guinness: it was too rich and too sour for his tastes. He took two sips, and decided he could just about finish it before buying himself something else. 'So . . .' he said, looking straight at Orla.

She brushed away some creamy foam that was resting on her red lips.

Then she reached out and touched Sam's hand, letting it linger for a fraction of a second longer than was necessary.

'Linke was an exhibitor at the 1904 World's Fair in St Louis, as you probably know.'

'Probably,' said Sam, with a slow smile. 'Although funnily enough it might have escaped my mind just recently.'

'It was a big deal for him,' continued Orla. 'The World's Fair was massive, one of the biggest events of its kind staged up until then. That song "Meet Me In St Louis" was written for it. And I believe the first ice cream cone was sold there. Anyway, it was good business for a man hoping to make some inroads into the American market like Linke. He took a whole collection of his furniture out there, bureaus, cabinets, the works, to put them on display.'

'Very interesting . . .'

'The point is, two pieces of furniture were stolen,' continued Orla. 'In 1908, a man called Martin Wood was convicted of a series of robberies from the fair. He died in jail – I couldn't get the precise date, but it was sometime in the mid 1930s – but his granddaughter still lives in his old house. I called her, and she told me there was a nice cabinet there that had been in the family for decades. We talked about it on the phone for a while, and from the description I don't think there can be any doubt about where it came from originally. It is ornately carved, made of polished wood, and dripping with gold leaf work.'

'It could be the work of any number of furniture makers,'

cautioned Sam. 'Maybe even some obscure American.'

'It has two Greek-style figures on it,' said Orla.

'Lots of people used those around that period.'

'In gold leaf.'

Sam nodded. 'And Linke loved his classical motifs. It was his trademark.'

'So I reckon it's a Linke,' said Orla. 'One of the two stolen ones.'

Sam had to admit she had a point.

Some obscure American cabinetmaker wouldn't have used gold leaf. It would have been too expensive for them.

Surely she hadn't found one.

It wasn't possible.

'But will she be willing to sell it?'

'I already asked her,' answered Orla. 'I mentioned a figure of $25,000 cash.'

'$25,000 for a Linke? That's robbery.'

'It's already been stolen once.'

'If it's genuine, how much do you reckon that Marchiony guy will pay for it?'

'At least £100,000,' said Orla. 'Sterling.'

She finished her pint.

'I've already booked a flight because I figured you'd want me to go and get it.'

# NINETEEN

**Tehran, 15 November**

Mehrak stepped through the familiar door.

The house in Vozara in the northern district was unchanged from the last time he'd been here a few days ago. The same flowers growing wild in the garden. The same musty smell of wax and dust in the hallway. But his mood was different, lighter. He'd secured the services of the Falcon.

*That was all that counted.*

Mohsen Farhadi, the head of the VEVAK, was already waiting for him. The villa had been built as a residential house in the days before the revolution, and had been designed for a large family. Off the main corridor, there were two sitting rooms, a library, and a dining room, while upstairs there were seven bedrooms and down below there were servants' quarters and kitchens.

Farhadi was sitting alone in what had once been the library. The walls were shelved, and the floor was made from polished oak. But the shelves were all empty now: the house had probably belonged to one of the Iran oil industry middlemen, and the man's tastes would no doubt have been too decadent and Western to survive the revolution. Some of the paint was starting to peel away from the shelving, and there was a smell of damp. The double French doors were open to the garden, but it was mostly a collection of weeds outside, advancing closer to the main body of the house with every season.

'We hired him,' said Mehrak, a soft purr in his voice.

'The Falcon?'

Mehrak nodded.

You could see the pleasure on Farhadi's face. His lips remained immobile, but his eyes showed a sparkle of recognition. Only one man could have recruited the Falcon for this job, thought Mehrak, and that man is me.

*With this under my belt, surely I can ask for anything I want . . .*

'He'll destroy an American plane?'

'So he told me.'

'And how much will it cost us?'

Mehrak hesitated for just a fraction of a second.

'$400,000,' he replied.

Farhadi was sitting in a comfortable armchair next to the French doors, but there was nowhere for Mehrak to sit. He was shifting uncomfortably from foot to foot.

'Where is the money being paid?'

Mehrak ran briefly through the details of the engineering company in Ghent to which the money was to be wired before it would finally end up in the Falcon's bank account. Inside a small notepad, Farhadi was jotting down the details. When he had finished, he looked back up at Mehrak.

'And when he's ready, will he contact you?'

Mehrak shook his head. 'The Falcon works alone,' he said. 'There will be no further contact with us. A plane will be crashed before Christmas. And that will be the first we know of it.'

'A civilian plane?'

Mehrak nodded.

'And he doesn't expect to hear from you again?'

Mehrak nodded again.

'Then your work is finished?'

Mehrak smiled. He had been thinking on the short flight

home from Damascus about what kind of reward he could ask for. An oil contract, perhaps? A new house? *Surely there will be very little I can't demand . . .*

'And we have no further use for you . . .'

It took a moment for the words to sink in.

At first, Mehrak thought he was just being dismissed. His job was done, he could relax for a while, and they could discuss his reward later. Then it struck him that maybe he was being told to leave the room.

And then it hit him.

*Surely they couldn't mean . . .?*

A man had already stepped in from the garden. Mehrak recognised him at once. Majid Kavousifar. A tall, wiry man, with cropped hair, and a short black beard, he was the main executioner for the VEVAK. He worked on internal security: the spies within the organisation who spied on the other spies. But Kavousifar didn't do investigations, or interrogations. He didn't do paperwork like the other agents. He just came in when that was all finished.

*He was the man who pulled the trigger.*

He took another step closer.

In his right hand, there was a Walther P88 handgun. Slowly he raised his hand, so that the gun was level with his eye. His arm and shoulders were rock steady, like a steel pylon. And the sights were pointed straight at Mehrak.

Mehrak could feel the sweat pouring off him.

Kavousifar never missed, he realised. Not at a hundred yards. Not at 200. And certainly not at five feet.

'Why?' he said, looking desperately towards Farhadi.

The head of the VEVAK remained impassive.

'I found the Falcon for you. The plane will be brought down, just as you asked . . .'

Farhadi stood up. 'And it must remain a secret,' he said. 'We don't want anyone to know we were behind this operation. And we certainly don't want anyone to know we had to hire a foreigner to do it.'

'My silence . . .'

He was spluttering over the words, unable even to complete a sentence.

'I promise . . .'

Farhadi raised a hand. 'No one's silence is ever guaranteed,' he said firmly. 'Not unless they are dead.'

He glanced towards Kavousifar. 'Finish him . . .'

# TWENTY

**London, 16 November**

Orla looked exhausted, noticed Sam.

Her eyes were strained, and her blue linen dress was crumpled. She was carrying a dark canvas bag under her arm, and a duty-free carrier bag with two bottles of Irish whiskey inside it.

'You could use a shower,' he said.

'And about a week's sleep,' replied Orla.

It was mid afternoon, and the shop was no busier than normal. Sam hadn't expected to see Orla for several days, a week at least. It was a nine-hour flight from London to St Louis. For her to have got there and back meant she only had ten hours or so in the country before turning around and coming straight home. She'd spent most of the last thirty-six hours in the air.

'Go upstairs and use the shower if you want.'

Sam pushed the keys across the desk to Orla. Next to the shopfront there was a side entrance to the apartment, up a single flight of stairs. Orla hadn't seen it yet: he'd still only known her for a few days. She was staying at a bedsit she rented by the week across the river in Battersea, but Sam didn't even have the address, and had no idea how far away it might be. Better if she cleans up here, he told himself. *I want to know whether she tracked down that Linke.*

'Thanks,' said Orla, taking the keys.

116

'I'll see you in a few minutes.'

She'd already left the room by the time he finished the sentence. There was a woman in the shop, asking about a gilt-framed mirror. Sam told her it cost £750. She asked if there was a possibility of a discount, but Sam wasn't in the mood for negotiating. He told her he'd take £700, but couldn't go any lower. She said she'd discuss it with her husband. Sam told her that was fine, flipped the shop's sign to 'Closed' and walked upstairs.

The flat was nice enough, but Sam had never got round to furnishing it properly. He'd taken it as part of his cover when he was still working for the Mossad: all of the five men in his unit needed somewhere discreet to live as they travelled around Europe tracking down the terrorists they were meant to eliminate. Elena and the kids had been living in Frankfurt through all of that, and they'd only spent a few months together here after he quit the Mossad before their marriage fell apart. If they'd stayed longer in London, they'd have found a bigger place in the suburbs, but now he was on his own again, the apartment was perfect. It had two bedrooms, a kitchen, and a sitting room that was big enough to store some of the pieces of furniture that didn't fit into the shop right now. There was a phone and TV and a shower, and most of the time that was all he needed.

Sam walked through to the kitchen. He could hear some singing from the shower room, and he didn't want to disturb Orla. He cooked an omelette with cheese and some herbs, made some toast, and brewed a fresh cup of coffee, black the way she liked it. By the time he took the tray through to the sitting room, Orla had already stepped out of the shower. She was dressed in a blue towelling robe, her hair still wet: she'd put a towel around her neck, and was combing it. She looked up towards Sam, smiling, and he was struck for the first time how like Elena she was: the same black hair, soft skin, sculpted nose and eyes: she reminded him of the teenager he first started dating at least fifteen years ago, back when they both lived in Tel Aviv.

*Maybe that's what I find attractive about her.*

'Thanks,' she said, looking down at the tray. 'I hate airline food. I don't think I've had anything proper to eat for the last two days.'

She took a slice of toast, spread it thick with butter, and took two mouthfuls of omelette, followed by what seemed like half a cup of black coffee taken in a single gulp. Already Sam could see some colour returning to her cheeks: the girl was resilient to the core, reflected Sam.

In a different life, she'd have made a fine agent.

'So how was St Louis?'

'It's a dump, I don't know how people can live in places like that.'

'But you found something?'

Orla nodded, wolfing down more forkfuls of omelette, chewing on a piece of toast. She swallowed, looking straight back at Sam. 'I rented a car, and drove straight out to this woman's place. Mrs Penny Strauss, she's called now, the granddaughter of Martin Wood, the guy we think stole the furniture back in 1904. I had to drink some really terrible coffee, and listen to the entire family history. Boring as hell it was too . . .'

'So what happened?'

'Wood went to jail and eventually died there, as we know. His wife remarried, and the crook she chose must have been a slightly more successful one, because the house is quite grand. A sort of mock-colonial place, on its own plot, in a town called Freeburg about ten miles east of St Louis. A dump now, but it had a tyre factory, so it was probably quite a prosperous place in its heyday. I guess the decent pieces of furniture came with him. There were two daughters, Eleanor and Louisa. Louisa married a guy called Jock, but he was killed in the Korean War, but not before she was pregnant with Penny. The old girl herself was never married, and she inherited the house and everything in it. So all the stuff belongs to her.'

'And you found . . . a Linke?'

'It's in the dining room, although I don't think anyone ever goes in there. The old girl doesn't throw many parties, I imagine. Doesn't have enough friends left alive. There's a big, polished table, and a gloomy grandfather clock, both of them worthless I guess, and then next to them, this beautifully ornate side bureau, laden with gold leaf and classical motifs. It was covered in black and white family photographs and ornaments and all the rest of it, but clear them away and its obvious what it is. A Linke . . .'

Sam could feel his pulse quickening. If she was right, and there was no reason to doubt her word, then it would be worth a fortune.

'I mean, I don't go for all the gaudy late Victorian rubbish myself,' said Orla. 'But when you see it close up, it's actually quite impressive.'

'She'll sell?'

'$25,000,' said Orla.

She beamed, her smile so bright it practically burst out of the room.

'Like you said, it was robbed in the first place,' said Sam. 'No reason not to rob it again.'

'That's what I thought,' said Orla. 'I used your credit card to arrange a cash transfer there and then, and I arranged for a shipper to come and collect it. Then I called Marchiony. He was delighted. And how much do you think he offered for it?'

'A hundred—'

'£125,000,' said Orla. 'I told him he was robbing me, of course, but because of cashflow, etc., etc., I'd be willing to take his offer. He'll pay cash by banker's draft on delivery.'

'Which is . . .'

'I told him that at that steal of a price I'd expect him to pay the transport charges as well,' said Orla. 'He's paying for it to go as cargo on the next flight leaving St Louis with space on it. Which by my calculations left about four hours ago, so it should be somewhere over the Atlantic by now. When it lands at Heathrow we just need to arrange for a van to collect it, and take it around to Marchiony's office.'

She finished the last of her omelette in a pair of final mouthfuls.

'We just made a profit of about a hundred grand,' said Orla. 'Split seventy-five, twenty-five, of course.'

You couldn't ignore talent when it was right in front of you, reflected Sam, and Orla had it in abundance. She could track anything down: so long as there was just a whisper, then she could follow it. It didn't matter what trade she was in, that was a valuable skill. The issue was whether he could afford to ignore it.

With Orla on board, maybe he could start making some serious money out of the antiques business.

'I already told you, it's too much,' said Sam. 'You could have collected all that money for yourself. I didn't do anything.'

'You made a nice omelette,' said Orla.

'I'm being serious.'

Orla paused, finishing her coffee. 'The deal stays as it is, seventy-five to your shop, twenty-five per cent to me.'

Sam shook his head. 'Like I said, it's too generous. It makes me feel uncomfortable.'

Orla stood up, walking closer to where Sam was sitting on the sofa. He could smell the fresh, clean soap still clinging to her skin. For a moment he was about to reach out and touch her. He sensed that she wanted him to, but then she turned away.

'That's why it works for me, because you're a man with a conscience,' she said. 'And sooner or later, that conscience is going to make it plain to you that since I've helped you, you have to help me as well.'

'You don't mind people doing stuff out of guilt?'

Orla laughed. 'I was raised by the Vatican. Why the hell should I mind that?'

Sam knew he was losing the argument. Maybe he should help her, he reflected to himself. He'd been thinking about that in the thirty-six hours she'd been away. What if her story was right? he wondered to himself. What if the Church was pretending to be broke so that it could avoid paying out compensation to the people whose lives it had destroyed? Then maybe something should be done about it.

'I don't get why you need me,' he said. 'Surely you can find anything you want yourself.'

Orla dismissed the sentence with a flick of her hand. 'Antiques! That's nothing, not detective work.'

She leaned over, so that Sam could see a few centimetres of cleavage where the robe was folded around her body. 'We're talking about tracking down the hidden wealth of the Vatican. That is going to take real talent.'

'Probably more than I have . . .'

'You were Mossad, Sam,' said Orla. 'Like you said, I'm good at tracking things down, it's my skill. I needed the best man at chiselling out secrets, and that led me to you. When you were in the Mossad you could find terrorists people believed had vanished forever. You discovered what happened to the billionaire Max Robertson after he drowned off a boat. And you can find out where the Vatican has hidden its assets as well.'

She paused. 'You and only you.'

The words struck home. Sam was never boastful about his achievements: he never needed to be. He knew there was more luck than ability in that line of work: you stumbled across things, made connections, saw things that had remained hidden, but you were always winging it, always hoping for a lucky break. There was no method, no plan, just persistence, determination and legwork.

Still, he made the breaks work for him more than most men could. He knew where to look, how to ask the right questions, how to be in the right place so that a crucial piece of information fell into your lap. And he knew how to stay alive as well.

So why not help her?

It's not as if the cause isn't a good one.

And let's be honest . . .

*It's not as if you don't want to . . .*

'You can make plenty of money all by yourself,' said Sam. 'You're a natural-born dealer. That's always lucrative. You don't need to go after the Vatican's money. You can make it for yourself.'

'But this isn't about money,' said Orla. 'It's about revenge for what happened to my brother.'

Her voice dropped to little more than a whisper.

'Surely you can see that.'

# TWENTY-ONE

**Beirut, 16 November**

There were alleyways that even five years working for the military, and another five years as a special agent for the CIA, had not prepared you for. You could feel the shadows closing in around you, and your blood started to run cold. It was your body's way of telling you that you were taking a risk, that you should turn back now. Before it was too late.

Ben Hanold stepped cautiously down the narrow street. It was filled with a few food stalls, selling *kibbee nayee*, the dish of lean raw lamb ground fine, pressed into a flat layer, and served with pitta bread, some vegetables and olive oil, that you seemed to find everywhere in the country. He passed a string of cafés, with old men sitting outside them, drinking endless cups of coffee, talking to one another, and arguing over the newspapers. Above them were row after row of tenement buildings, with tiny apartments packed one on top of the other, their occupants spilling out into the streets. There were kids running in and out of the narrow stairways that led into each block, mothers carrying their screaming babies, and men hanging out in the doorways, eyeing strangers suspiciously.

And somewhere inside this maze, he should find Hashem Akkad.

The first man who might give them a lead on where the hostages were.

Or at least talk to them.

Unlike everyone else in this damned country.

Americans, he noted grimly to himself, didn't usually walk through the Karantina district of Beirut. Not unless they were looking for a cheap and quick way of killing themselves.

It was the old slum district of the city – its name was a corruption of 'quarantine', since it was where all the sick people used to be hidden away – a place where even before the civil war the Lebanese government had never exerted much authority. From the 1970s onwards, it had been controlled by the Palestinian Liberation Organisation, but mainly inhabited by Kurdish and Armenian refugees. In 1976 it had been attacked by Christian forces, who fought a running street battle with the PLO, in which more than 1,000 civilians had died. Ever since then, rival forces had largely left it alone, making its narrow streets a perfect meeting point for the city's terrorists, criminals, and black markeeters. But they didn't like outsiders, no matter what the colour of their skin or their flag.

They particularly didn't like white CIA men.

Ben was dressed down for the trip. It was early evening, and cloudy, and he was wearing baggy white shorts, and a loose-fitting tee shirt. He didn't have a gun on him, but he had tucked a knife into the side of his belt. For the last twenty-four hours, the three of them had been talking to people, tapping into networks the agency was only loosely affiliated with. Whether the Beirut station had already talked to the same people didn't matter. Sometimes you had to squeeze a source again and again and again before you got any juice out of it.

It was often only on the fourth or fifth round of question-ing that you actually found out anything worth knowing about.

True, they hadn't come up with much so far. Jim was

spending this evening talking to a captain down at the harbour. It was possible the hostages had been taken to another country, and the safest way of doing that would be to slip them on to one of the fishing boats and get them out at night. For all they knew, they could be in Egypt by now, or Malta, or possibly even Spain. Who knows, maybe they were even being kept out at sea, in the hold of a cargo ship. There were few safer places. At sea, no one would hear a hostage scream.

If anything had happened around the docks, however, one of the harbour masters would know about it. By splashing some money around, Jim might be able to get a lead on it. If he could only get the right people to talk to him.

Meanwhile, Scott was off talking to one of the Libyan agents in the city, Massoud Arebi.

Officially, there were no contacts between the Americans and the Libyans. The two countries were sworn enemies: they didn't even have functioning embassies in each other's countries right now. But in the Middle East, there were always back channels, and Bill Horton knew how to operate most of them. He was the master of informal contacts between sworn enemies. Arebi was a senior intelligence official at the Libyan Embassy in Beirut, and he knew the power plays among the different terror groups. Sometimes the Libyans backed the PLO, sometimes Hamas, sometimes the Lebanese government. They were certainly an important conduit for arms and money – Libya was one of the few official states to deal openly with terrorists, whatever their nationality – and that meant they all wanted to keep them on side. That gave a man such as Arebi influence: influence which he could sometimes trade for information.

'He'll probably lie through his teeth to me,' said Scott, as he was leaving for the meeting. 'But who the hell knows?

Even while he's lying, he still might say something interesting.'

Ben had drawn what seemed the least promising lead of all.

The most chance of getting knifed in the back. And the least chance of coming up with the goods, he thought glumly to himself, as he pushed on into the shaded interior of Karantina.

Hashem Akkad was a relatively unimportant trader in information. The CIA used him sometimes for laundering money, and he could get hold of just about any weapon or transport you might need for a job as well. He got along with people, and he usually kept his mouth shut, and that made him useful, but nobody kidded themselves he was very important. Still, he was willing to talk, and for today that was enough.

Heck, no one else is talking.

Not yet anyway.

He lived by himself in an apartment halfway into the quarter, but had told Ben to meet him in a café just outside the building. As he walked through the narrow streets, Ben could feel the suspicious glances coming towards him, but he just ignored them, and quickened his pace. When Ben checked the café, the man wasn't there. He'd seen a picture of Akkad, and it didn't fit any of the guys sipping coffee. He checked with the waiter, and was told to try the garage, 200 yards down the road to the left. Ben kept walking. The place was just a rough workshop, its entrance dominated by a pile of old tyres, and with a pair of elderly Volkswagens being taken apart inside. The guy working there didn't speak any English, but Ben spoke enough Arabic to make it clear who he was looking for.

Out the back, the man told him. He pointed past a stack of exhaust pipes to a small doorway. Ben could feel a pair of men watching him carefully as he pushed the door open.

The yard measured just twenty feet by ten, with a high wall around it. There were yet more car parts: some doors, bumpers, and an oily engine block mounted on a wooden frame.

Ben stood still for a moment.

If you were going to kill someone, this wouldn't be a bad place to do it: quiet, not overlooked, and no doubt there was a sewer close by you could toss the corpse into.

Don't think about it, he told himself.

You'll just freak yourself out.

Akkad stepped forward. Ben's eyes flashed to his hands first, to see if he was carrying any kind of weapon. When he could see he was unarmed, he visibly relaxed. 'Ben Hanold,' he said, extending a hand.

Akkad didn't shake it. His expression was surly, nervous.

'My apologies for the meeting place,' he said softly. 'There is so much suspicion in Beirut right now that I can't afford to take any chances. You Americans are not very popular . . .'

'I know,' interrupted Ben.

'But we can talk all the same.'

'We need a lead on the hostages,' said Ben. 'Anything at all that will give us some clues as to where they might be. Or even who might be holding them. And, of course, we'll pay well for the information.'

Akkad lit up a cigarette, offered one to Ben, and looked surprised when he declined. 'I don't know where they are,' he said flatly.

'Any guesses? Maybe around this quarter?'

'In the Karantina? No.'

Akkad chuckled to himself, and tossed the match dangerously close to the engine block.

Ben stamped it out with his foot. He'd lose his life in a gun battle with Hamas if he had to to break the hostages out, but he didn't want to die because some idiot smoker didn't know any better than to toss around matches in a garage.

'There are no secrets in the Karantina. And these hostages are being kept very secretly.'

'In Beirut?'

'Within the city, I am certain of that much.'

'How certain?'

Akkad took a long drag on his cigarette, blowing the smoke out contemplatively, while scrutinising Ben's face. 'They are being moved every day,' he said. 'I know that much, because a cousin of mine is one of the men who have moved them.'

Ben had to restrain himself from punching the air. Maybe this could just be the breakthrough they were looking for, he told himself. One of those lucky slips of information that just drops into your lap. The hostages were being moved daily, from place to place: Bill Horton had told him he felt certain of that. The risk of that, however, was that several people a week had to be involved in transporting them, and that too created risks.

It only took one person to talk.

*And maybe I've found that person.*

'Your cousin . . .'

Ben didn't want to push the man. Reeling in a source was like reeling in a fish: you had to tug on it gently, making sure the hook stayed firmly stuck in the throat. Pull too hard, and it would start to struggle: that was when you might lose it.

'Distant cousin,' snapped Akkad. 'I have a big family.'

Ben could tell that Akkad didn't want to do this. The man was being tugged in two directions: his loyalty to his family and his people, and the raw, avaricious impulse that told him he could make a lot of money very quickly. Take this path, you could see he was thinking, and you would never have to set foot in a slum like the Karantina again. And yet, this same path meant you were cutting yourself off from everything you knew.

After all, a man who betrayed the location of the hostages to the Americans would be hunted down for the rest of his days.

Play this carefully, Ben warned himself.

He could switch to the other side of the coin in an instant.

'We'll pay him well.'

Akkad twisted the embers of his cigarette into the ground. 'It would be a big risk for him to take.'

'We could arrange safe passage out of the country,' said Ben. 'I'll speak to my office. Maybe even an American passport, so he could be set up somewhere quiet back in the States.'

'He has a wife,' growled Akkad. 'No children, not yet anyway, but a young wife who he cares about.'

'She could be taken care of as well. Nice house somewhere, a new kitchen, the works . . .'

'Where?'

Ben thought for a moment.

Where the hell would some jerk from a dump like this want to move to?

'California, maybe,' he said. 'Where the sun shines all the time, and the ocean is close by. Just like this place.'

'He'd like that.'

'And, if you arranged it, there would be a payment for you as well. We understand that.'

'How much?'

The textbook said you never made the first offer. It was up to the person putting the information up for sale to name their price. That way you could a sense of what it was worth to them, you'd know what they wanted, and you could start to haggle. There was no point in offering $100,000 when the guy would have only asked for $50,000, and settled for $40,000. But the manuals could be damned, decided Ben. They were written by desk cowboys back in Washington worrying about saving taxpayers' money. Not by the men on the ground, guys who had just fractions of a second to squeeze a source or else lose it forever.

Akkad needed to be convinced, and the only thing that was going to do that was money.

'We can pay your cousin $100,000,' said Ben. 'That's American dollars, paid into any account he wants. We'll pay $50,000 to you, for making the introduction. And in return, your cousin will tell us where the hostages are. Not the day after they've been moved. He'll tell us the moment they've been moved, so that we have enough time to assemble an operation to go in and get them out.'

Akkad nodded, making a careful mental note of the offer. 'It will be dangerous for me as well,' he said. 'A single word of this conversation leaks out . . .'

He ran a finger across his throat.

'I understand,' said Ben. 'I can probably make it $100,000 for you as well.'

'And a new passport? An American one . . .'

Ben nodded.

'And a house . . .'

'Like I said, in California.'

'With a pool.'

Ben nodded again.

Jesus, he thought.

This jerk will be specifying the colour of the curtains next.

Akkad took another cigarette from his packet, slipping it between his lips, but leaving it unlit. 'Is this from the drugs money?' he said. 'Or from Washington?'

'The drugs money . . .'

Ben stopped himself from completing the sentence. What drugs money? he wondered. What the hell is the man talking about? I should let him finish the sentence, and see where this leads.

'You didn't know?'

'I'm from the agency's head office, not the Beirut station.'

130

'I see,' said Akkad flatly.

He struck his match on the sole of his boot, putting the flame to the cigarette, then tossing it still lit on to the ground. This time Ben let it burn out naturally. Let him talk, he told himself. Don't distract the man.

'The Beirut office of your organisation has its own funds.'

'From drug running?'

Akkad nodded. 'They take shipments of heroin and cocaine, and they arrange for them to be taken to your country. They put it in the diplomatic bag, the one that flies from here to Washington every night, or so I'm told. Only a few people know about it. But it gives them a pretty big fund to finance their operations in this city.'

Shit, thought Ben.

*Can that possibly be true?*

'I didn't know about that,' he said calmly. 'Does it make a difference.'

Akkad looked at him sharply. 'If we do this deal, the money has to come from Washington,' he said. 'I wouldn't work with your Beirut people. You can't trust them.'

'It will come from Washington,' said Ben. 'I can guarantee it.'

'Then I will speak to my cousin.'

'When?'

Akkad tossed the cigarette to the ground. 'When we're ready, we will contact you.'

'I need to know when,' persisted Ben. 'There are arrangements to be made.'

'When it is you that's risking your life, then you can set the timetable,' said Akkad sharply. 'Until then we'll do this my way.'

# TWENTY-TWO

**London, 17 November**

Sam looked at the man across the desk. He was tall, elegantly dressed, in a blue pinstriped suit, with a white mono-grammed shirt, and gold cufflinks. His tie was made from blue silk, and his black brogues were so polished you could use them as a shaving mirror.

And Sam didn't trust him for a moment.

Edgar Samuels worked for the American Embassy in London as an economic liaison officer, but Sam was well aware that was just a cover. There were three men who counted at the American Embassy in London: the ambassador himself, the chief of staff, and Samuels, who, although he didn't put that description on his card, was the senior CIA officer for the whole of Britain. Of the three of them, Samuels clearly reckoned himself the most important, judged Sam. And, in fairness, he was probably right.

The CIA would never admit to spying on the British. They were meant to be allies. But, of course they did . . . they spied on everyone.

Sam had never met him before, but he had heard of him, and he knew he was an operator. When he came into the shop this morning, he hadn't hesitated to ask him into the back office for a private conversation. Samuels would know precisely who he was, Sam judged. There was no point in trying to trick him. Just find out what he wants.

*And how to get rid of him.*

'Nice shop, Mr Woolfman,' he said. 'If I wasn't so busy, I'd try and buy something.'

'Do that,' said Sam. 'Come back with Mrs Samuels. We're always open.'

Samuels smiled. He took a sip of the coffee Orla had just made, and waited until she had gone back into the shop and closed the door before speaking again.

'Bill Horton asked me to come and speak to you,' he said.

'The operation director?'

Samuels nodded.

They must be in deep trouble, thought Sam, if the operation director of the CIA is sending a man such as Samuels to see me.

'Perhaps he'd like to buy some antiques,' said Sam. 'An ornamental filing cabinet, maybe . . .'

Samuels didn't smile. He just leaned forwards, resting his arms on the desk, and looked straight into Sam's eyes.

'We know who you are, Mr Woolfman, and we know precisely what you are capable of.'

'Like furnishing an—'

'Don't play games, Mr Woolfman,' snapped Samuels.

'Or throwing people out of my office.'

Samuels fell silent. He examined Sam's face, as if scrutinising it for signs of weakness.

'It would be better if we tried to get along.'

Sam nodded. There was truth in that, he acknowledged to himself. The CIA bureau in London could make plenty of trouble for him if they chose to. So far, the British had left him alone, despite his past: they knew about it, but so far as they were concerned, the Middle East was a long way away, and they weren't going to worry about it.

But if the Americans started to lean on them, that could change very quickly. The British intelligence agencies didn't do favours for many people, but they did for the Americans.

133

'It's about the hostages, isn't it?' he said.

'They told me you were sharp.'

'Why else would a man such as Horton be interested in me?' said Sam. 'I can read the papers the same as anyone can. The Americans are in a deep hole. The press is screaming for something to be done about the hostages, but so far you don't appear to have a clue where they are. The CIA station in Beirut is a joke, everyone knows that. Even the press. They couldn't find the free toy in a Corn Flakes packet. So you aren't going to be getting any leads from them. In fact, there are only two organisations that have any real idea what's happening in the Lebanon, and that's the PLO and the Mossad.'

'And unfortunately neither of them are telling us what we need to know,' said Samuels.

Sam grinned. 'And you've probably got a better chance of getting a straight answer from the PLO,' he said. 'Which is why you are talking to me.'

'Precisely.'

'But I can't help you.'

Another pause, noted Sam. When Samuels heard something he didn't like, he just paused, hoping that in the awkward silence that followed the other person would change their mind. But not this time, he decided.

*My mind is already made up.*

'You haven't asked me what I want yet.'

Sam nodded. 'So tell me,' he said.

*Not that it makes any difference.*

'A way into the Mossad network in Beirut.'

'Who says we have one?'

Samuels smiled. 'I do,' he replied. 'We're well aware the Mossad had a network of sleeper agents inside Beirut. Even if we didn't know, then we could just assume it to be true. An agency of that power and resourcefulness isn't going to let a situation like that fester without keeping close tabs on it. So, the agents are there . . .'

Sam knew it was true. He'd even carried out a hit in the city, smuggled into the Lebanon by boat, then escorted through its streets by a series of runners so perfectly blended into the background no one would ever realise who they were working for. An Israeli assassin could be dropped into Beirut, complete a hit, and be extracted again within hours. He only knew three of the names: the identity of agents was so secret, their names were not revealed to anyone except those who absolutely needed the information. But he also knew how jealously the Mossad would guard that information. And he wasn't about to break any confidences now.

And certainly not for some jerk who just walked into his office.

'The trouble is, Tel Aviv won't help us,' continued Samuels. 'They won't admit it. But if they wanted to find those hostages they could. Now, we reckon there must be one or two of those agents who are getting close to their retirement age. Maybe they'd like a big boost to their pension, paid into a discreet offshore bank account. And I suspect you would know their names, and how to make contact with them.'

'And for me . . .'

'We could be useful to you, Mr Woolfman,' said Samuels. 'There would be a payment, of course. You could pretty much name your own price. Then, this could be the start of a relationship. We could work well together.' He smiled. 'Let's put it this way, the embassy could use a constant supply of antiques. And we have embassies right around the world, all of them needing—'

'I'll make some calls,' interrupted Sam. 'I can't promise anything.'

Samuels put a card down on the desk. 'You call me, Mr Woolfman. Trust me, you won't regret it.'

135

By the time Samuels had closed the door of the shop behind him, Sam had already tucked the card into the bottom drawer of the desk. He had no intention of making any calls. The Mossad had left him alone since he quit the service, but, although it was never spoken, he knew there was a condition to that. He would never meddle in their affairs, never contact any old colleagues, never trade on his Mossad connections. The rule was a simple one, and Sam wasn't about to break it now.

'So where do we start?' asked Orla.

'Same place you start any investigation,' said Sam.

He looked down at the card in the still open drawer of his desk. He'd call Samuels in a couple of days, tell him he'd left messages for a couple of guys and was waiting for them to call back: enough to string him along, and keep him from causing any trouble. Until then, he'd promised Orla last night he'd help her with tracking down the Vatican's money. That was one pledge he intended to keep.

'By asking the right questions?'

'Absolutely,' replied Sam.

They were sitting in his back office, with the door open through to the shop, so that they could keep an eye on any customers who wandered through. Orla had arranged for the Linke to be collected first thing this morning, and it had already been delivered to Marchiony's hedge fund. The profits had been securely banked, and Sam had written a cheque out to Orla for her share of the profits on the deal. She'd earned it, he reflected as he signed the cheque. Maybe it's time for me to earn my share as well.

'Which is where they've hidden the money,' she said.

Sam shook his head.

'Where they bank?'

'We know where they bank,' said Sam. 'The Vatican has its own bank.'

'The Istituto per le Opere di Religione, I know,' said

Orla. 'Or rather the Institute for Religious Works. It might sound like a charity, but actually it's the private bank of the Vatican city state. Its bank identifier code is IOPRVAVX if you ever happen to want to transfer some money. It's owned by the Vatican, but always run by a professional banker who reports to a committee of cardinals. It dates back to the original papal state before Italy was unified. And it's been involved in numerous scandals. Plenty of people reckon that a lot of the gold the Nazis looted across Europe ended up in the vaults of the Vatican bank, in return for providing safe passage for Nazi leaders out of Europe at the end of the war.'

'And they're saying they're broke?'

Orla shook her head. 'They're saying the Vatican bank can't be held liable for a civil action in the United States. It's the American Church that claims it's broke.'

'Which is rubbish,' interrupted Sam. 'The biggest organised Church in the richest country in the world. They'll have plenty of money, we can be certain of that.'

'But I need to prove it.'

'Like I said, by asking the right questions.'

Orla looked puzzled. 'Which, as I said a minute ago, is where have they been hiding it?'

Sam shook his head. 'The real question is, where are they getting the money?' he said. 'Find the source of a river and you figure out where it goes. Money is just the same. Work out where it comes from, and you'll soon find out where it is.'

# TWENTY-THREE

**Düsseldorf, 17 November**

Ahmed preferred Düsseldorf to Paris or Rome or Madrid. Of course, he knew that was a minority opinion. Most people found the grey German city in the Ruhr drab and soulless: a place dedicated only to industry and finance, with little space for fun or beauty or relaxation. But Ahmed liked its sense of purpose, the gritty functionality of its modernist streets.

In Düsseldorf, a man could get things done.

Just about anything.

Even blow up a plane.

He'd checked into the Marriott hotel on the Am Seestern, in the centre of the main business district that backed away from the Rhine, after arriving on a flight from Beirut late last night. He didn't like flying, but today there was no choice. It was a functional, commercial hotel, full of businessmen from around the world visiting the manufacturers that dominated the Ruhr. Even as he glanced around the room, Ahmed knew he would fit right in. There were Japanese, Chinese, Americans, Arabs, all sorts. So long as you had a suit and tie and an attaché case a man could blend right into the wallpaper.

This morning he'd hired a car at the Hertz desk, and driven straight out of town. He was travelling under the name of Moati Hegazi, using an Egyptian passport, and a credit card issued by the Hellanic Bank of Cyprus. It was one of five identities that he kept for when he was on the move: one British, one Greek, one Jordanian, and two Egyptian. He generally chose whichever one would draw least attention to himself. The Egyptians were often the best: after all, there were eighty million of them in the world, and the country excited no strong opinions one way or the other, so an extra one wasn't going to make much difference. Nobody paid any attention to Egyptians, which was the way Ahmed liked it.

He drove straight from town towards the small village of Neuss, in the direction of the Dutch border. It was flat, featureless countryside: pine forests, punctuated by well-tended fields, and every few miles, another factory. It was ten years since he'd last met Josef Muller, he reflected, as he steered the rented Audi off the main road and into the village. I've changed a lot in that decade. But I suspect that Muller has changed even more.

The house was the last in a row on a neat suburban street, a mile from the centre of the village. It was larger than any of the other houses on its block, but the high, well-trimmed hedges that surrounded it, and the modesty of its setting, disguised what an opulent property it really was. The house was less than a decade old, with seven bedrooms, three sitting rooms, a private cinema, a pool, and a gym. It suited Muller, decided Ahmed: he liked to live well, but he didn't want to draw attention to his wealth. After all, people might start asking where it came from.

And he wouldn't like that.

Maybe he should be an Egyptian, decided Ahmed with a smile to himself.

As Ahmed pressed the buzzer, the electric gates swung open, and he steered the Audi up the driveway. When he first met Muller, he was a peripheral member of the Baader-Meinhof group: he supported its ideology of visiting destruction on a capitalist society, but even then he was too smart to align himself too publicly to the cause. He was the engineer of the group, which, amid a collection of poets, politicians, and idealists made him unusual.

Like many Germans, Ahmed had observed from a distance, Muller was essentially a practical man. Germany was always a country that revered engineers, and, for all its radical pretensions, even Baader-Meinhof quickly settled into a very traditional German hierarchy, which placed the engineer right at its very apex. He was never officially a leader, but he was a dominant force in the group, organising its hits, developing the strategy of kidnapping prominent businessmen, and managing its money. As the operation grew, it became richer and richer, and so did Muller. But a decade ago, he stepped right away, claiming he was too old: in reality, so many of the leaders of the group were in jail, it didn't have the manpower to carry on. All the time, so far as Ahmed could tell, the German police had never suspected Muller's involvement: he'd stayed completely in the shadows, as Ahmed had known he would. We have much in common, he thought to himself. We know how to look after ourselves. And we know how to stay out of trouble.

'Business must be good,' said Ahmed, glancing across at the three different Mercedes parked in the carport.

'I'm getting by,' said Muller, offering him his hand.

He was greyer around the temples, and fatter around the waist, noted Ahmed. But he had the same expression of sleek confidence he'd had when he was younger. The only difference was that it was now backed up by more than a thin coating of prosperity. What precisely Muller did for a living now, Ahmed wasn't sure. All he knew was that you could call him, say you were looking to get a bomb made, and he'd tell you to come and see him. Which gave you the general idea.

He led Ahmed inside the house, poured some fresh

140

coffee, and led him into a private study towards the back of the house. In the distance, Ahmed could hear a dog barking, and a woman speaking on the phone, but Muller didn't want to introduce him to his family. The office was sparsely but expensively furnished. There was a glass-topped desk, mounted on two brass and leather stands, and a swivel chair upholstered in cream leather. There were a pair of modern pictures on the walls, but Ahmed didn't recognise them. On the desk, a computer.

'I thought you'd retired from . . .' started Muller, before pausing as he fished around for the right word. 'Our old trade.'

'This is business,' said Ahmed.

'A bomb? Unless you happen to be a defence manu-facturer, then buying a bomb isn't really a business deal.'

'This one is,' said Ahmed flatly.

He had no intention of telling Muller what he was planning: he trusted him, but not that much. He had to tell him what he needed, however. How else was the German meant to supply it?

'I'm being paid to bring down a jet,' he said, looking straight at Muller.

'And can I ask who's paying?'

Ahmed shook his head. 'No.'

'Or which jet?'

'No.'

Muller nodded. He wouldn't have expected that informa-tion, thought Ahmed. So he won't mind being refused.

'I thought you were out of . . . our old business, as well,' Ahmed said.

'Let us say, I have moved from retail to wholesale,' said Muller with a thin smile. 'After all, the product we're talking about never really took off here in Germany. The revolution never happened here, the way we once thought it might. And with the Wall coming down, and the country reunited,

141

I suspect it never will. Maybe you didn't know it at the time, but most of our funding came from the old East Germany anyway, so I think we can now assume that the overthrow of capitalism has been indefinitely postponed.' Muller shrugged. 'But the product has been doing just fine in other parts of the world. So, a bit like everyone else I was at school with, I've joined the great German export machine. Except that what I do is more profitable than the machine tools and chemicals and pharmaceuticals that they make. Less competition, I suppose.'

'I need a bomb that will do the job for me.'

'For a plane?'

'That's right.'

'Planes have always been difficult, you know that.'

'Of course,' said Ahmed. 'But, science moves on. There are new devices, new detonators . . .'

'You mean the Toshiba bomb?'

Ahmed nodded. The Toshiba bomb had acquired its name, not because it was made by the Japanese electronics manufacturer, but because the rough, early versions of them were placed inside Toshiba cassette players. Ahmed had learned about them after reading that a bomb-making house had been raided by the German intelligence foreign service, the Bundesnachrichtendienst, or BND, who'd discovered a range of sophisticated bomb-making equipment. Only the most scant details had been made available to the papers that Ahmed had read, but it appeared that the devices were triggered by a barometric pressure switch: that is, a device that measured the altitude, and, when it was high enough, it exploded.

It was perfect. Carry the device along at ground level, and it was perfectly safe. Take it up in the air, and it went boom. As soon as he'd read about it, Ahmed had known that was precisely what he needed. And since the arrests by the BND were all in the Ruhr region, it was safe to assume that Muller had links to whoever it was who knew how to manufacture such a device. This was his territory.

'That's what I'm looking for,' said Ahmed.

Muller nodded. 'I can supply one.'

'The BND didn't catch everyone, then.'

'Those fools,' answered Muller, with a dismissive shake of the head. 'They just busted a few harmless workshops. They didn't even find enough material to make any charges stick.'

Ahmed leaned forward. He knew he'd come to the right place.

'How much?'

'$50,000,' said Muller. 'No negotiations, and certainly no refunds.'

Ahmed hesitated.

'We used to read a lot of Karl Marx, back in the old days,' continued Muller. 'Monopoly capitalism, that's what he was always talking about.'

'I think you'll find that was Lenin.'

Muller smiled. 'Well, he was always the one you wanted to pay attention to, the practical man,' he replied. 'When it comes to Toshiba bombs, then I'm a monopoly. You can take my price, or you can go elsewhere. Except there isn't anywhere else to go.'

'How soon can I collect it?'

'Where are you staying?'

'The Marriott, in Düsseldorf.'

'I'll pick you up there tomorrow, at noon.'

# TWENTY-FOUR

**London, 17 November**

Sam liked libraries, always had done. He enjoyed the peace
and quiet, the politeness, and the way that no one ever raised
their voices. And he enjoyed the sense of being surrounded
by information. Maybe, he'd reflect sometimes, you could
just lie back, and let it all flood into you. And in time you'd
have the answers to everything.

He scrolled forwards through the pages of the *Boston
Herald*. Together with Orla, he was sitting in the library of
the American Embassy in London, making use of its
microfiche records of the major daily papers published in the
US. It had seemed to him the most natural place to start.
Boston was a Catholic city, one of the Vatican's power bases
in the United States, and you could be certain the city paper
would cover the affairs of the diocese in detail.

Including its financial affairs.

'So what exactly are we looking for?' asked Orla.

'Anything to do with the Church's finances,' said Sam.
'Just anything at all that looks expensive.'

Orla pointed out a story from a year ago about the
Church sponsoring a new school.

'That's spending money,' pointed out Sam. 'We're
interested in how they earn it.'

'From tithes, maybe,' said Orla. 'That's what they do in
Ireland. You're meant to give ten per cent of your income

144

to the Church. Most people don't give that much, of course, but a lot of people give something, and it soon adds up.'

'What else?'

'Well, people leave them money as well,' said Orla. 'It happens all the time in Ireland. Somebody dies, and a big chunk of their estate goes to the Church. Drives the kids crazy.'

'Maybe it happens in Boston as well.'

Sam scoured the paper. He checked the religious section, as well as the obituaries. He was a quick reader, but the print on the microfiche was small: even with the help of the magnifying glass supplied with the reader, it didn't take long before your eyes started to feel the strain. Most of the obituaries were either of national figures, or else of local politicians. But Boston had been a wealthy city for more than two centuries, he noted, and ranked second only to New York as a financial centre. There were plenty of rich families. He felt sure he'd find what he was looking for eventually.

'Here,' said Orla, pointing at her screen.

Sam glanced at the obituary. It recorded the death of Charles Stewart, founder of the Stewart, Robertson mutual fund company, which, by the time of his death, managed funds in excess of $10 billion. Sam leaned close into Orla's neck, aware of the way her breasts moved up and down as she breathed, and scanned the words. His hands rested on the soft skin of her shoulder, and she glanced back at him and smiled. He skipped past the description of his war service, his early banking career, the details of how he set up the mutual fund business in the late 1950s, and how he made his fortune.

'Here,' he said.

Orla finished the sentence for him, reading aloud. 'He left his estate to his two surviving children, James and Vivian, and to his local church.'

145

'Which church?'

Orla pointed higher up. 'It says here he's a Catholic.'

Sam nodded curtly.

'Note down his name,' he said.

He went back to scanning his own microfiche. Checking his watch, he saw it was just after four. They had been here for an hour: another sixty minutes passed before he came across anything else of interest.

'Here,' he said, nudging Orla.

He read out the details to her. Kenny Riley had set up a construction company, becoming a lead contractor on highways in five north-eastern states, as well as building homes and office blocks. By the time he died, he had an estimated fortune of $60 million. 'According to this,' said Sam, 'he left half to a series of charities and half to the church. In this case, the Catholic Church.'

'I've made a note of the name,' said Orla.

By seven in the evening, they had gone through the obituaries for the past five years, and collected a total of four names. In addition to Stewart and Riley, they had dug up the names of Carl Zeiss and Toni Bersani. Both men had built up substantial fortunes: one of them in real estate, the other with one of the early computing companies that had eventually been absorbed by IBM. Zeiss had divided his between his two children and the church, while Bersani had left all his money to the local diocese.

Sam guided Orla out of the library, just as it was closing. He bought a couple of coffees at the café across the street. Instinctively he knew they had stumbled across something. He could feel it in his gut.

But what?

'They are getting all this money left to them by these wealthy people,' said Orla. 'Fortunes are being poured into the organisation from these wills. But they keep insisting they are broke.'

'Of course they're hiding it.'

'Yes, but how?'

Sam shook his head. 'People leave them the money, but somehow it doesn't show up in the accounts of the diocese.'

'Maybe they just transfer the cash overseas,' said Orla.

'Too simple,' answered Sam. 'A lawyer could just issue a subpoena for their bank accounts. They'd have to disclose them if a judge supported the action, and then the records would show them transferring the money abroad.'

'Then . . .'

Orla paused, running out of ideas.

'What do we do next?'

'You get us up to Heathrow, and book us on to the next flight to Boston,' said Sam. 'I'll close up the shop and pack us a bag.'

'To Boston, now?'

Sam nodded. 'I thought you wanted to solve this mystery,' he replied.

# TWENTY-FIVE

**Beirut, 17 November**

Ben put three coffees down on the table.

He was nervous, he didn't mind admitting that to himself.

Because he had no idea how the others would react.

The apartment the CIA had assigned to them was far from lavish. It had a sitting room, three bedrooms, a bathroom, and a small kitchen. They'd brought in some breakfast, and reconvened at just after seven in the morning to compare notes on what they'd discovered the previous day. I've known these two guys for the last three years, Ben reminded himself. Maybe I wouldn't trust them with my life. But I'd trust them with just about anything else.

I have to tell them what I found out yesterday afternoon.

Scott was already running through what he'd uncovered. He'd pumped Massoud Arebi as hard as he could, spending three hours with the man, but so far as he could tell the Libyan didn't know anything more about the hostages than anyone else did.

He reckoned Hamas was facing a financial squeeze: they'd been trying to pump more money out of the Iranians for the last six months, but without much success. Their protection rackets in the city weren't as profitable as they used to be, and the crime networks they ran in the Palestinian communities in the cities of Western Europe weren't managing to make anything extra to make good the shortfall. Arebi figured it was more about the ransom money they were demanding than anything else, but he had no idea where the hostages were being held, or even who within Hamas had organised their capture.

'If there are any leaks, they sure aren't getting back to the Libyans,' said Scott. 'They know even less than we do, and I don't think they care much either.'

Jim hadn't got much further. He'd spent the day down by the docks, asking questions, and bribing some of the harbour masters to talk to him. If there were any suspicious movements around the docks, they would know about it.

'But nothing,' said Jim. 'I spent ten hours talking to five different guys, and I would have been better off fishing. Nobody saw anything, nobody heard anything.'

'They don't have to use the docks,' said Scott. 'They could take them up the coast, and just use a dinghy to get them out to a bigger boat.'

'Sure,' said Scott. 'Or they could knock them out with a tranquilliser, stick them in a cargo box, and ship them out that way. It's possible, and we shouldn't rule anything out. But I don't think so. I reckon there would be gossip if they'd been shipped out by sea, and these guys, even if they didn't see anything directly, would have picked up on the rumours.'

'They are in Beirut,' interrupted Ben.

Both Scott and Jim glanced towards him.

He started to explain about his meeting with Hashem Akkad, telling them how he had met the man, and a how a cousin of his was being used to ferry the hostages across Beirut. Whether they could trust him or not, Ben didn't know. Not yet anyway. But it was the closest thing they had to a lead so far.

'The trouble is, he wants $200,000,' said Jim. '$100,000 for himself, and $100,000 for his cousin. Plus a new identity and an American passport for the cousin.'

'Shit, that's a lot of money,' said Scott.

'I reckon the agency would pay up,' said Jim. 'So long as the guy was on the level.'

'But that's not the real problem,' interrupted Ben. 'They might pay up or they might not. If the guy checked out, and he could really tell us where the hostages were, with enough time to go and get them out before they are moved on again, then I reckon it would be worth it.'

He paused, looking at both his colleagues. 'There's something else.'

'Which is?' snapped Scott.

From his tone, it sounded to Ben as if he was starting to lose his patience.

'The Beirut office is involved in smuggling drugs back to the United States.'

There was a silence.

'Shit,' muttered Scott eventually.

'Christ,' said Ben.

'Akkad started asking whether his money would be coming from Washington, or from the funds the Beirut office was creaming off the drugs trade.'

'It could just be Beirut street gossip,' said Scott. 'All kinds of weird stories circulate about the agency in this part of the world.'

'I wasn't questioning him,' responded Ben. 'He just came right out with it. I don't know if it's true or not. But I could see this much. The guy I was talking to sure as hell *thought* it was true.'

'How would he know?' asked Scott.

'They could be sourcing the drugs here in Beirut,' said Jim. 'If they were doing that, then men like Akkad would know about it.'

'And how are they getting them back?' said Scott.

'In the diplomatic bag,' said Ben. 'That's the theory, anyway.'

He drained his coffee cup, stood up, and walked across to the kitchen. He poured himself some orange juice from the fridge, using the time to think.

'The question is, what are we going to do about it?'

'We were sent here to find the hostages,' said Scott.

'But maybe we've found something more important.'

'Than four innocent lives?' snapped Scott. You could hear the anger in his voice. 'I don't see what's more important than that, do you?'

'Shit, we're talking about shipping drugs into the United States via the CIA,' said Jim. 'That's pretty damned serious.'

'So what do you want to do?' said Scott.

'I reckon we investigate further,' said Ben. 'We'll talk to the agency and see if they'll authorise a payment to Akkad.'

He paused, weighing the next sentence carefully.

'In the meantime, let's see if we can find out more about these drugs stories. Maybe its just street gossip. But if it's not . . . we need to know about it.'

# TWENTY-SIX

**Boston, 18 November**

The Fairmont Copley Plaza was sited just back from Copley Square, and only a couple of hundred yards from Boston's Charles River. Sam had already taken two single rooms, one for each of them. The thought of a double room had flashed through his mind. It would save a lot of money, he reckoned. But he'd risk losing Orla with just the suggestion: no matter how much she might have rebelled against it, she was a still a convent girl from Ireland, and those kinds of girls stayed in singe rooms.

*She is too valuable a resource to lose now.*

Sam was sitting in the coffee room, waiting for Orla to finish changing: she hadn't brought any clothes with her, but she'd picked up a couple of things at the Gap down the road from the hotel. In a few minutes, they were meeting Richard Breedon, one of the best-connected antiques dealers in the United Sates, and a man Sam had already done business with several times. If anyone knew of any valuable items that had fallen into the hands of the Church in recent months then Sam felt certain Breedon would be the man.

The flight had been straightforward enough. Sam had gone back to the shop, persuaded one of the guys up the road to keep an eye on it for a few days, then tossed a few belongings into a bag before getting a cab out to Heathrow. Orla had already reserved them two seats on the ten o'clock flight from London to Boston operated by American Airlines. There was just time for a quick bite to eat and a glass of wine before boarding the plane. They'd talked for the first couple of hours, while Sam polished off a pair of whiskies: he'd learned more about her time with her brother, how she'd tried to protect him, and later on how she tried to help him recover from the years of abuse. It struck Sam how mature she seemed, like a girl who had grown up far too fast, and still wasn't sure what to do with her life.

She asked him some questions about himself. Clearly she knew about his past in the Mossad, and she was pressing him for details. She knew he'd been an assassin, and, like most people, she asked him how he'd felt about the work. They were criminals, he replied. They were enemies of my country, and I was a soldier, so I dealt with them, the same way any soldier would. It was the same answer he gave everyone. With Orla, however, he felt it was less than honest. The truth was, it wasn't quite like being a soldier. Armies fought in groups, surrounded by their own men, and when they killed it was in the heat of battle. Assassins worked mostly by themselves, or in small groups, and when they killed a man it was in cold blood. In time, that chipped away at you: you ended up feeling as much like a murderer as a soldier. It wasn't the kind of thing you could explain easily, reflected Sam. Maybe when I know her better.

'Another coffee,' said Orla, breaking his train of thought.

'I need something to keep me awake,' said Sam. 'I never sleep on planes.'

She looked as fresh as a newly picked flower, Sam noted, as she signalled to the waitress for another two coffees. She'd changed into a blue skirt, and a white blouse, and she'd pinned her slightly wet hair back with a hair clip, making her face appear thinner and older than before. And maybe even prettier, decided Sam. Unlike many women, she had the kind of beauty that will only improve with age.

Breedon was already walking across the reception. Sam had called him last night from the airport: they'd done enough good deals together, and he knew enough of Sam's reputation, that he didn't mind clearing out space in his diary to meet him the next day. Breedon had his own shop in Boston, and another in New York, but he mainly worked as a consultant, advising wealthy businessmen and some of the banks on how to furnish their homes and offices. There was plenty of old money even in this part of the world, reflected Sam to himself: but there was even more new money trying to look like old money. Breedon specialised in helping them complete the camouflage, and very lucrative it had proved so far.

He was a thin, elegant man, dressed in cream chinos, tanned leather loafers, a white linen shirt and a blue blazer. His clothes might be casual, but they looked expensive all the same, and on his left wrist, he was wearing the biggest, fattest Rolex Sam had ever seen.

'Aren't you going to introduce me to your young friend?' said Breedon, nodding in the direction of Orla.

In the few days he'd known her, Sam had grown used to the impact she had on men. It's not just me, he thought. He'd seen it at work in the shop as well. As soon as they saw her, and as soon as she smiled, men fell under her spell. It wasn't just the way she looked – she was a pretty enough girl, but nothing that amazing – but the way she seemed so full of life and energy. It was as if you could recharge your batteries just by touching her.

'Orla Sheehy,' she said, standing up, and signalling to the waitress to bring them another coffee.

'Welcome to Boston,' said Breedon.

'I've already lived her for a while,' said Orla.

'Then you won't need someone to show you the sights,' said Breedon. 'That's a pity.'

'I'm sure there are some I've missed.'

'A museum, maybe,' said Breedon.

'Or some restaurants,' said Orla brightly. 'I love seafood.'

'It's a date.'

Not for the first time, Sam felt needled by how easily she flirted with all the men she met: the older and the richer they were, the quicker she kicked into gear. He knew why she did it, of course. Or at least he hoped he did. It captured their attention. They wanted to please her, to flatter her, and prove their wealth and intelligence: it automatically gave her a certain power over them, and she certainly knew how to use that to get what she wanted. But it still grates, decided Sam. And I know why.

*Because I can't help suspecting she's been doing the same thing to me.*

'We're trying to get a lead on any items that might have fallen into the hands of the Church recently,' interrupted Sam.

Breedon sat down in a chair opposite Sam. He glanced through the lobby of the hotel: the Fairmont was the smartest hotel in Boston, and it was just the sort of place where he might bump into one of his clients.

'The Church?'

'The Catholic archdiocese, here in Boston,' explained Sam. 'Over the years, people have left them a lot of stuff in their wills. We already know about that. What we're looking for is something they've been left recently, something that hasn't come on the market yet.'

Breedon nodded thoughtfully. 'May I be permitted to ask why?'

Sam shook his head. It was what he referred to as his undertaker's look: an expression that conveyed sympathy, but no flexibility. 'Let's just say we'll treat the information discreetly . . .'

'And we'd be really grateful,' interrupted Orla.

She was twirling a finger in the froth of her cappuccino, noted Sam.

*And, as usual, it works . . .*

'Of course,' said Breedon.

He thought for a moment.

'You've heard of Amati?'

Sam was about to speak – to say that he hadn't – but Orla had already leaned forward.

'Most people have heard of Stradivari violins, but the Amatis are much older,' said Orla. 'Andrea Amati lived from 1520 to 1578, and his are the oldest violins that are still in use today. In fact, Andrea is credited with giving the violin its definitive modern shape. He had two sons, Antonio and Girolamo, but it is probably Girolamo's son Nicolo who is the most famous Amati of them all. He is credited with getting the tone completely perfect, and many musicians reckon that his instruments might have been equalled but they have never been bettered. Stradivari was one of his pupils, and although he refined the modern violin, it was really the Amati family that created it.'

'Beautiful and smart,' said Breedon, looking admiringly at Orla.

'Any Amati would be incredibly valuable,' said Orla.

'I know,' said Breedon.

'The Church has one?' asked Sam.

'Three months ago a man called George Turner died,' said Breedon. 'He was a banker here in Boston, a private operation, and he sold out about a decade ago to one of the big Wall Street firms. He was a fanatical collector of old instruments, and he owned an Amati. He left much of his estate to his daughter Eleanor, but the instrument went to the diocese.'

'A Nicolo?' said Orla.

'An Andrea,' said Breedon. 'Possibly the oldest violin you can still play anywhere in the world.'

'Will they sell it?' asked Sam.

'Of course, they need the money,' said Breedon. 'Or at least, they need the money a lot more than they need a 400-year-old violin.'

'How soon?' asked Orla.

'I believe it's on the market right now.'

'Believe?'

Sam looked straight at Breedon. 'Or know?'

'They have put the word out to a few upmarket dealers,' said Breedon. 'There aren't many people in the world that would want an Amati. And even fewer who would pay what they are demanding.'

He drained the last of his coffee. 'There is a man in the diocese office called Father O'Connell. He's handling the sale. In fact, he handles all the sales. I'll call him if you like, and say you might be interested.'

Sam nodded. 'We need to see him right away.'

'It's done,' said Breedon, standing up.

He looked towards Orla. 'You said you liked seafood,' he said. 'There are some marvellous seafood restaurants in Boston.'

# TWENTY-SEVEN

**Düsseldorf, 18 November**

Muller had collected Ahmed right on time. He was driving a new BMW 5 series, upholstered in thick black leather, with tinted windows. They drove mostly in silence, through the city, out into the industrial suburbs, and along the route of the Rhine, in the direction of Duisburg. They pulled off the main road, into the small town of Bilkrath, steering through the quiet suburban streets until they reached an industrial estate.

It was sleepy, suburban Germany, noted Ahmed, with the neatest lawns anywhere in the world: this was precisely the Germany that Muller and his friends had been trying to destroy during the 1970s, but now he seemed completely at home in it. He's probably even voting for Helmut Kohl by now.

'Here,' said Muller, climbing out of the car.

Ahmed followed him into the workshop. It measured about fifty feet by forty, filled with hi-tech engineering equipment and computers. There was a smell of smouldering irons, and of burnt electrical wires, but otherwise, the room was devoid of character, clean and functional.

A small man dressed in a white coat stepped forwards from behind a precision lathe, and glanced towards Muller. He had a bristly moustache, and a thin, yet friendly face. His black hair was short on top, then stretched down the back of his neck, making him look like the bass player in a not very successful heavy metal band.

'This is Hans Dittmer,' said Muller. 'He has prepared . . .' He paused, chewing over the word. 'The device.'

They walked in silence towards a small back office that sat behind the main workshop. On the desk, there were some papers, a diary, a half-drunk bottle of Diet Coke, and a computer with two monitors.

'One's for my work,' explained Dittmer. 'And this one . . .'

He pointed towards the second monitor.

'This one is for you.'

Ahmed looked at the device. It was a standard twelve-inch computer monitor, of the type that had become familiar on every desktop in the world since IBM launched the first of their personal computers a few years ago. There was a slight curve to the screen, and the monitor bulged at the back where the cathode ray tube stuck out, as well as a plug and some wires. To Ahmed, it looked just like an everyday piece of office equipment.

'How does it work?' he said, looking at Dittmer.

He withdrew a small screwdriver from the breast pocket of his shirt, and started to take the back off the monitor. 'Here,' he said, pointing towards the inside of the monitor.

Ahmed glanced inside. There was a tube, and a mess of wire, all enclosed within a metal frame to which the plastic casing was attached.

'We're actually using a slightly smaller than usual cathode ray tube which I made here,' said Dittmer. 'That frees up some space for us. But it also means the monitor will still work, should anyone become inquisitive and decide to switch it on.'

Ahmed nodded.

'Around the core of the tube, I've packed in 300 grams of

159

high-grade Semtex. As I am sure you know, that is by far the best type of explosive for a job of this sort. This batch was produced by VCHZ Synthesia, based in the town of Pardubice in the Czech Republic, where, of course, the explosive was first developed, so it is of the highest quality. Semtim, as you may know, is a suburb of Pardubice, and that's where it gets its name from. These days they add ethylene glycol dinitrate to the mix, which gives a smell that the airport scanners can detect, but this batch was made five years ago before they started doing that. And, since Semtex has a shelf life of twenty years, it is as good as the day it was made. It has no smell, so the sniffer dogs won't detect it. It should be more than enough to blow a decent-sized hole out of the fuselage of any aircraft.'

'How big?'

Muller leaned forwards on the desk. 'This should punch a hole of at least a foot in diameter,' he said. 'That's assuming it is placed at the centre of the cargo hold. If it is close to the skin of the plane, the hole will be bigger.'

'But a foot is enough,' said Dittmer. 'Even on a 747, the largest plane in commercial service, that will critically destabilise the plane. The pressure set off by the blast will literally start to tear it to shreds. The pilot will lose control within seconds. Within less than a minute, the plane will be plunging to the ground.'

'And how do we set it off?'

'The problem with putting a bomb on a plane is not usually getting the explosives on board,' said Dittmer. 'We can pack some Semtex into a monitor such as this one, or a television or a cassette player, without much risk of it being detected. The problem is setting it off.'

'If you use any kind of radio device, it will be detected by the airport security staff,' said Muller. 'And anyway, how are you going to send the signal? After all, you wouldn't want to be in the plane yourself.'

160

He laughed, but no one was sharing the joke, and he quickly fell silent again.

'You could use a timer,' said Dittmer. 'But plane schedules aren't reliable enough. If the bomb just goes off in the hanger, that's not going to have the impact you are looking for.'

'So we've fitted a barometric device,' said Muller.

With his screwdriver, Dittmer pointed to a tiny pressure gauge, attached to a detonator, and four slim pencil batteries, inside the monitor. A thin strip of wire attached the detonator to the Semtex. 'The barometric gauge has a small vacuum chamber,' said Dittmer. 'Once that falls to 950 millibars, it flicks this switch here.' Again, he pointed with the screwdriver. 'That is attached to a timer, set for forty minutes. The pressure will only drop to 950 at about 2,500 feet. The aircraft should reach that within about six or seven minutes after take-off, and the bomb will explode forty minutes after that, which should be once it is up to its cruising altitude.'

'Does it ever fail?' said Ahmed.

'We've tested this one dozens of times, without the Semtex attached, of course, by putting it through a pressure chamber,' said Dittmer. 'It works perfectly.'

He leaned forwards. 'You just have to switch it on, using this lever here.'

Ahmed tried it three times, making sure he knew exactly how to activate the device.

'You can transport it quite safely back to Beirut,' said Muller. 'Unless it is activated it, there is no possibility of the device exploding. Nor should it be detectable by any airport authorities.'

'Thank you,' said Ahmed, shaking Muller's hand. 'You won't be hearing from me again.'

Muller smiled. 'Why not?'

'Because after this job, it will be too dangerous for me to work again.'

# TWENTY-EIGHT

**Boston, 18 November**

Sam didn't much care for the Catholic Church. He was Jewish, a Mossad man in spirit if no longer in service, and he knew the Church had never been any friend of the state of Israel. They might have dropped the older form of the Latin mass – the one that spoke about 'delivering the Jewish people out of their darkness' – but there had always been a tension between the two religions. And that historical record would take a long time to address.

Still, decided Sam, you couldn't question the beauty of their cathedrals.

The Cathedral of the Holy Cross wasn't the most stunning he had ever seen: it certainly wasn't a match for the Spanish, Italian, or French cathedrals that filled the main cities of Europe. But it was among the finest anywhere in North America. Located in the city's South End district, it had been started in the 1860s, and the dedication had been performed by Boston's first archbishop, John Williams, in 1875. It was built in the Victorian Gothic style. Indeed, reflected Sam, as he glanced up at its imposing spire, if the building was located in London, you might well assume it was a railway station.

It was quiet at this time of the morning. As he pushed the door ajar, and stepped inside, Sam could feel the sombre silence all around him.

Father O'Connell was seated on the tenth row back from the altar, on the left-hand side of the main aisle. Sam could feel the cool air all around him as he walked through the building: blue and red lights were streaming through the stained-glass windows, and, off to the right, you could smell the soft scent of the candles. Sam could see now why O'Connell had suggested they meet here when he phoned this morning. It was a far more impressive display of the Church's wealth and power than the diocese's rather modest administrative office a couple of blocks away. It was a way of letting him know exactly who and what he was dealing with.

And in its own way, he admitted to himself, it worked.

Sam paused for a moment, allowing himself time to take in the atmosphere, before approaching O'Connell. Boston, although originally a Protestant city, had become one of the main centres of Catholicism in the United States, he recalled. People put that down to the waves of Irish immigrants who arrived in the nineteenth century, but in fact there were just as many Poles and Germans in the city as there were Irish. It had been made an archdiocese by Pope Pius IX in 1875 in recognition of its growing power, and today, it covered nearly two million Church members, of whom 300,000 attended regularly. It was the richest diocese in the richest country in the world, and that gave it a special position within the Catholic hierarchy that outweighed the actual size of its congregations.

'Mr Woolfman,' said Sam, leaning forward from the pew behind where O'Connell was kneeling.

He looked around. O'Connell was a pale-faced man, with grey hair, and gold-rimmed glasses. He was wearing a dark blue suit, and a striped tie, with a white shirt. His expression was kindly yet authoritative, like a schoolteacher's.

'Let's take a walk,' he said softly.

There was a garden directly opposite the cathedral,

although at this time of year there weren't any flowers in bloom, and the leaves had all fallen from the trees. Sam followed him through the gate, and remained silent as they stepped along the path. He suspected that Father O'Connell wanted to put some distance between himself and the cathedral before he started talking about money. Let him play it his way, decided Sam. I'm here to learn, that's all.

'You come highly recommended, Mr Woolfman,' said O'Connell.

'I'm pleased to hear it,' answered Sam.

'London must be a good place to deal in antiques,' said O'Connell. 'The English value the past, not like us Americans. Here people want everything to be new.'

'Surely not everyone?'

Father O'Connell shook his head sadly. 'Maybe a generation ago, there were plenty of rich men who valued antiques, art . . . but not so many anymore.'

Sam shrugged. 'There are still plenty of them in Europe, at least.'

Father O'Connell stopped and turned around to look at Sam directly. 'And you know who they are.'

'I have a number of wealthy clients,' said Sam. 'I source valuable items for them. If they want them, then they don't mind paying what they are worth.'

'Such as?'

'I heard the diocese was left a violin, an Amati,' said Sam.

He could hear the wind starting to whistle in the trees all around them.

'And that it might be for sale.'

'Ah, but it's a lovely instrument,' said O'Connell. 'You should hear the tone on it, like a bird singing it is. Can you imagine it, Mr Woolfman? A 400-year-old piece of carved wood, and it can still sing to us exquisitely. Through all those centuries.'

'Amazing,' said Sam. 'And valuable, no doubt.'

'And you know someone who wants to buy it?'

'Indeed,' answered Sam. 'There aren't many people who collect Amatis. But the right person would pay handsomely for the right piece, I feel certain of it.'

Father O'Connell kept walking. 'Where are you staying, Mr Woolfman?'

'The Fairmont.'

'Then you'll be hearing from me before the day is done.'

# TWENTY-NINE

**Beirut, 18 November**

Ben sat silently in the car, looking at the clock on the dashboard as the hours ticked by. Waiting was part of an agent's job, he knew that by now, but he still found it boring. You sat, and sat, and sat . . . and most of the time nothing at all happened.

He glanced across to the drab office building. The CIA bureau was on the third floor, as he knew from his visit there earlier in the week, but it was just after eight in the evening now, and he was well aware that probably most of the few staff that worked there would have already gone home. They might be in the middle of a hostage crisis, but when you worked in Beirut, Ben reflected, there was always some kind of crisis, so not many of them would be staying late.

*And it looks like they might have more profitable things on their minds.*

He was waiting in a black Volkswagen Golf, the most anonymous car he'd been able to rent at the Hertz office in the centre of the city. He'd been sitting here for an hour already, ignoring the traffic all around him. The three of them had agreed yesterday morning that they would do what they could to establish whether the agency's Beirut bureau was really trading in drugs or whether it was just street rumours.

If we can't stand it up in forty-eight hours, Ben had told Scott and Jim, we'll just let it drop.

An elderly but well maintained grey Audi pulled up outside the building, its driver taking care to park discreetly behind a blue van. Ben watched carefully as one man climbed out of the car, and stepped into the foyer, while another man stayed at the wheel, keeping the engine ticking over. Ben started up the VW, and kept his hands on the wheel. Less than a minute later, the man emerged, carrying a crate. He placed it on the back seat, then climbed into the car, shutting the door carefully behind him.

The diplomatic 'bag' hadn't actually been a bag since the days when they carried messages around by horseback, Ben reminded himself. This one was more like a crate, made from metal and measuring four feet by two, with enough room to store several folders of diplomatic files. Whether anyone ever read the stuff, Ben wasn't sure. Probably Bill Horton does, and no one else. Still, it was what they were paid for, and the bureau dutifully churned out files every day. And the crate was flown home, unopened by anyone on the way, just like hundreds of crates arriving in Washington every day.

Except – maybe – this one was different.

He pulled the VW away from the kerb, following the Audi at a discreet distance. He was careful always to keep at least three cars between himself and the target. The Audi drove through the diplomatic quarter, past the gigantic Omari Mosque and the old Parliament Building, then started to head out of the city towards the suburbs.

A taxi slipped between them at one stage, then paused for more than two minutes while a woman climbed out and fumbled in her purse for her change, but Ben managed to keep the Audi within eyeshot. In total, the drive took about fifteen minutes, before the car pulled up outside an apartment block and a row of local shops in the Naccache district. A man stood up from one of the cafés, left his newspaper and coffee behind, and walked across to the car, exchanging a few words with the driver. They seemed to be joking about something, because both of them were laughing, noted Ben, maintaining a discreet distance twenty yards back. They obviously knew each other well, and were relaxed in this routine. Then the man went back inside the café, and returned with a large black sports holdall. They opened up the crate, and placed three bags inside it. Another joke, more laughter, then the Audi pulled away from the kerb again.

Ben steered his VW back on to the road. This time, the car seemed to be heading towards the airport, and the traffic was getting heavier. It was just after six in the evening, and people were heading home from work. Staying in touch with the Audi was getting harder. Beirut didn't have the calmest drivers even at the best of times, reflected Ben. In rush-hour traffic they were snarling into one another like wild dogs.

A couple of times he lost sight of the Audi for a few moments, only to pick it up again on the highway. Eventually it pulled up outside the cargo bay of the airport. Ben hung back, watching from a distance. Both men climbed out of the car, showed a set of ID papers to a uniformed guard, then carried the crate into the building. There was a wait of three minutes, then the men came outside, got back into the car, and drove away. Time for those guys to get a beer, Ben told himself.

And for me to go to work.

He parked the VW into the bay, and stepped towards the cargo building. When the guard stopped him, Ben fished out his CIA identification badge. He had a shoulder bag on his left arm, and he patted it. 'There's some important stuff left out of the American diplomatic bag,' he said. 'I need to add it.'

The guard pointed inside.

Ben stepped through the doors. There were two more uniformed guards, and a row of airline desks, handling the different airlines. The diplomatic bag, he'd established, flew on a Lufthansa flight from Beirut to Frankfurt, and from there was placed on to Pan Am Flight 103 that flew from Frankfurt to Washington via London. The Lufthansa desk was manned by a uniformed local.

'I need to see the American diplomatic bag,' said Ben, putting his ID down on the desk.

'Your name?' said the official.

'Ben Hanold,' he replied.

The official pushed across a form, taking a note of Ben's agency ID, and also his passport number. 'Sign here.'

Ben scrawled his name. He knew he was leaving a paper chain: if anyone wanted to find out later on whether he been checking on the diplomatic bag, then it would be a simple matter to retrieve these records. But the risk was low, he judged. The bag was flown out of Beirut every night. He hadn't been spotted following the Audi. There was no reason why anyone from the Beirut bureau should be investigating whether anyone looked at today's bag.

'That way,' said the official.

The crate was sitting just behind a partition screen, close to the loading bay where it would be driven out on a trolley to be put on to the aircraft. A guard was standing close to him. 'This is official,' said Ben. 'I need to be alone.'

The guard stepped away, behind the partition. As he did so, Ben opened up the crate. It was secured in place by two simple catches: there was an electronic code to open the catches, consisting of four digits, but Ben had already called Washington to ask what the code was for the Beirut bag. Inside was a collection of official papers.

And three bags, made from strong, black plastic.

Using his fingers, Ben deftly opened one of them up.

169

Inside there was white powder.

From his pocket, Ben took out a clean cotton handker-chief. He folded a sample of the white powder into it, and tucked it back into his pocket.

Sure looks like cocaine, he told himself.

He folded the crate shut, then walked back outside the partition.

'All done,' he said to the official. 'Thanks for your help.'

# THIRTY

**Beirut, 19 November**

Ahmed checked the package.

He had just collected it from the Federal Express office in Beirut, after it had been delivered overnight on a flight from Frankfurt.

He opened it up carefully in the apartment he had rented for a few days.

The monitor was there, intact.

Using a screwdriver, he undid the back. The Semtex was neatly packed into the sides of the cathode ray tube, just the way Muller had said it would be. The barometric device had been set so that it would only trigger the detonator the third time the device was lifted above 2,500 feet, as he had requested.

You can't beat German efficiency, he told himself with a thin smile.

All he had to do now was make sure it got on to the right plane at the right time.

And he already knew how he was going to do that.

He walked out of the apartment, and down on to the street. It was a one-mile walk to the café where he usually met Hussein Gezairy. Like most of Beirut's businessmen, traders, and traffickers, he maintained an office, but preferred to hold his meetings in the open, on the streets and over a cup of coffee.

*Maybe he likes to keep tabs on his enemies.*

If that is how he wants it, that is okay with me, decided Ahmed.

Just so long as no one overhears us.

The clouds had lifted this morning, and Beirut was bathed in the warm, hazy sunshine of late autumn. Ahmed walked slowly, not in any rush. He'd landed in the city last night after catching a train from Düsseldorf down to Frankfurt airport, then getting a last-minute seat on the Lufthansa flight into Beirut. The airlines weren't full into this city anymore, he noticed. Even the German businessmen with their cars and chemicals and machine tools weren't so keen on doing business in Beirut now.

Not with the kidnapped hostages still making headlines all over the world.

'Life is treating you better, I hope,' said Ahmed, sitting down at the café next to Gezairy.

He was early, he noted, glancing at his watch. They'd arranged to meet at eleven, but Gezairy was already there, even though it was still only ten forty-five. He looked worried, like he had just received some bad news, but Ahmed knew better than to enquire. If he had any problems, he wouldn't expect to be told what they were.

'I can't complain,' said Gezairy.

But he had the look of a man who would complain at length if only he was given the chance.

'I have something for you,' said Ahmed.

Gezairy looked up, as if he was expecting yet more bad news.

Ahmed opened up the shoulder bag he was carrying, and took out an envelope. He pushed it across the table.

Gezairy waited for the two coffees they had just ordered to be put down on the table. He watched the waiter disappear back into the café before picking up the envelope. His eyes started to brighten as he surveyed its contents.

$10,000.

In crisp, fresh notes, straight from the bank.

'What's this for?' he asked.

'I need something done.'

'What?'

There was a tone of suspicion in his voice, noted Ahmed. To a man such as Gezairy, when somebody needed something, it nearly always meant trouble.

'I want to know the precise route that the drugs take to the United States.'

Gezairy took a sip of his coffee. His expression switched to one of conspiratorial confidence as he pondered his reply.

'The bag goes on the Lufthansa flight from Beirut to Frankfurt,' he said. 'When it arrives at Frankfurt airport, the bag is transferred on to Pan Am Flight 103. Nobody touches it en route. That plane takes off for London, then flies on to Washington late in the evening. It flies overnight, then arrives the next morning.'

'The same route every time?'

I need to know precisely how this works, Ahmed reminded himself.

Nothing must be left to chance.

Gezairy nodded.

'They are scheduled flights with reliable airlines,' he said. 'We've been doing this run every day for more than a year now, and it is always the same.'

'When the drugs are put into the diplomatic bag, I want to put something else in there as well.'

'What?'

Ahmed leaned forward and tapped the envelope with the money in it.

'This gives me the right not to have to answer any questions.'

Gezairy smiled.

At least I'm talking a language he understands, decided Ahmed.

'There is a café in Naccache,' he said. 'The bag is collected every night from the CIA bureau in Beirut. The drivers go via the café. The drugs are planted inside the bag at that point. Then they drive on to the airport, and hand it across to security. There is a code on an electronic lock, but our men have that so that the drugs can be put inside.'

'I'll go to the café, and instead of drugs, I'll put a different item in the bag,' said Ahmed.

'What's in it?'

Ahmed patted the envelope with the cash inside.

'Like I said, what I'm buying with this money is the right not to have to answer any questions.'

Gezairy stood up and tucked the envelope with the cash inside it into his pocket.

'Consider it done,' he said.

# THIRTY-ONE

**Boston, 19 November**

Orla was wound up like a coiled spring, noted Sam.

You could see the tension within her. She was pacing around the room, drinking endless cups of coffee, picking up a book, then putting it down again after reading less than half a page.

Nothing seemed to calm her down.

They had spent the day sightseeing in Boston. She'd been out to dinner the night before with Breedon, and Sam didn't mind admitting he'd felt angry with her for going. He ate alone in the hotel, then waited for her in the lobby, drinking two whiskies in a row, watching for her to return. She'd finally showed up about eleven, complaining about how she had to spend most of the evening slapping the man's hands away from her thighs.

'Are all antiques dealers like that, Sam?' she asked, after he'd ordered her an Irish whiskey as a nightcap.

'The real ones, yes,' said Sam. 'You should stick to the spies who just pretend to be dealing in antiques. We keep our hands to ourselves.'

This morning, there had still been no word from Father O'Connell, so they'd taken themselves on a tour of the city. Orla knew it intimately, but Sam had only ever drifted through it. She took him to the Boston Museum of Fine Arts, to look at its Titians, Van Goghs, and Dürers, then they

175

had some pasta overlooking the Charles River. But he could tell she was on edge. She picked reluctantly at her food, whereas usually she wolfed down anything that looked edible, and she resisted several invitations to show off how much she knew about the paintings in the museums. Investigations are like this, he tried to explain to her over lunch. He could tell she was nervous about when Father O'Connnell would call, about when they could take the next step. But there was no point in rushing it: do that and you could blow everything. Try to hurry O'Connell, he explained, and the man will just become suspicious. On every investigation, a lot of the time you are just hanging around, waiting for things to happen.

You just have to get used to it. *It never changes.*

'There is a message for you, Mr Woolfman,' said the receptionist, as Sam picked up his key from the desk.

Sam was aware of the way Orla was looking at him expectantly as he opened up the envelope he'd just been handed. He slit open the paper, glanced inside, then looked up at Orla and smiled.

'Father O'Connell wants me to call him,' he said.

He could see the excitement on her face. They took the lift to Sam's room, and, while Orla shut the door behind her, Sam dialled the number noted down on the slip of paper.

'Father O'Connell,' he said, when the phone was answered on the third ring. 'Sam Woolfman here.'

He listened closely as O'Connell spoke.

Then he turned around to look at Orla.

'There's a man called Reto Ziegler in Geneva,' he said quietly. 'He's been finding buyers for anything that falls into the hands of the diocese.'

Orla leaned across, and kissed Sam on the cheek.

It seemed to him the kiss lingered slightly longer than necessary.

*But maybe I'm just imagining that.*

'We should get to the airport, and get ourselves back to London,' said Sam. 'When he rings, we don't want to miss that call.'

# THIRTY-TWO

**Beirut, 19 November**

Ben put the sheet of paper down on the table. On top of it, were a few traces of white powder.

The test results were clear enough.

'Cocaine,' he said, looking across the small apartment at Scott and Jim. 'The bastards are smuggling cocaine. I reckon there might be heroin in that other bag as well.'

Jim looked down at the sheet of paper. In his first year working for the agency, he'd spent a year down in Colombia, fighting the drug cartels that were shipping narcotics up from that country into the United States. He'd been out in the villages where the crop was grown, harvested, and processed. He fought the men who organised the trade, some of them in hand-to-hand combat. He knew what cocaine tasted and smelled like, and he knew as the kind of damage it could inflict on the streets of the ghettos.

And this was cocaine.

'It's a betrayal of everything we've fought for,' he said quietly. 'Guys from this agency are out fighting and dying to stop this kind of shit getting into the country. And the Beirut bureau is shipping the stuff into the country on the damned diplomatic bag.'

'The question,' said Ben, 'is what are we going to do about it?'

All three men fell silent.

It was early in the morning. Ben had got back from the airport with the sample yesterday evening. It had taken a few hours to get the kit together, then to complete the test. He'd done it three times. With evidence like this, there was no way you could afford to make any kind of mistake. He'd let the others sleep, grabbed a few restless hours in bed himself, then presented them with the evidence this morning.

'We go home and blow the whistle,' said Ben.

Scott shook his head.

'We speak to Horton first.'

'They aren't going to let this come out,' said Ben. 'Who knows, maybe they'll even cover the whole thing up. You know what the agency is like.'

'Horton has a right to know,' said Jim. 'He runs the Middle East desk. And he's the operation director. If we tell him what the Beirut bureau is up to, then he'll move in and stop it. He's a decent guy.'

'Like hell he will,' said Ben.

'We need one more piece of evidence first,' said Jim.

Both men turned to face him.

'What more do we need?' said Ben. 'We found the damned drugs in the diplomatic bag heading for Washington.'

'We need to know who's collecting them at the other end.'

'And how are we going to do that?' asked Ben.

'We need to follow Flight 103,' said Jim.

Light was starting to pour in through the apartment's windows, and you could hear the bustle of people going to work outside.

'We need to be on that flight, then see what happens to the bag at the other end,' persisted Jim. 'That way we'll know precisely who is collecting the drugs. After all, right now we don't even know for sure whether anyone in Washington is involved. Or whether the drugs are just passed on to a local dealer.'

179

'Then we catch the Lufthansa flight first,' said Ben.

Jim shook his head. 'That would create too much suspicion,' he answered. 'I reckon we should fly to Cyprus first, then get to Frankfurt from there. That way no one in the agency will suspect what we are up to.'

Scott stood up and looked towards the window.

I don't like the plan, he told himself.

*I don't like it at all.*

# THIRTY-THREE

**CIA Headquarters, Langley, 19 November**

Bill Horton put the phone down.

He stood up, and walked across to the window. It was early morning here, and the office was largely empty. Horton always made sure he was here at six sharp: unless he was at his desk by that time, he couldn't study all the overnight briefings before the morning round of meetings kicked off at eight. There were a few people starting to pull up in the parking lot, and the gardener was starting to sweep up the autumn leaves that had fallen over the pathways. But this was the quietest Langley ever got.

But in Beirut it was mid afternoon.

And his three agents were already on the way to Cyprus.

*With some stupid story about drug trading in the Beirut bureau.*

Problems, thought Horton to himself. Nothing but damned problems.

The file on the hostages was still on his desk.

A rescue squad had been assembled, on the orders of the president.

A battle cruiser had been sent to the Mediterranean, and was equipped with two Chinook helicopters. A unit of five Navy Seals was ready to go in and attempt to break the hostages out. They had been briefed on the mission. A pair of advisers had been drafted in, one from the Israeli Defence Force, and the other from the British Special Air Service, the two military units with more experience of getting hostages out alive than any others in the world. They were on permanent twenty-four-hour standby.

But so far they still didn't have a clue where they were.

The Beirut bureau was claiming not to have any fresh leads. So far, they had spent nearly $100,000 on informants, but most of the money looked to have been wasted. They had been sold a series of dud informants. None of the tip-offs had led anywhere: some of them even turned out to be traps, and one agent had been badly injured when he went to talk to an informer, and was met instead by a hail of gunfire. The reality was they had no more idea where the hostages were than they did a week ago.

And now this.

Scott had just been on the phone.

He had slipped away from Ben and Jim to tell him that the three of them were coming straight back to Washington.

They had evidence that the Beirut bureau was smuggling drugs. And using the diplomatic bag.

Horton sighed.

It might be true, he reflected to himself. He'd never liked Foley. The man had been a political appointment, when they should have put a professional agency staffer into such a sensitive post. There was no more important bureau than Beirut. He'd tried to explain that to the director general, but the man hadn't listed to him. The budgets were strictly controlled. So much money had been wasted on covert operations over the years that the Beirut station was kept on a tight leash. Maybe they were raising extra cash to spend on their operations. Maybe they were creaming the money off for themselves, stashing it away in some tidy little retirement fund in the Cayman Islands.

*Who the hell knows?*

I know one thing for certain, thought Horton.

The agency can't afford a scandal like this.

182

*I can't afford a scandal like this.*

Not at this time.

Horton wiped his brow.

A bead of sweat was running across his forehead, he noticed. And he was a man who never sweated.

He could already imagine the field day that the press would have. As four innocent hostages were kept captive in Beirut, the CIA bureau was channelling drugs back into the United States.

They would be demanding that heads rolled.

And the operation director, the man with control of the agency's Middle East operations, would be the first with his neck on the block.

*That's me.*

Horton turned around, walking back to his desk. His first meeting of the day started in half an hour. They would be demanding to know what was happening to the hostages.

But that hardly mattered anymore.

I have to find a way of stopping those three men touching down in Washington, he told himself.

*This secret has to remain buried.*

And it doesn't matter what I have to do to make sure that what they discovered in Beirut is never revealed.

It will be done.

# THIRTY-FOUR

**Beirut: 19 November**

Ahmed sat quietly in the café.

He was wearing dark glasses, and he was concentrating on the newspaper laid on the table. Not many people knew him in Beirut. But he certainly didn't want to be recognised.

Not this evening.

Not when he was so close.

He glanced up and down the road. It was just after seven in the evening and the suburbs were starting to fill up with people. Some of them were coming home from work. Others had knocked off early, and were going out for the evening with their wives and girlfriends. The café was starting to get crowded, mostly with men, but a few women as well.

None of them, thought Ahmed, with a brief smile to himself, have any idea what is about to happen.

The Audi pulled up at the kerbside.

A man climbed out, and started walking towards the café. He went up to the waiter, and they exchanged a few words. He seemed to be laughing about something, noted Ahmed.

About what, he couldn't tell at this distance.

The waiter nodded towards Ahmed, and the man walked across, so that he was standing directly in front of him. 'You have something for us I'm told.'

Ahmed stood up and walked towards the car. He lifted up the boot, and looked down at the crate inside. The man leaned forward, keyed in a four-digit digital code, and the case sprung open. Ahmed lifted up his own blue plastic sports bag, and took out the monitor. He'd already set the barometric device perfectly, and screwed everything back into place. To anyone who examined it – and there was no reason why anyone should, since diplomatic bags were never opened – it would look just like a normal piece of computer equipment.

*It shouldn't arouse any suspicions at all.*

He slotted the monitor into position, towards the edge of the crate, next to a pile of papers tucked up inside thick white envelopes. For a brief moment, he decided it might be amusing to take some of the papers. After all, it wasn't often you got to read the confidential analysis the CIA bureau in Beirut was sending back to their head office. There were people he knew who might pay handsomely for that material, he reflected. And it wasn't as if anyone would notice. This crate was going to be blown to pieces some-where over the North Atlantic. They wouldn't ever discover a missing envelope.

But no, he told himself.

You never take any risks you don't have to.

That's how you have stayed in this game for so long.

He sealed the crate down shut, and watched as the man slammed the boot of the Audi.

'This is going straight to the airport?'

The man nodded.

'On to the Lufthansa flight?'

'Right now.'

Ahmed shook his hand. 'That's all,' he said curtly.

He watched as the car pulled away, then walked across the street to where his own driver was waiting in the Mercedes he used for long trips. He pulled open the door, and climbed into the back seat, telling the driver it was time to leave for Damascus.

Ahmed lay back.

Try to rest, he told himself.

You've done your job. And by the morning, several hundred Americans should be dead.

# THIRTY-FIVE

**Cyprus, 19 November**

The Skettos Travel Agency was located on a small side street just off the Kanlidere River that ran through the centre of Cyprus. It was a small operation, run by Grigorios Petrakis. He'd inherited the business from his father-in-law ten years ago, and had run it competently enough, even if he'd never made as much money as either the old man or his wife thought he should. It employed two part-time staff, both of them women who worked alternate shifts, but both of them were away today: one of them was looking after her sick mother, the other was stuck at home with a brood of children who had come down with chickenpox.

That meant it was just Petrakis in the office this morning.

But that didn't matter very much, he decided.

It was late November. From March through to October, Nicosia was always bustling with tourists. British and German and Dutch mostly. But there was also a sprinkling of Americans, plus some Greeks from the mainland. There were always plenty of people who needed to get home quickly, who needed train or plane reservations, or were moving on from Cyprus to the Greek Islands and needed a hotel booked: enough of them would drop into the travel agency to make a decent living. But by November, the tourist traffic dropped off dramatically. Nobody wanted to come to Cyprus in the winter. It was too quiet and too cold. You could spend the whole day in the office, and only deal with one or two bookings.

Which is why, he reflected, it was unusual to see three Americans.

Particularly ones who had money to spend, decided Petrakis. I'll owe myself a good lunch on the proceeds from this. *And a decent bottle of wine to go with it.*

Ben Hanold was booking the tickets.

He sat in front of Petrakis and gave him the precise details.

He needed three seats booked on Flight 103, leaving Frankfurt later tonight, heading for Washington via London.

'What class?' asked Petrakis.

'Doesn't matter,' said Ben. 'Whatever is available. Economy if you have it.'

'I'll check.'

Petrakis put through the call to the reservations desk. Seats from London to Washington could be difficult to get hold of at short notice: it was always a busy route, particularly in the run-up to Christmas.

'You're in luck,' he said, looking back up at Ben. 'There's plenty of space. I've reserved three seats in economy.'

'And three tickets to Frankfurt,' said Ben. 'So we can make the connection.'

Petrakis made another call. There was a flight leaving in two hours that would arrive at Frankfurt Airport just before six, leaving another two hours to make the transfer on to Flight 103.

'Book it,' said Ben crisply.

Petrakis pushed a piece of paper across the desk. The total bill for all the tickets combined came to $4,655. Of that, he reminded himself with a smile, his commission would be slightly more than $200.

Ben paid him with a credit card, collected the tickets, and walked across the street to the café where Scott and Jim were waiting for him. 'We're on our way home, gentlemen,' he said. 'And we're going to blow the Beirut drug-running operation wide open.'

Both Scott and Jim finished their coffees, then followed Ben towards the taxi ranks. It was only a twenty-minute ride to Nicosia's airport, but there was no point in wasting any time.

Petrakis was watching from the window.

He picked up the phone, and dialled a number in Athens.

The city's CIA bureau.

His father-in-law and his wife might not think he ran the business that well, he reflected. But they didn't know the deal he'd done with the CIA in Greece. He ran the business as a front for the agency, arranging tickets for its people around the Mediterranean, and reporting on anyone suspicious booking tickets in Nicosia.

The agency knew that if anything illegal happened anywhere in the world – a terrorist conspiracy, a military coup, a fugitive on the run, an agent defecting – a travel bureau was usually involved somewhere along the line.

They were one of the best sources of information in the world.

The CIA maintained agencies as fronts in every major city in the world. It was a giant machine, and Petrakis was just one cog within it. But a cog all the same.

'Three American guys just booked tickets in here,' he told the duty officer in Athens in the phone. 'The names are Jim Prentiss, Scott Valentin, and Ben Hanold. They'll be on Flight 103 leaving Frankfurt tonight, heading for Washington.'

As he put the phone down, Petrakis permitted himself a sigh of quiet satisfaction.

A commission for the tickets.

A commission from the agency.

Business was good.

Now, he thought, surely it's time for lunch. And to decide which wine to have with it.

# Part Two

# The Investigation

# THIRTY-SIX

**London, 20 November**

Sam was sitting alone in his apartment, his eyes fixed to the television screen. The news was the same, whichever channel you switched to, the tragedy unfolding minute by minute.

An American Boeing 747 had crashed in the small Scottish village of Lockerbie.

Flight 103 from London to Washington.

The news reports coming through were still patchy, noted Sam. The plane had crashed only forty minutes into its overnight flight. All 270 people on board had been killed: many of them were young American students going home for the Christmas holidays, although in total there were twenty-one different nationalities on board the plane.

Another eleven people had been killed in Lockerbie itself, caught by falling debris from the plane. Winds of a hundred knots were blowing across Scotland that night, scattering victims and debris across an eighty-one mile corridor, a total area of 845 square miles. The worst damage had been at 13 Sherwood Crescent, hit by a wing section that was travelling at more than 500 miles an hour: the impact of the collision created a crater fifty yards wide and seventy yards deep. All four members of the family living in the house were killed instantly. A huge fireball had risen up from the houses, and flickered across the nearby A74 that ran from Glasgow to

Carlisle. Bodies were still strewn across the village, but the police and firemen who had taken control of the village were saying that they couldn't be moved yet, because they still needed to gather forensic evidence detailing what part of the plane had hit them.

Seen from a helicopter that was broadcasting back to the studio, there were still smouldering fires all around the village.

And the cause of the explosion?

Nobody yet knew.

But the experts were already saying that all the evidence pointed to a bomb.

'Bastards,' muttered Sam under his breath.

It never ends, he realised.

We kill them, then they kill us.

So we kill them some more.

*At least I'm out of that game.*

He finished his coffee, and walked downstairs to the shop. It was just after nine thirty in the morning: Sam had skipped his usual jog around Battersea Park, staying glued to the news reports from Lockerbie instead.

Orla had already opened up. There was some late autumnal sun shining this morning, and the light was pouring in through the window, making the antiques glimmer. There was the Alphonse Tahan desk that Sam particularly liked sitting in the main window, which used bronze to imitate bamboo, and the light caught it brilliantly for a moment as Sam stood to admire it. Maybe that's what appeals to us about antiques, he wondered: the way they can age so perfectly, becoming more brilliant as the decades go by, even as everything around them decays.

'Terrible news,' said Orla.

Sam nodded. She was wearing a new outfit, he observed: a short black leather skirt, with a red jacket with prominent gold buttons, and black shoes with an inch of heel on them.

194

They had arrived back from Boston late, then taken some time off to try and rest, and she had clearly used some of the money she earned in the last week to buy herself some new clothes.

'Do you think it was a bomb?'

Sam looked away. It was probably a bomb, he reflected. All the evidence pointed that way. He knew from the years he'd spent working for the Mossad that the Arab terrorist groups had been plotting to put bombs on planes for years. El Al had been one of their main targets, but the security was always too tight. They tried it in the early 1970s, but backed away because the technical challenges were too great.

But they'd be back, the Mossad always knew that. Technical challenges were always overcome eventually. It was just a matter of time.

But why an American plane over Britain, he wondered?

That didn't make any sense.

'We've got our own case to solve,' he said.

He could see a smile brightening up her face. Orla was determined to track down what had happened to the Boston diocese's money, and Sam could understand that. They had a lead into Ziegler. He was the man who appeared to be organising the sale of any valuable items that fell into the hands of the diocese.

But so far they knew very little about him.

The phone rang in the corner.

'Mr Woolfman?'

Sam recognised the accent: Swiss. Like the country itself, the tone of voice was a hybrid of German and French cultures. It had the clipped, metallic precision of a German, but also the reserved indifference of the French.

'My name is Herr Ziegler,' he said. 'Father O'Connell in Boston called and suggested that I give you a ring.'

'Of course,' said Sam. 'I was speaking to him earlier this week.'

'I'm told you might be interested in an Amati violin, if one was available.'

'On behalf of a client, yes,' answered Sam.

'But you can't tell me who it is?'

'My client is my client . . .'

'I understand . . . but he would need to be a rich one.'

'How rich?'

'The violin is worth at least $500,000,' said Ziegler. 'We couldn't sell it for any less.'

'That wouldn't be a problem.'

There was a pause, and a hint of static on the line between London and Switzerland. Sam wondered if he answered that question too quickly. $500,000 was a lot of money. Not many people spent it that quickly, not even on a four-centuries-old violin. It might not ring true: and that would make Ziegler suspect that he was being set up.

'I'll need to make some enquiries, Mr Woolfman,' said Ziegler. 'I'll call you to arrange a meeting shortly.'

Sam put the phone down and glanced across at Orla. 'We're close to buying a violin,' he said.

And yet as he walked out into the shop, he wasn't so sure. Maybe I've blown it, he wondered to himself. Maybe I played that conversation too confidently. And maybe they'll realise I'm investigating how they hide their money.

*And then I'll have the Vatican to add to my list of enemies.*

# THIRTY-SEVEN

**London, 21 November**

Sam enjoyed Sundays. The apartment was strewn with papers, nearly all of them devoted to the terrible crash up in Lockerbie. Orla had come round, cooked up some omelettes for breakfast, and later today they were planning to browse the antiques fair at Chelsea Town Hall before maybe catching a movie somewhere, and getting a bite to eat.

Sort of like a date, wondered Sam to himself.

Christ, I haven't been on one of those for years.

He flicked over a few more pages of the paper. The stories were full of speculation about the crash of Flight 103. The theory was hardening that a bomb had detonated on board the aircraft, but nobody had any clear idea yet who had put it there, or who had managed to get it through the airport's security measures.

Theories were being thrown around: the IRA, the Libyans, the Iranians, or one of the radical Palestinian groups.

But nobody had any firm evidence.

Not yet.

He sat down at the table, taking a bite of the omelette Orla had just finished cooking. She was dressed down today: blue jeans, a white tee shirt, and flat suede shoes. The food tasted good, better than his own omelettes. Sam enjoyed cooking, but he was never sure he was very good at it, whereas Orla threw herself into it with the same passion that she approached everything.

'How long before he calls?' asked Orla.

'Who?'

'The Pope, stupid.'

'You mean Ziegler.'

Orla nodded, brushing her black fringe out of her hair as she did so.

'It could be two or three days,' he said. 'I made some investigations. It seems some of the antiques dealers around London know of him. Sotheby's and Christie's know who he is as well.'

'And so who is he?' said Orla, leaning forwards.

'He lives in Geneva,' said Sam. 'He's about fifty, and works alone, and always has done. He's a middleman basically. There are stories he used to work in the arms trade, but switched to art and antiques about a decade ago. Probably safer. More lucrative as well, the way prices have been going up.'

'And who does he trade with?'

'Anyone who wants him, from what I'm told,' said Sam. 'There's a rumour that he's done some fencing. You nick a high-end piece of furniture, and Ziegler is the man who will get it back on to the market for you, with fresh provenance, so that the top-end auctioneers will take it on to their catalogues without kicking up a fuss. And then it can be sold to one of the wealthy collectors, and they can kid themselves that it's a legitimate piece.'

'The Vatican is working with a thief . . .'

Sam shook his head.

He'd started out thinking that, but now he wasn't sure.

'A guy at Christie's told me there had been plenty of suspicion about Ziegler but nothing anyone had managed to make stick. It's like that whenever anyone seems to have access to a lot of high-end stuff. There are always rumours they are fencing it for a gang of robbers, and sometimes it's even true. But not in this case. I think Ziegler is working for the Vatican. We know he's working with Father O'Connell in Boston, but why would it stop there? Maybe there are fifty different dioceses around the world, maybe a hundred, and all of them hiding their assets in the same way. That would explain how Ziegler has access to so many high-end items, why he works alone, and why he works in secret.'

'So he is a kind of fence?'

'Meaning?'

'For the Vatican.'

Sam smiled. Nothing got past Orla.

That's what he liked about her.

In the corner of the room, the phone was ringing. Sam walked across to answer, aware that he was feeling nervous as he did so. Elena usually called on Sundays: it was the day the kids wanted to speak to him. Usually, he wanted to speak to them. A few minutes of banter on the phone once a week was the only contact he had with them right now. But he felt uncomfortable with Orla in the room. How she might react, he couldn't be sure, and he wasn't certain he wanted to find out either. Not today.

'Mr Woolfman?'

'Yes,' replied Sam.

Not Elena, he noted with relief.

This was an American accent.

'My name is Carter Jenas.'

Sam nodded. The name meant nothing to him.

'I'm the head of security here at Pan American,' he continued.

Sam paused.

Pan Am?

It was Pan-Am Flight 103 that crashed in Lockerbie.

*Why the hell is its head of security calling me?*

'I was sorry to hear about the crash,' said Sam. 'Terrible news, really terrible.'

'Thanks.'

Jenas hesitated.

'I need your help.'

'My help?'

The surprise was evident in Sam's tone of voice.

'I can't talk on the phone,' said Jenas. 'There's a United flight leaving Heathrow this evening at eight for New York. Can you be on it?'

'But—'

'I'll pay you $50,000 just for taking the conversation.'

'Can you send a car to meet me?'

'Done.'

'And make it two tickets.'

'Done.'

'Then I'll see you tomorrow.'

Jenas paused for a moment. 'Thanks, Mr Woolfman, I appreciate it.'

Sam looked around at Orla. 'Let's pack a bag,' he said. 'We're catching a flight to New York.'

'For New York?'

'There's a job . . . Flight 103.'

'I thought you were out of that game?'

'I am . . . but . . .'

But what? thought Sam.

I don't know.

Not yet anyway.

'Two hundred and seventy people died,' said Orla suddenly. 'You have to do this.'

# THIRTY-EIGHT

**New York, 22 November**

The drive in from John F. Kennedy airport to Manhattan
was, Sam judged, one of the most spectacular in the world.
From other airports, you made a short subway ride, or drove
through anonymous suburbs. But from JFK, you turned the
corner, and looked into the magnificent skyscape of
gleaming towers, rising up out of the ocean. It was, he
reflected, the only airport drive that actually made you feel
glad you'd arrived.

Orla was resting on his shoulder, in the back of the silver-
grey chauffeur-driven Lincoln that Jenas had sent to collect
them at the airport.

'Why are you doing this?' she asked.

Sam had asked himself the same question, in the small hours
of the night, 30,000 feet above the Atlantic, leaning back in a
first-class seat on a United Airlines 747. The money was
useful, that was one answer. $50,000 was a lot to make for a
breakfast meeting, even if you did have to fly across the
Atlantic to get there. No doubt they would pay even more if
he agreed to help them with their investigation into what
happened to Flight 103. But that wasn't really the answer.
With Orla's help he was starting to make some proper money
from the antiques trade. There was something else.

I'm doing it to impress her, he reflected to himself.

Surely she knows that.

While Orla slept, and the plane's four huge General Electric CF6 engines powered relentlessly through the night sky, Sam's mind wandered back to school, and the words he'd been taught of Rabbi Hillel, a preacher who'd taught at the time of King Herod and the Emperor Augustus. 'If I am not for myself, who will be? If I am only for myself, what am I? And if not now, when?'

That's why I joined the Mossad, he reminded himself.

And that's why I'm on this plane.

'Someone has to do it,' said Sam, looking back at Orla.

The Lincoln pulled up just after the turning into 34th Street. Sam hadn't been sure what to expect. Probably not the airline's own office, he reminded himself. The building would be besieged by reporters this morning, and if anyone came into the building, they would want to know who they were. He could see why Jenas would want to hold the conversation off premises. Still, Mario's Diner hardly looked promising. A greasy, sweaty-looking place, there were a dozen workmen eating big cooked breakfasts, but the office workers collected their orders without lingering any longer than they had to.

'You stay here,' said Sam to Orla as he climbed out of the car. 'I'll do this by myself.'

'But—'

'In my experience, these kinds of conversations are confidential,' he said firmly.

Sam felt bad about leaving Orla behind, but he felt he had no choice. Jenas asked to see me . . . not me and some Irish girl. If nothing else, her presence there would make him feel uncomfortable.

He stepped into the diner. In the far corner, close to the window, a man nodded in his direction. About forty, black, with a strong, lean face, and piercing eyes, he already had a cup of coffee in front of him, but signalled to the waitress for another.

'Mr Woolfman,' he said, standing up, and shaking Sam by the hand. 'Thank you for coming.'

'Call me Sam,' he replied.

He sat down opposite him in the narrow booth.

'Flight okay?'

Sam tried to smile. 'Half empty.'

'People are too frightened to fly,' said Jenas. 'All the airlines are going to get hammered, but this one in particular.'

'I can imagine.'

Sam glanced up at Jenas. At a guess, he'd say the man hadn't slept for forty-eight hours, but he still looked calm, and in control of the situation. His face was strained, but there was no trace of panic: he must have come from a background where you got used to handling stress. A soldier maybe? Or a policeman?

'We need you to find out who brought down our plane,' said Jenas, looking straight at Sam. 'And we need you to do it as quickly as possible.'

'You're sure it was brought down?'

Jenas nodded.

'Have you found the black box?'

Jenas shook his head. 'The debris is scattered over a huge area,' he answered. 'We have a team out looking for it. But the box isn't much bigger than a car battery, and we're searching an area that looks to cover about half of Scotland.'

'So . . .'

'We know it was a bomb, Mr Woolfman.'

'Sam.'

Jenas nodded. 'Okay, we know it was a bomb, Sam.'

'How?'

'Flight 103 was a fully maintained Boeing 747-200, only four years old,' he said. 'It had four GE engines on it, and they were only four years old as well. That kind of kit has a life expectancy of twenty-five years minimum. For an

203

aircraft, it was basically as good as it gets. Old enough for any problems to be detected and fixed, but still basically a new plane. It was flown by an experienced pilot with an unblemished safety record. There were no unusual weather conditions.'

He paused, looking straight at Sam.

'Our engineers know a Boeing 747 inside out. We were the launch customer on that plane, and they don't just suddenly blow to pieces in mid-air for no apparent reason. So it was a bomb, okay . . .'

'The question is, who put it there?'

'Absolutely.'

'And you want me to find out.'

Jenas nodded.

'Why?'

Jenas leaned forwards. The waitress was just pouring some coffee into Sam's cup. 'Something to eat, honey?' she said, glancing down at Sam.

He shook his head.

Then he looked back at Jenas. 'Why?' he repeated.

'We're taking a beating,' said Jenas. 'This airline could be bankrupted unless we can find out who did this to us.'

'There's the police, the FBI, your own security department,' said Sam. 'Then there's the British police, their security services . . . I would have thought there would be plenty of people crawling all over that question by now.'

'I'm told you're the best,' said Jenas. 'You can find out things that are buried where no one else can see them.'

'Who told you that?' said Sam.

'I've asked around.'

'I'll take the case,' said Sam. 'But only if you level with me.'

Jenas paused. 'The Mossad,' he said. 'We need someone with Mossad connections working on this case for us. It's the only agency that understands the Middle East.'

'The plane was flying from Frankfurt to Washington via London,' said Sam. 'It didn't go anywhere near the Middle East.'

'But it wasn't a German terror group,' said Jenas. 'The Baader-Meinhof gang folded years ago, and anyway they never attacked planes.'

'The IRA?'

'It's an American plane, and this is where most of their money comes from,' said Jenas. 'If they had the ability to get a bomb on to one of our planes, they could have got it aboard a British Airways flight just as easily. They would have done that. So that leaves the Middle Eastern terror groups. All I need you to do is find out which one.'

He had a point, Sam decided.

Not many organisations would want to blow up an American plane.

And nearly all of them were in the Middle East.

'Do you know anything about the bomb?'

Jenas shrugged. 'From what they've discovered on the scene so far, our experts reckon the bomb punched a twenty-inch hole in the side of the aircraft, about a third of the way down. That's right next to the P in Pan Am on its side.'

'And that was enough to cause the crash?' said Sam.

'What are you getting at?'

'There could have been a second bomb? Or maybe a terrorist on board?'

'The way our experts say it happened is like this,' said Jenas. 'On a 747, the nerve centre, where all the navigation and communications systems are placed, is two floors under the cockpit, partitioned off from the forward cargo hold by a bulkhead wall. We reckon that the explosion broke through that wall, shaking up all the flight-control cables and causing the front section of the fuselage to start to pitch and roll. The plane would have started to move about very violently, snapping the reinforced belt that holds the front section to the main body of the aircraft.'

He took a sip of his coffee.

'At about the same time, the shock waves from the blast would have ricocheted back from the skin of the aircraft, and met up with pulses from the initial explosion. That produced shock waves with about double the power of the original explosion, which rippled back up into the plane. The roof would have literally started to peel away, like the lid coming off a tin can. After that it had no chance. The aircraft just started to break up, then drop from the sky.'

'So the bomb was in precisely the right position?'

'I guess.'

'And you have no idea how it was triggered?'

'Except for the fact that the people involved obviously had a good idea what they were doing then no, we have no idea.'

Sam hesitated. There wasn't much to go on, he reflected.

'Any warnings?'

Jenas shook his head.

'Blackmail threats? Disgruntled employees?'

Jenas laughed, but quickly stopped when he noticed someone at the counter of the diner looking at him. 'We're an airline, and I guess plenty of our staff are pissed off, just like any big company,' he answered. 'That doesn't mean they are going to start blowing up aircraft, even if they knew how to do it.'

'Then we don't have much to go on.'

'Which is why I've turned to you.'

Sam nodded.

'You *are* taking the case?'

'What's the pay?'

'We'll pay your expenses, and give you all the help we can, plus we'll pay you $500,000 for delivering the answer.'

Sam drained the last of his coffee.

'I need two things,' he said. 'I'll need some expenses upfront so I can vanish off the face of the earth. I don't want anyone to know who I am, or where I've gone.'

'Done,' said Jenas.

'And I want a list of everyone on that plane.'

'You think . . .'

'I don't think anything,' said Sam. 'I just need leads to follow, that's all.'

Jenas stood up. It was just after nine in the morning. 'Done.'

He put a ten dollar bill down on the table. 'And thank you, Mr Woolfman.'

'Sam.'

'Thanks, Sam.'

'One other condition,' he said. 'You'll hear from me when I've found something, or if I need some help.'

'Call me, anytime of the day or night.'

'Right,' said Sam. 'But until then, I don't exist.'

# THIRTY-NINE

**Geneva, 23 November**

A gentle afternoon breeze was blowing across Lake Geneva. Sam sat for a moment, admiring the view around the bay. It was late autumn, and the mountains in the distance were covered with a thick layer of snow, but down here by the lakeside the temperature was still mild enough to sit in your shirtsleeves.

'His house is about two miles away,' said Orla, returning from the phone box where she had just made the call. 'He'll be there anytime until six.'

Sam checked his watch. It was just after two in the afternoon. Plenty of time for some light lunch, then they could get a cab up to Ziegler's house.

They had landed in Geneva this morning, after yet another overnight flight. The only plane out of New York they had managed to get at such short notice flew directly to Frankfurt, but from there they'd managed to get seats on a Lufthansa flight for the forty-minute hop down to Geneva. They checked into the Hotel des Bergues, the finest hotel in Geneva, with rooms directly overlooking the lake. The last time Sam had been there, he'd been kidnapped and abducted by the Mossad, soon after discovering the real secret behind the death of the billionaire publisher Max Robertson. At least this time, no one is holding me prisoner, he reflected to himself.

*Not yet anyway.*

The plan had been to stay in New York for a couple more days, but when he checked his messages at the shop in London, it turned out that Ziegler had been in touch, and was willing to see them tomorrow. There was no time to lose. Jenas had supplied him with a list of all the passengers on Flight 103, and Sam had studied it on the overnight flight. So far, none of the names meant anything to him.

'Let's go,' said Orla impatiently, as she finished off the last of her club sandwich.

Sam took a last bite of his own sandwich and stood up. The taxi rank was right across the road. To Ziegler's villa was a ten-minute drive along the road that twisted along the back of the lake. Whatever the nature of his business, noted Sam, as the taxi delivered them outside an impressive pair of gates, it was clearly paying well. The driveway led back from the lake, but the six-bedroomed villa was built into the hillside, with a long terrace looking straight out over the water. He pressed the buzzer on the intercom.

'Mr Woolfman?' said the man who answered it, and as soon as Sam had replied, the electronic gates swung open.

After they had landed in Geneva, Sam had bought himself a new shirt, a new Hermes tie, plus matching cufflinks. He'd told Orla to spend at least a thousand dollars in the Chanel boutique across the road from the hotel, and she'd come back with a perfectly tailored two-piece black suit plus a cream and blue striped blouse that made her look even more elegant than usual. Geneva, Sam reminded her, was probably the best-heeled city in the world: if you didn't look smartly turned out, people would be instantly suspicious.

Sam walked up the drive. The villa looked Edwardian, built from red brick, with a long white terrace, and well-tended gardens. There were two BMWs parked on the thick gravel of the driveway. The front door was already open, and a man was stepping out to greet them. Sam assumed it was Ziegler. He looked around fifty, with greying hair combed back over his forehead, and a thin, pinched face. He wore glasses that were perched on the end of his nose, as if his normal position was to look down on things. 'Mr Woolfman?' he asked.

Sam nodded, and shook his hand. 'This is my assistant, Orla Sheehy.'

Ziegler nodded, glancing admiringly at Orla, and clearly enjoying the bright smile on her face. Among Swiss businessmen, judged Sam, 'assistant' probably meant 'mistress'. And, in truth, in her Chanel suit, Orla looked like she might well have fitted into Geneva's circle of kept women: younger perhaps, but every bit as polished and groomed. Ziegler looked back at Sam. Lucky bastard, the smile in his eyes appeared to be saying.

'It's a fine afternoon,' said Ziegler. 'We can talk on the terrace.'

As they sat down, a woman appeared from nowhere, with a tray of tea and biscuits. 'Have you ever heard an Amati played, Mr Woolfman?' said Ziegler, pouring tea first for Orla then for Sam.

'The Maggini String Quartet in London used to use one,' said Orla. 'You can hear it on any of their recordings from the 1970s and 1980s, and it's particularly good on the Bach. The tone of an Amati is much sweeter than later violins, so it was better suited to vinyl, analogue recordings, than it was to CDs, which of course have a much harsher sound.'

Sam could see Ziegler looking at her, thinking the same thing they all think. Beautiful *and* smart.

'Or, of course, live,' he said.

'Naturally,' replied Orla. 'For a live performance, it would be unmatched.'

'Do you have the violin here?' asked Sam.

Ziegler smiled. 'I'm afraid I don't want to install those kind of security systems,' he answered. 'An Amati is far too valuable to keep here. There is a safe down in Geneva, at one of the banks.'

'My client would be happy to buy it,' said Sam. 'So long as he can be provided with a history of its recent ownership. And so long as he can remain anonymous.'

'The price would be $500,000.'

'Agreed,' said Sam.

'With half upfront, and the rest on delivery,' said Ziegler.

'As you wish.'

Ziegler nodded, taking a sip of his own tea, and toying with a biscuit between the thumb and index finger of his right hand. 'Then I think we have an agreement.'

'Where shall I transfer the money,' said Sam. 'I think my client would prefer it was a Swiss bank, since he doesn't want to be traced.'

'The Bank Laboucherd in Lucerne,' said Ziegler. 'It's a private bank, not very well known, but always discreet.'

'I'm familiar with it,' said Sam.

'Then as soon as the initial transfer of funds is completed we have a deal,' said Ziegler. 'Once the balance is received, you'll be given the violin, plus of course its full background.'

He stood up. 'It's a pleasure doing business with you, Mr Woolfman,' he said. 'And I hope you have a good flight back to London.'

'Likewise.'

'And you too, Miss Sheehy,' he said, looking towards Orla.

Orla smiled bashfully. 'Just one thing . . .'

'Of course,' said Ziegler attentively.

'There is a Jean Miro painting that was recently bequeathed by the Rebolledo family,' she said. 'I was wondering, on behalf of another client of ours, whether it might come on the market.'

'A Miro?'

'From when he was living in Paris in the 1920s,' said Orla.

211

'Some of the City guys are really getting into the surrealists.'

'I'll see what I can do, Miss Sheehy.'

Orla flashed him a bright smile, then walked alongside Sam back down to the lakeside. It only took a few minutes to find a taxi to take them back to the hotel.

'He's dealing for the Vatican, I'm certain of that,' said Sam as they arrived back. 'The Amati was left to the Boston diocese, and now we've bought it in Geneva.'

'He says it's in a safe deposit box here,' said Orla.

'I think he was lying about that,' said Sam. 'I reckon the way it works is like this. The Church is left valuable items all the time, and then Ziegler is tasked with finding buyers for them. He doesn't advertise his service, but enough collectors know who he is, so he doesn't have to. When he finds a buyer, the item is shipped straight to them. And then the funds he collects are all banked here in Switzerland.'

'Like the Miro . . .'

'What was that all about?'

'Juan Rebolledo died last week,' said Orla. 'He ran one of the largest construction companies in Mexico. A devout Catholic, like most Mexicans. He left a Miro in his will, apparently, although the report I read didn't say who it had gone to.'

Sam smiled. 'So if Ziegler calls us and says he thinks he can get it for us, then we'll have proof that he's dealing for the Vatican,' said Sam. 'And not just for Boston. For the whole Church.'

'Exactly,' said Orla.

Sam thought for a moment. 'You need to go to Lucerne,' he said. 'It's not far on the train.'

'Why?'

'To investigate the Bank Laboucherd,' said Sam. 'That's where Ziegler told us to pay the money for the violin. We need to find out more about the accounts he keeps there.'

For a moment, Sam could see from her expression that

Orla was worried. He'd seen a lot of different expressions on her face: anger, excitement, amusement. But he didn't think he'd ever seen her look worried before. Up until now, he'd imagined that Orla was completely fearless. But, of course, that's not true, he reminded himself. She's afraid of every-thing, just like all of us. She just doesn't like to show it.

'And where are you going?'

'Scotland,' said Sam. 'To Lockerbie.'

She drew closer to him. 'I don't want you to go, Sam,' she said.

He could feel her arms wrapping around his chest, and, close to his, feel her heart thumping. 'I'll be back in a couple of days,' he said quietly.

# FORTY

**Scotland, 24 November**

It was a struggle to find a place to stay in Lockerbie. Sam had tried all the local hotels before eventually he found himself a room in a farmhouse in Middleshaw, about five miles away on the A74. There area was still swarming with journalists. Sam had caught a flight from Geneva to Edinburgh this morning, then hired a car and driven the fifty miles south to the village. There were camera crews parked along the main street, and police cordons around the roads.

And it wasn't hard to see why, noted Sam.

The scene, even days later, was still one of total devastation. It reminded Sam of the war zones he'd witnessed when he was still in the Israeli Army. Except this wasn't the Middle East. This was a sleepy Scottish village.

What the hell happened here? he wondered to himself.

Four different craters had been blown into the heart of the village by debris from the aircraft. Bulldozers had been moved into position because one street was so badly damaged it had to be demolished. Police teams were still recovering forensic evidence. And teams of salvage experts were still picking up pieces of broken fuselage, and carefully taking them away for examination, both by the police, and by the airline's own investigators.

Sam knew precisely what he had come for.

To witness the scene for himself.

And to see what evidence he could pick up on the spot.

*Evidence that everyone else might have missed.*

Dusk had already fallen by the time Sam arrived in the village. It grew dark early in the afternoon in Scotland in the winter, and a light rain was falling, which made it even darker. There was a sombre mood. Not surprising, reflected Sam to himself, when you thought about how many people had just died here.

He started out by talking to a couple of the salvage operators. They had collected most of the aircraft from the ground, despite the distance it had travelled, but nobody knew yet whether the black box had been discovered. There wasn't so much as a rumour. Nobody wanted to talk to him much. They were busy with their work, and they had already been besieged by reporters from just about every newspaper and television station in the world. They didn't want to talk to yet another investigator. And certainly not one who couldn't even offer them any credentials.

Sam tried some of the policemen manning the cordons, but they treated him with the suspicion he would have expected. They weren't there to make conversation, and they weren't about to reveal any information.

Draw too much attention to myself, and it might be me that is put under investigation, Sam warned himself. The police have no idea who bombed this plane or why. They won't be treating any strangers turning up in the town sympathetically.

He arrived back at the farmhouse at just after ten, after grabbing a bite to eat at one of the local pubs. Sam was starting to wonder if he should call Jenas. It wasn't fair to take his money if he wasn't going to be able to tell him anything new.

And so far today, he'd come up with precisely nothing.

Patrick McKenny, the owner of the farm, was only forty, but he looked at least ten years older. It must be the weather up here, decided Sam as he spoke to the man in the kitchen. The winds across the North Sea blew straight down into this region, blowing hard across the hilly countryside. It was enough to age any man, and McKenny was no exception.

There was a bottle of whiskey on the table, and Sam took a glass gratefully. McKenny didn't usually rent out rooms, but he'd noticed the sudden influx of people following the crash, and the farm didn't earn so much money that he could afford to pass up the opportunity to make some spare cash. All the farmers within a ten-mile radius were doing the same thing, the bookings co-ordinated by the receptionist at the Townhead Hotel in Lockerbie, which was already charging triple rates for each of its thirty rooms. Sam was paying £60 a night for a small spare room carved out of a corner of the attic: there was a Norwegian journalist sleeping next door who he believed was paying even more.

'What are you doing in Lockerbie, Mr Woolfman?' he said, pouring a generous measure of whiskey into his own glass, and pushing the bottle across to Sam.

'The crash, of course,' said Sam.

'A newspaper, is that who you work for?'

Sam shook his head. He wasn't about to tell the truth, but he didn't want to stray too far from it either. 'Insurance.'

McKenny growled. 'Trying to wriggle out of the payments, eh?'

Sam shook his head. 'There will be a lot of claims on this one,' he replied. 'The plane, the houses in the village, the cancelled flights, and then of course a lot of the people on board will have life policies as well. Most of the bills will end up back with Lloyd's of London, because that's where most insurance claims end up, and that's who I work for. We're just trying to get all the facts straight so we know who to pay and how much.'

McKenny took another hit of whiskey, making his weather-beaten face even redder.

'Then who were the men who descended right after the crash?'

'What men?'

'The way I heard it, it was like this,' said McKenny. 'Straight after the plane came down, we're talking about the first ten, maybe fifteen minutes after the explosion woke up everyone around here, a helicopter rolled up out of the sky. Six men dropped out of it, all of them dressed in black. I even heard that they were American soldiers.'

Sam was tired from the flights, and from the day spent trudging around Lockerbie not finding anyone who wanted to talk to him. His body was telling him it was time to try and grab some sleep. But this sounded interesting. American soldiers dropping from the sky in the immediate aftermath of the crash? Why the hell would they be doing that?

'You're sure they were Americans?' said Sam.

McKenny shrugged, knocked back his whiskey, then generously refilled his glass. 'I'm not sure of anything because I didn't see it,' he said bluntly. 'You'd need to speak to Barry McDonnell. His farm is about three miles from here, and the main fuselage of the plane came down in one his fields. Killed eight of his sheep, I believe, so I suppose your insurance company will be hearing from him soon enough.' He chuckled to himself. 'Not that sheep are worth very much right now.'

'And he saw it?'

Sam wanted to press the point. He certainly didn't want to talk about the price of sheep.

'So he tells me, and Barry is the straightest, truest man for miles about,' continued McKenny. 'He heard the explosion the same way we all did, then he came out of his bed, and started walking across the fields to see what happened. That's when he saw it. A chopper comes down, hovers above the ground, and six men climb out of it all dressed in black. They spent about five minutes on the ground searching for something.'

'What?'

'How the hell should I know, I wasn't there.'

'And he thought they were Americans?'

'So he says.'

'They could have been the British police, or the army,' said Sam. 'They could have been part of the rescue effort.'

'But Barry knows about military hardware,' said McKenny. 'He reads books, and builds model tanks and planes. And this was a Black Hawk. Only the US military fly those.'

As he finished the sentence, Sam's fellow guest, the Norwegian journalist, Lars Enoksen, was just coming into the room. He looked exhausted as well, noted Sam. It was raining hard outside now and the man's hair was wet through. He'd been sent over by his paper because a Norwegian couple had been on Flight 103, but so far there was no trace of the bodies, nor were they expected to be found. About two dozen corpses had been collected by the police so far, some of them still strapped to the seats that had been blown straight out of the plane. Some of them, according to the forensics team, might even have been alive on impact: they would have lost consciousness as their seats were ripped from the plane due to the rapid change in air pressure but a few of them might have regained it during the three or four minutes it took them to hurtle to ground. One woman had even been found strapped to her seat, and clinging to a crucifix around her neck: she must have been conscious when she smashed into the ground to do that.

But the Norwegians were not among them. And the police were starting to draw the search to a close: most of the debris had scattered across open farmland, and if they hadn't been found by now, it wasn't likely they would be found ever. They would be among the dozens of people incinerated in the sky. Enoksen had filed a final piece for his paper, the mass circulation *Dagbladet*, and was planning to go home tomorrow.

The Lockerbie story was already starting to die down.

A few more weeks, thought Sam, and it would just be more stale news.

Except to the friends and family of the people that died.

'We were just talking about the Black Hawk, Mr Enoksen,' said McKenny.

He pushed the bottle of whiskey across the table. Enoksen took a generous glass, drained most of it in a single gulp, then refilled it. McKenny must be making a tidy profit on these rooms, decided Sam. Enough to be generous with his whiskey, anyway.

'A few of the journalists have been talking about that story,' said Enoksen.

He was a thin man, with long, blond hair tied back in a ponytail. He was wearing a dark green rainproof jacket and sturdy boots, but the weather had still seeped into him. He looked wet through.

'Do they think it's true?' asked Sam.

'McDonnell swears its true, and someone else says they saw the helicopter.'

'Who?'

'Sandy Teller,' said Enoksen. 'Retired schoolteacher. She lives in a cottage, about a mile from McDonnell's house. Her story pretty much backs his up. Except she doesn't know anything about military hardware, so she can't tell you what type of helicopter it was.'

'And are the journalists following it up?'

'There have been some questions put to the police, and also to the Ministry of Defence down in London,' said Enoksen. 'The response has been a flat denial. There are no American air bases nearby. Machrihanish in Argyll is the closest one, but that is a top-secret facility, and they claim there are no Black Hawks stationed there.'

'Then there's no story?'

'None that anyone in the media can follow up,' said Enoksen. 'If you run with it, and it gets denied, then you just end up looking stupid.'

'What are the latest theories?' asked Sam.

'The police don't appear to have any clear idea,' said Enoksen. 'No one is claiming responsibility, and that in itself is unusual. Why go to all the trouble of blowing up a plane, and then not tell anyone you did it? It doesn't make any sense.'

Sam drained his whiskey glass, and, warmed by the alcohol, climbed upstairs to bed. The room was built into an alcove, with sloping roofs, and just a tiny, dormer window looking out into the countryside below. The rain was lashing hard against the glass, and clattering against the slates of the roof, just a few inches above him.

A Black Hawk, he wondered to himself.

Just a few minutes after the crash.

It might have been denied by the police and the military, but that didn't mean it wasn't true.

After all, there were two witnesses.

But what could they have been looking for? Sam asked himself.

Or who?

From his attaché case, he took out four sheets of closely typed paper. It was the list of names Jenas had given him of the passengers on Flight 103.

He read through them for the tenth time.

And asked himself the same question again: What was the Black Hawk looking for?

Or who?

# FORTY-ONE

**London, 25 November**

Sam looked down at the papers on his desk. He filled in the final numbers. Then he walked across to the fax machine that sat in the corner of the office, keyed in the number for it to dial, then pressed send. Slowly the five sheets of paper slid inside the machine.

During the course of the last decade, he reminded himself, the Caribbean had become one of the leading financial centres in the world. The Bahamas led the way, along with the Cayman Islands. They had a robust legal system, based on English common law, and they had stable governments. They were close to the United States, and they were accessible on a seven-hour flight from Europe. There were even some fine beaches if you wanted a break from your work. But most of all, they were committed to total secrecy.

The Swiss were slowly compromising on banking secrecy, giving in to the demands of European Union regulators that they open up their secret bank accounts.

So too were Luxembourg and even Liechtenstein.

But in the Bahamas, no one asked any questions. Which was why Sam had chosen it for this operation.

Heck, I've always wanted to own a bank, thought Sam to himself.

*And now I've got one.*

He travelled down from Edinburgh this morning on the

first flight he'd managed to get a seat on, and made his way straight to the shop. Sam was still determined to try and find a way into the mystery of Flight 103, but he didn't feel he was going to find out anything more in the village itself. He'd tried speaking with the farmer who'd seen the Black Hawk, but his wife was fed up with journalists calling, and was slamming the phone down on anyone who rang the house.

Anyway, whoever had planted a bomb on the plane, they hadn't done so in Lockerbie, and it wasn't the Scottish village they were attacking. You could be sure of that much. The answer was somewhere else. At Heathrow, where the bomb must have been planted, he wondered to himself? Or in the Middle East, where the plot must have been hatched? Right now, he had no idea, but he intended to find out.

He still needed to crack the mystery of where the Vatican was hiding its money.

That's why he'd set up a bank in the Caribbean.

Yesterday, Orla had taken the train from Geneva to Lucerne. She made some enquiries about the Bank Laboucherd, but so far she hadn't managed to discover anything that you couldn't find out just by looking at its brochure. It had been owned by the Laboucherd family since it was founded in 1893: the current chairman Henri Laboucherd was the fourth in a series of family directors. It was a tiny, intensely private operation, which even eschewed branches in Geneva or Zurich. You needed an introduction just to open an account there, and if your credentials weren't impeccable, they turned you straight down. They weren't about to tell Orla anything about their accounts. That was to be expected. A banker from Laboucherd would rather boil their own children in oil than betray one of their clients.

When he spoke to her this morning, Sam told her not to worry.

He'd thought of a way through.

'Banks don't like to talk to people,' he reminded her. 'But they talk to other banks.'

'What do you mean?' she asked.

'Just give me twenty-four hours,' he said. 'Then I'll come out and join you.'

As soon as he got off the phone, Sam had called David Soloff. He'd first got to know Soloff in the Mossad, when David was working there as a financial analyst. While Sam and his unit had been tracking down actual terrorists, Soloff had led a small team that traced their finances. He created a shadow financial network with accounts across Europe, including a front bank in Cyprus where the PLO even set up an account. Once you got a lead on the money, you could very quickly find the man: that was the thinking behind the creation of the unit. Twice, Soloff's team had come up with the locations of terrorists on Israel's most-wanted list, and Sam's unit had been able to move in and complete the execution. Four years ago, Soloff, like Sam, had grown tired of the Mossad and moved into the private sector. He'd set up an office in Nassau in the Bahamas, and now advised multinationals on how to shift their assets from one country to another so as to end up paying virtually no tax. But Sam still spoke to him occasionally. And like most refugees from the Mossad, he would seldom refuse a favour to a friend.

'I need a bank, David,' said Sam, when he got him on the phone.

'They've got plenty of those in London.'

'My own bank,' said Sam.

'What name?' he said crisply.

You got the impression, reflected Sam, that people called him all day long asking for a bank to be set up.

Sam thought for a moment. 'The United Dominions Bank,' he replied.

It was the first thing that had come into his head.

*But it would do.*

'I'll check whether it's available,' said Soloff.

It turned out to be surprisingly easy. In the Bahamas you could set up your own bank for a one-off payment of $5,000. It came complete with a licence from the Bahamas banking regulator, a board of directors appointed by a local law firm, and a certificate of incorporation. Most crucially of all, it came with an IBAN (International Bank Account Number) number and SWIFT (Society for Worldwide Interbank Financial Telecommunications) code: the two vital pieces of information that would convince every other bank in the world you were a legitimate financial institution.

An IBAN number was a complex collection of information, agreed by an informal convention of global banks. It could be up to thirty digits long, and included a country code, a numerical bank identifier, a branch code, and an account number. There were standard digits for each country, rather like the phone system, and an agreed algorithm for turning the name of the bank into a series of numbers.

The SWIFT code was just as important. A co-operative society of most of the world's banks, it was registered in Belgium, and headquartered in Brussels, and it set the standards by which money was transferred electronically from bank to bank. The first electronic transfer had been sent using the system in 1977, and by now it was processing millions a day.

Soloff had faxed through a series of papers that Sam needed to sign, and a credit card slip. Within twenty-four hours, he assured him, the United Dominions Bank would be up and running. He could even have a chequebook if he wanted one.

Next, Sam called Michael Boaz. He'd left his number on his card, and had been meaning to get in touch with him.

'Hey, Sam,' said Michael, when he picked up the phone.

'Are you planning to join us in Russia? I thought you'd change your mind. Even you aren't quite stupid enough to pass up on an opportunity like this.'

'One day, Michael,' said Sam tersely. 'But not today.'

'Then what do you want?' said Michael. 'Sam Woolfman never makes social calls.'

It was true, reflected Sam. He called people when he was involved in an investigation. Otherwise, he kept to himself. He started to explain. There was a list of names, and he wanted to know if any of them meant anything. It was, of course, the list that Carter Jenas had given him, the same list he'd reviewed again in Scotland. Buried inside that long roll call of the casualties, Sam felt certain there was a clue: some key that would start to unlock the mystery. He faxed the list through to Michael, allowing him time to study it before calling him back.

'I'm sorry, Sam, none of them mean anything to me,' Michael told him.

'Thanks for trying, anyway,' he said.

'Who were they?'

'The passengers on Flight 103,' replied Sam.

'Christ, you're looking into that? And I thought you said you were out of that game.'

Next, he took a cab across to the City. Maurice Dowler was another former Mossad man, who'd left the service and set up Merriman & Dowler, an upmarket financial investigations agency. After struggling for a few years, it had made a name for itself during some of the big takeover battles of the 1980s. Several tycoons had retired wounded from the battle after Merriman & Dowler had dug up details of Liechtenstein trusts, illicit tax deals, or mistresses living luxuriously on the company payroll. If you need some dirt dug up, Maurice Dowler could supply some men with shovels. It was Dowler who had put Sam on to the Max Robertson case, and although that hadn't worked out the way either man expected, he was still pleased with the results. His door was always open if Sam needed some advice. *Like today.*

'Is life treating you okay?' said Dowler as he showed Sam into his office.

Dowler shook him warmly by the hand. He was a short man, running to fat as he moved towards the end of his fifties. His hair was gone, and the thick black spectacles he wore turned his face into a series of circles. But his smile was genuine. 'Okay,' answered Sam. 'You?'

'At least we're not working on the Robertson case anymore,' said Dowler. 'For that at least we can be grateful.'

'I wanted to show you a list,' said Sam.

He pulled the sheaf of papers from his case, giving Dowler a chance to read it while he sipped on the coffee his secretary had just brought into the room.

As he looked up, he could see Dowler scanning the names on the list. His glasses were squashed tight to his eyes, and his finger was tracing down the list. Dowler was an experienced investigator, Sam reminded himself. *More experienced even than I am.* He knows that often you just have to keep looking and looking at the same information until you find the nugget that everyone else has missed.

'It's Flight 103, isn't it?' he said, glancing back up at Sam.

'How'd you know?'

'I recognised some of the names,' said Dowler. 'They've been in the papers for the last few days, along with their pictures.'

He sighed, putting down the list. 'Terrible business.'

'But do you recognise any of them?'

'Apart from the names I've seen in the papers?'

Sam nodded.

'What are you looking for exactly, Sam?'

'You know how it is, you track every lead until you find something.'

'You think it was an attack on an individual, not the plane,' said Dowler. 'Is that what you're saying?'

'Anything's possible.'

Dowler looked again at the list. 'I suppose anything is possible,' he said, 'But if you wanted to target an individual, surely there must be an easier way of doing it than bringing down a whole 747.'

He took off his glasses and put the list down on the table. 'You're working for the airline.'

'They gave me the list.'

'Do you think it could have been one of their rivals?'

Sam shook his head. 'Competition can be cutthroat, but surely . . .' He paused, thinking through the whole issue. 'Surely it would damage the whole industry too much.'

'I'm just trying to think outside the box,' said Dowler. 'How about a religious extremist?'

'A Christian? Or a Muslim?'

'Either,' said Dowler. 'There are some apocalyptic Christian sects becoming active now that the millennium is drawing closer. Some people believe the Muslim fundamentalists are going to start attacking the West one day. The United States in particular . . .'

'But they'd claim responsibility.'

Dowler nodded. 'Which is why you come back to murder.'

Sam drained the last of his coffee. 'If it's terrorism, why not own up to it?' he asked. 'Terrorists are looking for publicity, for acknowledgement of their power. Unless you claim it, however, you haven't achieved anything.'

Dowler circled a name with a black fountain pen. 'Check out this man,' he said.

Sam looked across. The name was Oleg Borrodin. 'I've never heard of him.'

'You would have done, if he'd lived,' said Dowler. 'He's only thirty-two, a Siberian by birth, but a Muscovite really.

His family have been well connected in Russia for generations. He's been buying up the oil industry over there piece by piece. Russia has a lot more oil than anyone yet realises, it's just that the Communists were so useless at getting it out of the ground. There are going to be some very rich Russian oil barons in the next decade, and Borrodin would have been one of them. If he'd lived . . .'

'So it could be murder?'

'I'm just speculating,' said Dowler.

Sam took the sheaf of papers off the desk. 'Nobody else on the list?'

Dowler shook his head. 'Just Borrodin, I'm afraid.'

The two men shook hands, exchanged some pleasantries about how they must have lunch sometime, and Dowler told him how welcome he was to come and work for his firm one day. As Sam took a cab back to the shop, he was thinking over the Russian angle. There was a brutal new generation of oligarchs stealing Russia's mineral wealth amid the collapse of the old Soviet Union, he was well aware of that. Plenty of them wouldn't think twice about assassinating a rival. But bringing down a 747? That was an extreme way of murdering a man. Even if you didn't have any qualms about killing 300 innocent people at the same time, you'd be nervous of the global investigation into what caused the crash that was now underway. It was likely to catch up with you. He needed to add it to the list of possibilities, but Sam wasn't sure it made much sense. And how did it square with the American Black Hawk that descended on the crash site minutes after the plane came down?

When Sam got back to the shop, there was a message for him. Michael had called. 'I've got something for you,' it said simply.

Sam punched out the number on the phone. 'Did you hear something?' he said, as soon as Michael picked up the phone.

'About Flight 103?'

'Yes,' said Sam tersely.

'Just this,' said Michael. 'It's just a rumour, and I don't know whether it's true or not, but I've heard that American Embassy staff around the world were warned not to travel on that flight.'

'Warned? How?'

'I'm getting this second and third hand,' said Michael. 'But there were discreet notices up in many of the embassies around the world, and a lot of last-minute cancellations. A lot of American diplomatic staff used that flight, apparently, but not many of them were on board when it came down.'

'Any idea which embassies?'

'Most of the European ones, so I'm told,' answered Michael. 'Like I said, this is second and third hand. I just thought you'd be interested.'

'Thanks.'

Sam paused.

'One more thing,' he continued. 'While you've been working in Russia have you heard of a guy called Oleg Borrodin?'

'Big player in the oil industry,' said Michael. 'He's been buying up the oil wells in Siberia. There are about six different groups trying to get control of the Russia oil industry and they all hate each other's guts.'

'He died on Flight 103.'

'I know,' said Michael. 'It's been reported over here. There were three Russians on the plane. Borrodin, his chief accountant, and his bodyguard.'

'Reckon he could have been the target?'

'You bring down the plane to get Borrodin?' said Michael. 'Why not just shoot him in Moscow? Sounds too complicated to me. The Russians know the basic rule of assassinations as well as you and I do. Keep it simple. That way there isn't so much to go wrong.'

True enough, thought Sam. 'Thanks for the tip on the embassies,' he said, putting the phone down.

Why would American diplomatic staff be warned off the flight? he wondered to himself.

As well as a Black Hawk retrieving something from the wreckage.

Finally, he called Orla. 'We're getting close,' he told. 'And I'll see you tomorrow.'

As he put the phone down, he just hoped it was true.

# FORTY-TWO

**Bern, 26 November**

The American Embassy in Bern was a solid, white stucco-fronted building, built at the turn of the century. It dominated the square, dwarfing the buildings around it in both size and presence. Sam paused for a moment, glancing at the security guard, before stepping inside.

This morning, he'd taken the first British Airways flight he could get a seat on to Zurich, moved swiftly through passport control, then caught the one-hour train connection from the airport down to the Swiss capital Bern. He arranged to meet Orla in Lucerne later on today. But there was one more thing he wanted to do first.

Check out the American Embassy.

And find out if what Michael had told him was true.

From Bern station, he caught a cab that took him up past the Parliament building, and then on to the Jubilaumsstrasse, where the embassy was located. The stars and stripes flying above it made the embassy building instantly recognisable.

Before he left, Sam had done some research. He had a list of consular officials, so that he knew which name to ask for. He walked inside, and went up to the desk.

'I'm here to see Jacob Rosen,' he said.

Rosen, according to the directory he'd consulted in London, was the deputy undersecretary for cultural affairs. He'd been at the Bern Embassy for five years, a career diplomat who'd also had postings in Bonn and Madrid. His job was to promote exchanges between arts and literary organisations in Switzerland and the United States. Every embassy had them, Sam reminded himself. And they were so far down the hierarchy, you could be sure that no one paid any attention to them.

'And you are?'

According to the name tag, the girl at the desk was called Liza. She spoke perfect English, with just traces of a German–Swiss accent. As she spoke, Sam noticed one of the security guards glancing in his direction: a tall, thin man, in a blue uniform, he was standing right next to the entrance, scrutinising everyone who presented themselves to the reception desk. He was looking at Sam, but it would be an exaggeration to say he was suspicious. He was just keeping an eye on him, the way he did on everyone.

'Mr Woolfman,' said Sam. 'I'm from the European Library Association. I have an appointment at eleven.'

'Please take a seat.'

Sam nodded, looking around.

'May I use the Gent's?'

'Take the corridor on the right,' said Liza. 'It's the third door on the left.'

Sam started to walk. Every embassy, just like every office building, had a staff noticeboard: a place where anything the employees needed to know could be posted. You usually found them either near the foyer, or close to the canteen: the two places in the building you should be able to guarantee most of the staff would walk past every day. But so far, Sam had seen nothing in the foyer.

He walked past the toilets, and kept on down the corridor. At the end, there was a junction, with two corridors leading away from it. Sam could see the canteen at one end: even before you saw it, you could smell coffee and sandwiches. He quickened his pace, checking his watch as he did so. He'd used up a minute so far, and reckoned he had three minutes to play with before anyone became suspicious. 120 seconds to go . . .

The noticeboard was right next to the canteen. To his left, a couple of men in suits were chatting about their plans for Christmas as they ordered their coffees but they paid no attention to Sam. He scanned the noticeboard. There were notices about teenage daughters available for babysitting in Bern. There were a couple of chalets to rent up in some of the nearby ski resorts. And there was a notice about the upcoming Christmas party.

Then he saw it. The words at the top of the single-sided sheet of A4 paper simply stated: 'Pan Am Flights to the US: Security Advisory'.

Sam looked again to the left. The two guys in suits were stirring sugars into their coffees. They moved on from Christmas to complaining about the ambassador's chief of staff, a woman who, in their view, had clearly been promoted way above her level of minimal competence. Sam resisted a smile: it's the same rubbish in every organisation, he reflected to himself. He reached forwards, unhooked the pin, and took the sheet of paper off the wall, folding it once, and slipped it into the inside pocket of his jacket. He started walking back, checking his watch. Two minutes down, he noted, as he quickened his pace. Sixty seconds left.

*I should be okay.*

'Mr Woolfman . . .'

Liza was looking straight at him as he stepped back into the foyer.

'I'm afraid Mr Rosen has no record of the meeting,' she said.

The tone was apologetic.

But the guard was still looking at him suspiciously.

'But I'm sure my secretary fixed the meeting a month ago,' said Sam.

'Perhaps you could wait,' said Liza. 'I think Mr Rosen could come down and see you before lunch if you wouldn't mind waiting.'

'No, no,' said Sam, threading a tone of irritation into his voice. 'I have a meeting at the French Embassy at twelve. I'll have to get my secretary to rearrange.'

He stepped out of the office and started to walk down the Jubilaumsstrasse. It was getting closer to lunchtime, and the streets were starting to fill up with shoppers. A few office workers were emerging for lunch. It took a few moments to find a cab. When he did so, Sam told it to take him straight to the train station. It would take him an hour to get to Lucerne, on the train that ran through from Geneva, and if the taxi was fast enough he should be able to catch the train that left at five past twelve. It was only when he was sitting in the back of the cab that he unfolded the single sheet of paper in his jacket and started to read.

'Pan Am Flights to the US: Security Advisory', it started. 'Embassy staff are warned that a security threat exists at this time to Pan Am Flight 103 flying from Frankfurt to Washington via London. Until the full scope of this threat can be quantified, staff are advised to reconsider taking this flight, and should make alternative travel arrangements.'

Sam looked up at the train station just coming into view as the taxi turned a corner.

Why would the US Embassy staff be warned off the flight? he wondered to himself.

And if there was a threat to Flight 103, why hadn't they warned the airline itself?

Or all the other people travelling on it?

# FORTY-THREE

**Lucerne, 26 November**

The Grand Hotel National on the shores of Lake Lucerne had been built by César Ritz and Auguste Escoffier in the 1870s, but it had been modernised every decade since then, and its business centre was equipped with everything Sam needed.

He sat down at the desk, inside the private cubicle he had asked for, and checked that everything was in place: a phone, a computer with a modem connection, a telex machine, and a fax. Then he glanced across at Orla.

'You ready?'

A smile creased up her bright red lips. 'Sure,' she replied.

Sam had all the papers laid out in front of him. The United Dominions Bank had its own IBAN and SWIFT codes. Sam had already transferred $10,000 from his own account in London into the bank, then bounced $5,000 into an account he maintained in Tel Aviv and back again. His purpose was to make sure the bank was familiar to the computers that governed transfers within the global banking system, so that any more transactions he put through wouldn't be refused.

So far, everything was working perfectly.

Next, he asked Orla to call and get the IBAN and SWIFT numbers for Bank Laboucherd. When a receptionist from the bank picked up the phone, Orla said she was calling from a law firm in London, and needed to organise a transfer for a client. A secretary read out the information for her: that kind of information was never secret, because banks make thousands of transactions with one another every day.

Once the numbers were written down in front of him, Sam went across to the telex machine. He made up an eight-digit account number, then imputed a transfer of $100,000 to Bank Laboucherd. 'Now we wait,' he said, glancing across at Orla.

'For what?'

'For the payment to be rejected, of course.'

It took fifteen minutes.

Sam looked across at the telex machine. The message was from the computer system at Bank Laboucherd, and said simply that the account number had been rejected.

Picking up the phone, Sam punched through the number. 'May I speak to accounts, to someone who speaks English?' he said.

His tone was official, but impatient: the voice of a man who had more important things to do than track down rejected payments.

He waited, listening to the hum of the phone system as the receptionist transferred him. When the phone was picked up again, he said: 'I'm calling from the United Dominions Bank in Nassau. I've been having trouble making a transfer.'

He rattled off his IBAN and SWIFT numbers, and waited while the clerk checked the system.

'For $100,000, yes?' asked the clerk.

'That's right,' answered Sam.

'Who's the payment to?'

'Reto Ziegler.'

Another pause. Thirty seconds ticked by then a minute as the clerk went back to the main bank computer. 'You have the wrong account number.'

'Can you give me the right one?'

'Eight, four, two, seven, one, seven, nine, two.'

Sam scribbled down the number on a piece of paper and read it back to the clerk to make sure he'd got it right. 'Thanks for your help,' he said cheerfully. 'I'll put the payment through again later on today.'

Then he looked across at Orla, a smile on his face. 'Like I told you, banks don't talk to people, but they do talk to other banks,' said Sam. 'We have the account number for Ziegler.'

'Well done,' said Orla.

From the look on her face, Sam could tell she was impressed.

'Next we need to know how much money is in it, and who controls it.'

'And how the hell are you planning to do that?'

'I'm not,' said Sam. 'But *you* are.'

It took ten minutes for Sam to rehearse all the lines with Orla but when they had finished, she was word perfect. She knew exactly what to ask for, and how to put each question. 'Why me?' she asked, when Sam had finished explaining how the deception would work. 'Surely you could do this?'

'But people automatically trust a woman more than a man,' Sam replied. 'That's just human nature.'

Orla picked up the phone and dialled the number. When it was answered, she asked to be put through to the person who dealt with credit card authorisations.

'My name is Miss Rachel Evans, and I'm calling from the United Dominions Bank in Nassau,' she said when Herr Gerber picked up the phone. 'I need to check some details on a credit card application.'

Sam had told her it was unlikely the earlier call from United Dominion had been logged, so no one would know there had been two calls supposedly from Nassau in the space of one day. She rattled out her IBAN and SWIFT numbers to prove the credentials of her bank.

'What name?' asked Gerber.

'Reto Ziegler.'

'And his account number?'

'Eight, four, two, seven, one, seven, nine, two.'

She could feel her heart thumping in her chest as she read out the digits.

We are so close . . .

'And what is it you need to know?'

'A balance on the account, so that I can authorise the credit limit for this card.'

There was a pause on the line. Banks talk to other banks, that was what Sam had told her. They called each other all the time, checking on customers, accounts, movements of money: by always co-operating with one another, they could minimise fraud, and that helped all of them make more money.

'As of yesterday, 3.7 billion Swiss francs,' said Gerber.

Then, with the closest to a trace of humour in his voice that a Swiss banker could manage, he added: 'I think you'll find he qualifies for a gold card.'

'I believe so,' said Orla. 'And is there another signatory, in case I need to issue a second card?'

'Withdrawals have be co-signed by a Father Alberto Trapini,' said Gerber. 'Now is there anything else I may help you with Miss Evans?'

'That's all, thank you for your help.'

'My pleasure.'

Orla put the phone down. She looked across at Sam. 'You were quite right,' she said. 'A bank will always talk to another bank.'

'How much does he have?'

'The bastard has 3.7 billion Swiss francs deposited in the account,' she said.

238

Sam was scrawling on a piece of paper. 'That's $2.4 billion,' he said. 'So that's what they do with their money.'

'There's another name on the account,' said Orla. 'A guy called Alberto Trapini.'

Sam walked up close to her, glancing down at the piece of paper. 'I've got an idea where we might find him.'

'The Vatican . . .'

'Precisely.'

There was a brief look of sadness in Orla's eyes, noticed Sam. A look people sometimes get when they finally achieved something they've been pushing for for a long time.

'We found their money, Sam . . . the money they said they didn't have.'

She put her arms around him. Sam could feel her skin against his, and feel the warmth of her breath on her chest. 'I knew you could do it,' she said. 'I just knew.'

'I need to go up to my room and change,' said Sam, reluctant to let her leave his chest. 'Which one did you reserve for me?'

'I only booked one room,' said Orla.

'They didn't have two?'

Orla shrugged. 'I didn't ask,' she said, with a sly smile.

They moved upstairs likes a couple of teenagers who'd just realised their parents were away for the weekend. By the time Sam had shut the door, and opened up a bottle of champagne from the minibar, she was already in his arms. He could taste the champagne on her lips, and smell the perfume on her skin. Her arms were wrapped around him, and his lips were sliding down the side of her neck, until his tongue was flicking against the edge of her nipples. She took a sharp intake of breath, then shuddered, before pushing him down on the carpet. 'Fuck me,' she muttered, her voice slurred slightly from the alcohol. 'Fuck me right now.'

It lasted an hour, maybe an hour and a half: Sam wasn't

keeping track of the time. She made love the same way she talked: with a brutal, unsentimental intimacy. By the time he was finished, Sam felt drained and exhausted, his muscles still rippling with pleasure.

'What shall we do next?' asked Orla.

'First we eat,' said Sam. 'And then we book two tickets to Rome.'

'You forgot something,' said Orla, rolling on top of him.

'What's that?'

'First I'm going to fuck you again.'

Sam grinned, pulling her body down close to his. He lashed his tongue on to her nipples, feeling them stiffen at his touch. 'Now the Vatican really is going to be pissed off with you.'

# FORTY-FOUR

**Rome, 27 November**

Offices didn't come much more imposing that the suite of buildings occupied by the Vatican's Secretary of State, decided Sam as he glanced up at its sombre stone facade. They had walked into the tiny city state via St Peter's Square, after taking a flight from Zurich that lasted less than an hour. The magnificent facade of St Peter's stretched out before them, and, even though it was still only eleven in the morning, and November was hardly the high season for tourists, there were still flocks of people moving towards its entrance. You had to push your way through the crowds to get anywhere.

Behind St Peter's there was the massive papal garden, and to the right the Vatican museum. Sam and Orla walked past the museum, and into the tightly packed enclave of offices and apartments that filled the narrow streets behind it. It was here that the real heart of the Vatican lay: the offices that controlled not just the state itself, but the entire Catholic Church.

The Secretary of State's office was towards the back of the Vatican, itself backing on to the wall that partitioned the state from the rest of Rome. A high, six-storey building, it had been extensively rebuilt in the mid nineteenth century, with an imposing wooden door, opening on to a narrow, dark hallway.

Most people thought of the Pope as the leader of the Catholic Church, and while that was true in spiritual matters, the mechanics were controlled by the Secretary of State: he was, in effect, the prime minister while the Pope was the president. Each Pope chose his own Secretary of State, a cardinal, who managed the finances, controlled the monasteries, and who handled diplomatic relations with other nations. With a staff of 300 on the premises, all of them apart from the secretaries ordained ministers and fiercely loyal to the Church, he ruled the bureaucracy with an iron hand. Ministers in democracies, and even most dictators, reflected Sam, had to compromise and negotiate. But not the Secretary of State. He could do absolutely as he wished, and no one apart from the Pope himself was permitted to criticise him.

Sometimes not even the Pope.

Sam looked across at Orla. 'You feel ready to talk to them?' he said.

'Let's go,' she said simply.

He could spot the frailty in her voice, but Orla was a woman who kept her anxieties to herself, Sam reminded himself. Maybe it was because she grew up in an orphanage.

They stepped into the building. Sam didn't speak any Italian, or Latin, but it was a safe assumption they would speak some English. At the entrance to the office stood two uniformed members of the Swiss Guard, the Vatican's own private army. There had been four separate guards – the Swiss, the Corsican, the Noble, and the Palantine – but three of them had been abolished by Pope Paul VI in 1970. The Swiss Guard remained. The force dated back to the Swiss mercenary armies who roamed Europe in the fifteenth and sixteenth centuries. In 1527, 147 of the 189 guards had died during a desperate last battle during the sack of Rome, while the remaining forty men had helped Pope Clement VII escape from the city. Even today, the entry requirements for the Guard were stiff. Members had to be Swiss, of the Catholic faith, unmarried, and have completed basic training with the Swiss Army. Today, the Guard numbered 135 men, led by a commandant, bearing the rank of *oberst* or colonel, plus a chaplain, three officers, one sergeant major (known as the *feldwebel*), thirty NCOs, and ninety-nine 'halberdiers', a rank equivalent to private in a conventional army (they took their name from their halberd, a traditional, heavy Swiss weapon that was part sword, part axe, and part spear).

Sam glanced at the guard at the doorway. He was dressed in full ceremonial costume, combining blue, red, orange, and yellow, and there was a sword in a sheaf hanging from his belt. Sam was well aware that the man on the door was about as important to the security of the Vatican as the guards in red uniforms who posed for the tourists outside Buckingham Palace. There was plenty of back-up behind that facade. Ever since the assassination attempt on the Pope in 1981, the Swiss Guard had beefed up its weapons training, and the Vatican was now one of the most heavily fortified places in the world.

As Sam walked into the foyer, he noticed that the temperature dropped a couple of degrees. There was bright sunshine outside, but the office building had small windows, and thick walls: built in the days before offices had air conditioning, it was designed to allow the Vatican's machinery to keep working through the fierce heat of the Roman summer. In July a building such as this would be comfortable, but in the autumn it was chilly.

At the simple wooden desk that stood at the front of the small foyer there was a man about forty, with a thick black moustache, and a harsh, unforgiving face. Sam stood in front of the desk. 'I'm here to see Father Alberto Trapini,' he said.

Once they had the name, it hadn't been hard for Orla to track down Trapini's function. He was listed in the Vatican's directory of key officers as assistant to the Cardinals Directorate. He was the bureaucrat's bureaucrat, a lifetime Vatican staffer who had spent his whole career tending the Vatican machine. He was born, according to the brief biography Orla had found of him, in Milan in 1930, the youngest of four brothers in a banking family. Two of his older brothers were killed in the Second World War, while the one surviving brother was now a senior official in the Bank of Italy.

Alberto had joined the Church straight after school, completed his training for the priesthood, and was then placed within the Vatican. Every year, a small number of young priests, all of them Italian, were told that their career would not be in a church or a monastery, but within the machinery of the Church itself. They were chosen for their brains, and their determination, and although they knew they would never quite get to the top of the organisation, they would always be very close to it. Few of them ever regretted their choice: they were men who believed that a strong Church was vital for the world, and strength required organisation, discipline, and money, as well as faith.

'And you have an appointment?'

The man behind the desk didn't have a name tag. And he didn't smile much either.

'Tell him that Sam Woolfman and Orla Sheehy are here,' said Sam firmly. 'And that we need to speak to him about Reto Ziegler.'

If the name meant anything in the Vatican, it clearly hadn't percolated down to the front desk: there wasn't so much as a flicker of recognition. The man picked up the phone, spoke a few sentences in Italian, then looked back at Sam. 'Wait here,' he said.

Sam backed away a couple of steps, so that he was standing next to Orla. It was busy within the offices, but not bustling. Down the corridor, Sam could hear the sounds of a quiet conversation. A few people came in and out, but none of then did anything more than flash their security badges at the guard.

'You said your name was Mr Woolfman?'

Sam looked up. A man had appeared as if from nowhere, and was standing right next to Sam. He was more than six foot tall, with an imposing build, thick black hair, and was wearing a dark grey suit, white shirt, and deep blue silk tie. He spoke in a clipped Germanic accent.

'That's right.'

'And you wish to see Father Trapini?'

Sam nodded towards the man at the desk. 'I already told him that.'

'You don't have any appointment.'

'I don't need one,' Sam snapped.

The man paused. 'The Father is very busy.'

'So am I,' said Sam.

He took a step forwards, so that he was just a few inches from the man's face. 'Tell him that I need to talk to him about Reto Ziegler,' he said. 'Tell him that if he doesn't talk to me in the next five minutes then I'm going to talk to the newspapers instead.'

'But—'

'Five minutes,' growled Sam.

'I—'

'I make it four minutes and thirty seconds,' said Sam. 'If you want to be the guy responsible for bringing down a Pope, and plunging this organisation into the greatest financial scandal of the century, then that's your choice. If you don't want to, I suggest you go and tell Trapini to come and speak to us right now.'

The man turned on his heels, and started to walk back down the corridor. Sam waited. He had a feeling that before long he'd be seeing him again. He glanced across at Orla: for just a second he could see the nervousness in her expression.

You caught glimpses of it occasionally, like a small, dark cloud drifting across a blue sky, but it quickly disappeared, replaced by a mask of implacable determination.

An older man was walking towards them. Sam recognised him from the picture they'd seen in the directory. Thin, with a long, Roman nose, close-set eyes, and a wiry, imposing face, he was looking straight at Sam.

Trapini.

Sam felt certain of it.

'Come this way,' he said quietly.

They walked along a corridor leading away from the entrance hall for twenty yards before Trapini stopped. He opened a door, and showed them inside. It wasn't his office, noted Sam. Just a meeting room. It measured ten foot by fifteen, and was painted cream, with a wooden table and six chairs down the centre. There was nothing on the walls, and nothing to drink on the table. In the centre of the ceiling, there was a single lamp, casting a pale light down into the room. There was one narrow window, but it was so high up you couldn't see out of it.

I know what this reminds me of, thought Sam.

A military interrogation room.

I've been in these before.

*When the Mossad wanted to beat something out of me.*

'I don't even know who you are, Mr Woolfman,' said Trapini. 'And yet you come in here demanding a meeting with me.'

'We know about the account.'

'Who are you Mr Woolfman?'

'The account with Bank Laboucherd.'

'I said, who *are* you?' snapped Trapini. 'I won't talk to a man who won't even tell me who he is or why he's here.'

At that moment, Orla stepped forward. 'Let's start with me,' she said. 'My name is Orla Sheehy, and I was raised by your Church.'

'What do you mean?'

'The Order of St Luke's in Leighlinbridge in County Carlow in Ireland,' she said. 'I was taken in there as an orphan along with my brother Rory after my parents died. We were both just kids. Rory was systematically abused. Eventually . . .' She stumbled over the worlds, noted Sam. 'Eventually he killed himself.'

Trapini remained silent. He was standing at one end of the table, while Sam and Orla stood at the other, the strip of wood all that separated them. 'The Boston diocese denied everything, but I got a judgement against them, making them culpable for Rory's death. There were damages against them—'

'I know about the case,' interrupted Trapini. He looked up at her, his eyes suddenly full of venom. 'So you are the girl.'

'That's right,' snapped Orla. 'And you won't get rid of me as easily as you got rid of Rory.'

Trapini shrugged. 'You have your judgement,' he said. Then he glanced upwards. 'But there is, of course, only one judgement we care about in here, and it doesn't have anything to do with a court in Boston.'

'They claimed they didn't have any money,' said Orla.

'We are a poor and humble Church,' said Trapini, with a thin smile. '"Sell your belongings and give alms. Provide money bags for yourselves that do not wear out, an inexhaustible treasure in heaven that no thief can reach nor moth destroy." Luke—'

'I know the quote,' snapped Orla. 'Chapter twelve, verse thirty-three.'

For the first time since they'd come into the room, Sam noticed, Trapini looked taken aback: on his face, you could see the suspicious respect of the man who realises he has underestimated his opponent.

His eyes darted from Sam to Orla, then back again. 'If the

Boston diocese has no money, then I trust they have been using it to help the poor, as of course they should.'

'They've been hiding the money,' said Orla.

'We've tracked it down,' said Sam. 'The diocese is left a trove of valuable treasure, and they use a dealer in Geneva called Reto Ziegler to sell it for them. The money is paid into an account held with Bank Laboucherd in Lucerne. We know the precise details of the account, and we know exactly how much money is in it.'

'3.7 billion Swiss francs,' said Orla.

'That's too much money to come from the Boston diocese,' said Sam. 'I reckon you've been pulling the same trick all over the world, and using Ziegler to hide the money for you.'

'It's just conjecture,' said Trapini. 'You can prove nothing.'

'We've identified the money.'

'And a Swiss account remains secret, you know that,' snapped Trapini. 'The judgement against us in Boston is a civil one, but in truth whether it is a civil or criminal verdict doesn't make any difference. A Swiss bank is not going to disclose the details of one of its accounts, not on the orders of an American court, or anyone else. You can make all the allegations you like. People have been levelling charges against this Church for 2,000 years, and many of them are far darker than storing some money away in a Swiss bank account, I can assure you of that. So if you think of this is of any concern to me, then you are very much mistaken.'

He started to walk towards the door, brushing past Orla with a contemptuous sneer.

Sam could see that he was right.

If they revealed the details of the account, the bank would just deny it.

That was the way Swiss banks operated.

They never revealed anything.

It certainly wouldn't be obliged to respond to a demand from an American court. And in the face of a denial from the bank, what did they have?

Just conjecture?

It was time to take a chance – or lose everything.

'We know about the other documents you store with Bank Laboucherd,' he said.

Trapini already had his hand on the door handle. He paused, then looked around. 'What documents?' he said quietly.

If they kept a fortune hidden there, why not some documents as well? figured Sam. The Vatican was full of secrets, and no doubt many of them would be buried off the premises.

'From the bad old days,' said Sam. 'Documents you would prefer were buried forever.'

'You're bluffing,' said Trapini.

Sam could see Orla glancing in his direction. What the hell are you talking about? her eyes appeared to be saying. Fortunately, Trapini is looking at me, noted Sam. If he glanced at Orla, he would know I was winging this. But his eyes are fixed on mine. And I'm giving nothing away.

'It can be all over the papers in a couple of days,' said Sam.

Trapini released his fingers from the door handle. 'I hope you know what kind of forces you're up against, Mr Woolfman.'

'You want to settle?' growled Sam.

There was brief moment of hesitation.

'Because you sure as hell don't want the existence of that document revealed.'

'How much?' snapped Trapini.

Sam glanced at Orla, then back at Trapini. 'The judgement was for $500 million,' he said. 'We want it paid in full.'

Another silence.

Sam was already wondering what he would do next. He'd played his cards. There was nothing left in his hand if Trapini said no.

'Give me forty-eight hours,' he said.

'We want the money transferred to the lawyers who brought the case,' said Orla.

'It will be done,' said Trapini quietly.

'I think you'll find you've made the right decision,' said Sam.

But Trapini had already walked from the room. With Orla at his side, Sam walked back to the foyer, and out on to the street outside. Both of them remained silent as they pushed their way back through the crowds thronging through St Peter's Square. Suddenly Sam felt the need to be off the Vatican's soil.

He quickened his pace, relieved when he was back in Italy itself.

'What the hell was that all about?' asked Orla.

'The document?'

Orla nodded.

'I reckoned that if they hid their money in that bank, they would probably have hidden documents in there as well,' said Sam. 'Documents that were so sensitive that they couldn't even be kept in the Vatican.'

'And you didn't know what they were?'

Sam shook his head.

'Christ,' muttered Orla. 'We could have ended up looking really stupid.'

Sam took her in his arms, and hugged her close to his chest. 'It doesn't matter now,' he said. 'We beat them, and that's all that counts.'

# FORTY-FIVE

**Tel Aviv, 28 November**

Zvi Imer greeted Sam warmly, the same way he always did.

Now in his seventies, a thin and wiry man with chestnut brown eyes, Imer had been the head of training for the Mossad up until six years ago when failing health had finally forced him out of the service. He had taken Sam as a raw recruit straight out of the army, and spent a year turning him into an agent. It was a process that was as much psychological as physical: Imer took his recruits apart piece by piece, then re-engineered them as the perfect servants of the Israeli state.

Imer, Sam sometimes felt, had Israel in his blood: cut open his chest, and his heart would be shaped like a thin slither of land nestling precariously on the edge of the Mediterranean. He'd been born in the Ukraine in 1927, a fact that he would often refer to with a hollow laugh. 'Imagine it,' he'd say, as they shared a meal after a long day of training. 'A Jew born in the Ukraine in 1927. Can history deal a tougher hand to play than that? And you boys think you have it tough when I make you do fifty press-ups before breakfast. I tell you, you don't even know how to spell the word tough.'

There was much truth in that, Sam would later realise, as he gradually learned the truth about Imer's life. The man himself never spoke about it, but Sam put together some of the details from talking to his father and his friends among Israel's old warriors. As a child, Imer lived through the collectivisation of the farms in the Ukraine, and the famine that followed it: then the purges of the 1930s that saw millions deported to the camps: then the Nazi invasion that swept brutally through the country: then the round-up of the Jews in Nazi-occupied Ukraine. Imer himself was sent to Dachau, and managed to survive there for two years, until the camp was finally liberated by the Allies. He was one of just a handful of Jews left alive at the end of the war. From there, he made his way to Palestine, and joined the fighters battling to found an independent state. He was wounded twice, but both times went straight back into action.

Sam's father, himself a Mossad agent, had told him it was not surprising that the man was prepared to fight to have a country where he could feel safe among his own people. Nor that he expected others to do the same.

For that generation, reflected Sam, there could be no compromising on the security of the Jewish homeland.

Sam had spent the night with Orla at the Grand Hotel Plaza, a ten-minute walk from Rome's Spanish Steps. They had much to celebrate. From nothing, they had forced the Vatican to capitulate. There was a lightness to Orla's mood, noted Sam, that came from knowing she had avenged her brother's death. The Church had been forced to pay a price, and that was some measure of consolation. Maybe now, she'd told Sam, she'd be able to get on with the rest of her life.

This morning, they'd taken a flight from Rome to Tel Aviv. With the Vatican case wrapped up, Sam wanted to push on with the mystery of what happened to Flight 103. And Sam instinctively knew that the next clue was most probably not in Lockerbie, nor in New York.

But in Tel Aviv.

After touching down at the airport, Sam and Orla checked into the Optima Tower Hotel, a functional modern block close to the centre of the city. Orla had stayed behind, while Sam headed out across town to see the one man felt certain might be able to help him find a way into the mystery.

Imer.

The block where he lived was close to the Yarkon Park, on the northern edge of Tel Aviv. Along the way, he'd passed St Antony's Church on Jeffet Street, one of only four Catholic churches in the whole of the city, and Sam found himself wondering about Trapini's threat. He made it just as they were leaving the building. The Vatican was a powerful enemy and the money hadn't been paid over yet.

And if something happened to us, they wouldn't have to pay out $500 million.

One more reason to be careful.

Sam checked the passage leading up to the apartment block before stepping inside. Whether there were any other old Mossad men living here, he had no way of knowing, but it was a possibility. Everyone likes to stick with their own kind, Sam reminded himself, and of no breed of men is that more true than old soldiers.

The passage was empty. It was just after two in the afternoon. There were some bikes parked in the hall of the concrete apartment block, and some cheap cars in the parking lot outside. But at least half the spaces were empty. This was one of the roughest areas of town: anyone who had the money for a decent car would be living somewhere else.

Imer lived on the eighth floor. Sam took the lift upwards, then turned left. He only had to knock once on the door before Imer opened it.

'Sam,' he said, a broad grin breaking out on his thin and leathery face. 'Come in, come in.'

It was two years since he had last seen Imer: not since he'd closed the file on the Robertson case. Sam had always suspected that retirement aged a man, yet he had never seen the evidence so clearly demonstrated as it was now. Take away a man's purpose, and the life started to drain out of him. Last time Sam had seen Imer, he was a fit, if ageing man, his skin polished, and his eyes bright and alert. Now his skin was grey, the stubble was spiking his chin, and his eyes were shot with exhaustion. 'Here.' he said. 'I'll get you something to drink.'

Sam followed him through the hallway. The apartment had just one room. There was a kitchenette off to one side, and next to that a shower room in which a man could just about stand. There was a single living space, with a television and radio on a stand, a small writing desk, and a futon laid out on the floor to sleep on. The only ornament was a picture of Imer's two daughters: Katie, who now lived in Boston, and was married with two children; and Hannah, who was working at one of the American investment banks in London. Imer, Sam knew, had divorced almost twenty years ago, and the girls were the only family he had, yet he hardly ever saw them.

Just like me, Sam reflected sourly.

*I guess the Mossad and marriage don't mix.*

The only luxury was a noisy air-conditioning unit stuck through the single front window.

So this is what a lifetime in the service of the Mossad gets you, Sam reflected as he cast his eyes around the apartment.

*Absolutely nothing.*

At least I got out while there was still a chance.

'You're still freelancing?' said Imer. 'You should be back in the service. Israel needs you . . .'

'They wouldn't have me back,' said Sam. 'Not now . . .'

'So what do you want?'

'I need your help.'

'And this time it's . . .'

'Flight 103.'

'A tragedy,' said Imer.

'I know,' said Sam. 'But also a mystery.'

From the small kitchenette, Imer had brought out two steaming hot mugs of coffee. They sat down at the small wooden table. He might be old and frail, but Sam knew that Imer was still plugged into the Mossad network. He had trained a whole generation of operators for the service. It's not just me that regards him as a surrogate father, it's a whole generation of them, and they all drift through this apartment, bringing slithers of gossip from the front line.

'It was a bomb, wasn't it?' said Imer.

Sam nodded, taking a first sip of coffee. It was the cheapest, own-label instant you could buy in the local supermarket, and it tasted terrible, but at least there was some caffeine in it.

'Then it must be our friends over the border, the Palestinians,' said Imer. 'They are the only people who bomb planes.'

'Except . . .' Sam paused. 'Except for two things.'

'Which are?'

Sam told him what he heard in Lockerbie, about the Black Hawk swooping down on the crash site minutes after the plane came down. Then he told him what he'd found in Zurich, the warning to embassy staff about not flying on Flight 103.

'So what are you saying?' said Imer.

'Just that there seems to be a lot of unexplained American activity around this plane.'

'And . . .'

'And I want to know why they were so interested in Flight 103.'

He pulled out the list of names Carter Jenas had supplied him with, and placed it down on the table. 'These were the people on the flight,' he said. 'I need to know more about the names.'

Imer started reading.

His lips were moving slightly, and his brow was furrowed in concentration. 'These three,' he said finally.

'Who?' asked Sam, leaning forwards.

Imer was pointing at three names halfway down the passenger list.

'Jim Prentiss, Scott Valentin, and Ben Hanold.'

'Who the hell are they?' growled Sam.

'They are CIA men,' said Imer. 'Three of their best special agents. They were sent to Beirut to work on freeing the four American hostages beings held there.'

'Why would three CIA men be on board the plane?' asked Sam.

Imer shrugged. 'Maybe they'd been called back to head office.'

'But embassy staff were warned not to travel on that flight.'

'So maybe the message didn't get through to the CIA,' said Imer. 'Government agencies don't trust each other. It happens in Israel, and it probably happens in the US as well.'

'But if you piece it all together . . . there's a pattern.'

'Maybe,' said Imer. 'Or maybe just a series of coincidences.'

'I have no idea.'

'I need to find out,' said Sam.

# FORTY-SIX

**Tel Aviv, 28 November**

Orla was waiting for Sam in the room at the Optima Tower Hotel. As soon as he stepped into the room, Sam could sense she had something to tell him. She'd been on the phone to the law firm in Boston. 'And it's amazing,' she said. 'They settled just like that.'

'What did they say?' asked Sam.

He poured himself a whiskey from the minibar. It was already after six in the evening and it had been a long day. The flight from Rome had taken over an hour, and he'd spent two hours talking with Imer. He was still trying to puzzle his way through what he'd learned. Why would three high-ranking CIA men be on that flight? Just going home? Possibly . . .

'The Boston diocese has been in touch with the lawyers,' she continued. 'They said it was all a mistake, and the assets were there after all. They've offered to pay the entire amount in cash as soon as the paperwork is drawn up.'

'And how long will that take?'

'A week, at least.'

'That long?'

'They have to lodge papers with the court stating that the claim has been fully settled.'

She could see that Sam was looking worried.

'But at least we won . . .'

'So long as we stay alive.'

Now it was Orla's face that was flushed with fear.

'What do you mean?'

She's just a kid, thought Sam. Smart and beautiful, but a kid all the same. She has no idea of the forces at play in the world.

'If we die before the money is transferred, then the case dies with us.'

'They wouldn't . . .'

'People have died for a lot less than $500 million.'

She stepped closer to Sam, resting her head against his chest. It had never occurred to her what she was taking on, Sam realised. Or what the cost of the fight might be to her personally. Her fingers were trembling and her skin was suddenly cold. Sam looked down, and kissed her on the lips. 'It'll be okay,' he said. 'We just need to be careful, that's all.'

He stepped away, draining the last of his whiskey. 'Did you find anything from Carter?'

'I spent two hours in the business centre, using the fax and the phones,' she said.

'And?'

Orla laid out a series of sheets of paper on the desk.

'He faxed through a list of the cancellations from Flight 103,' she said. 'It is basically a business route so they get about twenty per cent cancellations on every flight. That's normal. In fact, the system allows them to sell a 110 per cent of the seats because they can assume plenty of people will cancel at the last minute. So Carter warned me not to get too worked up about it. Cancellations are normal in the airline business.'

'But this was higher than normal, right?'

Orla nodded.

'How much higher?'

'More like thirty per cent,' said Orla. 'That's partly why

there were so many students on the flight. They were all on standby, and because there were so many cancellations, a lot of them managed to get seats at the last minute.'

Sam peered down at the list of names.

'So who are all these people?' he asked.

'I've been working the phones,' said Orla.

'And?'

'In total, there were seventy cancellations from Flight 103,' said Orla. 'Of those, thirty-one were standard business and leisure travellers. Guys working for American corporations in London, City guys going to the States for a meeting, that kind of things. But thirty-nine worked for the American government.'

'Shit,' muttered Sam.

He looked up at Orla. 'Which branch?'

'Twenty-one were American Embassy staff, from London, Bonn, and a couple from Ireland who'd caught a feeder flight from Dublin and were scheduled to get on to the plane at Heathrow.'

'And they all cancelled?'

Orla nodded.

'Another five were American military personnel stationed in Germany.'

'And?'

Sam sensed he already knew what was coming next.

'Thirteen of them were officials with the CIA.'

'You sure?' said Sam.

'I've checked and double-checked,' she said, pointing to the list of names. 'And if you call the switchboard at Langley, you get put through. So yes, they are all CIA staffers.'

Sam looked at the list again, this time running his eyes down the names of the passengers who died. 'So I wonder how many of these people worked for the American government?'

'So far as I can tell, none of them,' said Orla.

'Except for these three,' said Sam. 'Jim Prentiss, Scott Valentin, and Ben Hanold.'

'Who are they?'

'Special undercover agents for the CIA,' said Sam. 'They won't appear on any records, so you wouldn't have come across them in your search.'

'But they were agency?'

Sam nodded. 'They were sent to Beirut to try and free the American hostages being held there,' he said. 'So the question is, why were so many American government staff pulled from Flight 103? And why weren't these three guys?'

'Maybe there just wasn't time to get through to them.'

'Maybe . . .'

But Sam wasn't sure.

There was something else.

He looked across at Orla.

'Do you get seasick?'

She shook her head. 'Once you get used to the Irish Sea, your sea legs are fine.'

'That's good.'

'Why?'

'Because we're going to Beirut,' he said. 'Tonight.'

# FORTY-SEVEN

**Beirut, 29 November**

The dawn was just breaking over the shoreline, sending shafts of pale orange light out across the sea. Sam held Orla close to him. It was chilly out on the Mediterranean, and fishing boats don't come equipped with heating. He could feel the cold air wrapping around him, and his skin was wet from the spray splashing up across the boat's deck. Looking out, he could see the port drawing ever closer. In a few moments, they would be on dry land again.

The trip had been simple, if expensive, to arrange.

When he was still in the Mossad, Sam had made three sorties into the Lebanon to take out Palestinian terrorists, and each time he'd gone into the country by boat. The land border between the two countries measures less than a hundred miles, and is heavily fortified. There is barbed wire along its entire length, all of it heavily patrolled by armies from both sides, and even if you attempt to sneak through in one of the more remote areas, you are at risk of triggering a landmine. But both countries had coastlines that stretched for hundreds of miles, and opened on to the Mediterranean, one of the busiest seaways in the world. There were ferries, cargo boats, and fishing fleets. The sea was impossible for anyone to police, and that was the simplest way to get from one country to the next without having to show yourself to the border police.

From the hotel, they had travelled down to Netanya, a small port town located on the seafront between Tel Aviv and Haifa. There they had met up with David Tobin, who ran a small fishing fleet in the town, but was also the man the Mossad used for its covert drops into the Lebanon. He remembered Sam from the old days, and for a $2,000 fee was happy to make the couple of phone calls necessary to arrange the trip.

Together, Sam and Orla lay down on the bench in Tobin's office to catch a few hours' sleep before the journey would begin. They were woken at four in the morning, and taken on board a small fishing steamer heading out into the Mediterranean. It was crewed by eight Israelis: all of them knew the drill by heart. They assumed that Sam and Orla were working for the Mossad and knew better than to ask any questions. At four thirty, they were far enough out to sea for the transfer to be made. Another vessel, run by a Lebanese fisherman called Marwan Hamadeh, stopped twenty feet away, and a small dinghy, steered by Tobin himself, took Sam and Orla across and deposited them on Hamadeh's boat. Another $2,000 changed hands. You had to catch a lot of fish to make that much money. It was split equally between the six Lebanese crewmen, and the money bought their silence. They had been dropping Mossad men into the country for years, and so far they had not been discovered.

For the next two hours, Sam and Orla stayed in the hold of the small, sturdy vessel. Returning without any fish would be suspicious, so it was part of the routine that they always sailed back into harbour with a full haul. Hamadeh's boat specialised in the anchovies and sardines that were common in this part of the Mediterranean, and over the next two hours hauled in catch after catch until the deck was slippery with tiny, wriggling fish.

'Jesus, I don't think I'll ever eat sardines again,' said Orla as the boat finally headed into the port. 'Poor little guys . . .'

They landed at Damour, a small port village, about twenty miles due west of Beirut. From there, they grabbed some coffee and a roll from a local café, then caught the first bus up to Beirut. They were dressed simply, so as to blend in with the locals, but Sam bought Orla a bag and a camera so that she would look like a tourist: with her white skin and pale eyes, she was never going to pass for an Arab even if her hair was jet black. By the time they arrived in Beirut, it was just after nine in the morning. Sam got them a room at a small hotel in the backstreets behind the port. It was one of the dozens of hotels in a maze of streets where the sailors stayed between jobs. They took cash, and didn't ask for any papers, and that suited Sam just fine. He didn't want anyone to know he was in the country. Beirut wasn't a safe city for most people anymore, and certainly not for a former Mossad agent.

There were plenty of people in Beirut who wanted to see Sam dead, and he wasn't planning on meeting any of them.

'So what do we do now?' asked Orla.

'We talk to the Mossad men here, and see what the hell we can find out,' answered Sam.

The Mossad maintained a network of undercover agents in the city. There were layer upon layer of them: the agency had always regarded the Lebanon as the greatest potential threat to the state of Israel, and infiltrating every aspect of Lebanese society had always been one of its highest priorities.

The agents could be found in every rank of Lebanese society. It was rumoured within the Mossad that at least one cabinet member was an undercover agent, although Sam had no idea which one it might be. There were senior bankers, businessmen, and diplomats. Then, as you went further down the chain, there was a network of traders, ship brokers, travel agents, arms dealers and gangsters, all of whom could be relied upon to provide advance warning of

263

any sudden, unexpected movements of money, men, or weapons that would alert Israel that an attack was imminent. Right at the very bottom were newspaper vendors, ticket clerks, and cleaners: people with their eyes on the ground.

Some of them were men who had been turned for money. In any country – and in the Lebanon more than most – there were always people for whom a couple of thousand dollars paid into a foreign bank account every month would be very useful. Sometimes you just had to make one discreet phone call every couple of years to justify your existence.

Then there were the Kesaria, which together with the Kidon (the assassination units, to which Sam had once belonged) were the most highly prized with the service. The Kesaria were Jews of Arabic origin, and who spoke fluent Arabic, who were planted in Arab societies, and who would live their entire lives as loyal citizens of those countries while secretly feeding information back to Israel. Known as 'combatants' – or *lohamim* in Hebrew – they were men of exceptional discipline and bravery. Everyone knew they were out there – even the PLO had been infiltrated – but nobody ever knew who they were.

That was their strength.

They spent their whole lives in the shadows.

Sam didn't know the details of more than a fraction of the network. But he knew enough names to make a start.

As soon as he stepped out of the hotel, Sam took a cab down to the Karantina district. He'd been here twice before. Once during his training for the Mossad, he and one other former soldier had been told to go and retrieve a document from an agent: it was part of a series of training exercises, designed to test the resourcefulness and resolve of the recruits. The second time he'd been sent to track down a Hamas terrorist the Mossad knew was holed up in its narrow streets. The first time he had been successful. The second time he'd been lucky to escape with his life: that mission had ended in a shoot-out, in which Sam had been badly outgunned and outnumbered, and it was only the twisting alleyways of the district that gave him the opportunity to escape.

The third time?

If he was honest with himself, Sam wasn't taking any bets.

It took a special kind of cunning to survive in the Beirut arms business: Munir Ghanem, however, had plenty of that. Aged thirty-five, he was a thin and wiry man, clean-shaven, with his hair worn untypically long. He ran an electronics shop on the western edges of the Karantina. Sam paused outside the crowded entrance. It was stacked high with reconditioned fridges and air-conditioners that spilled out on to the alleyway, while, as soon as you stepped inside, it was packed from floor to ceiling with kettles, fans, and TV sets. Sam was aware that this was the place to come if you wanted to buy a weapon – for cash, of course – with no questions asked. Beirut had plenty of gun runners, but all of them were affiliated to one faction or another in the country's endless civil war. They'd sell you a gun, but only if you were shooting at the other side. In a city of partisans, Munir was the only independent: the only side he was on was his own.

'I was looking for one of the back-room items,' said Sam.

He delivered the sentence confidently but he didn't feel that way. He was aware that equipping yourself with a weapon on hostile territory was one of the most delicate parts of any mission: there were plenty of dealers who would sell you a gun for a few hundred dollars, then collect a few hundred more by turning you in to your enemies.

'And you are . . .?' said Munir.

He was standing just a few inches away from Sam. He had suspicious eyes that no doubt had good reason to be mistrustful.

'I'm a roll of banknotes,' said Sam.

Whatever else he did, Sam wasn't about to tell him who he was, what he was here for, or who he used to work for. The Mossad wasn't about to win any popularity contests in Beirut. He wanted a gun. But he didn't want it that badly.

'Mr Banknote? Now that's a guy we can always do business with,' said Munir crisply.

He led Sam through to a back entrance. Switching on a light, Munir pulled aside a curtain, revealing a neat stack of weapons. There wasn't a huge amount of choice, reflected Sam, but like a good French restaurant, a short menu was more than made up for by the quality of what was on offer. Beretta, Heckler & Koch, Browning, and Colt were the four manufacturers Munir stocked. He had handguns, sniper rifles, assault rifles, and range of plastic explosive. Sam ran his eyes across the shelves before he saw what he wanted: a Beretta M591 handgun. It wasn't the greatest weapon in the world, but Sam had trained with it when he first joined the Israeli Army, and he knew the gun intimately. He took it down off the shelf, and took a moment to assess its weight and balance. It was brand new, which was not the way Sam liked his guns: like a car, a weapon was better when it had been run in. But it would work well enough. 'I'll take it,' he said.

'$800,' said Munir.

Sam attempted a smile. 'Robbery.'

Munir shrugged. 'The reason we do business with Mr Banknote is because he doesn't haggle.'

Sam reached into his pocket, and counted out the notes. You could buy one of these wholesale for a $100. Maybe I should be a gun dealer, he reflected to himself. The margins are a lot better than antiques.

Slipping the weapon into his jacket pocket, Sam walked quickly through the streets until he found a taxi. The Beirut Bank of Global Commerce was next port of call.

It occupied a palatial office on Hamra Street, right in the centre of the city's business district, and was run by Arslan Sinno, one of the best-connected men in Beirut. The BBGC was one of the few financial institutions trusted by the city's Muslims and Christians alike. It only had one office, but it had excellent contacts with all the main banks in London, Zurich, and Frankfurt, and for money coming into and out of the country, it was usually the main conduit.

Arslan Sinno had run the bank for twenty years, building it cautiously into one of the most trusted in Beirut. He was born into a Lebanese family in Geneva, educated there and in Paris, and had worked at Credit Suisse before moving back to the Lebanon to set up the BBGC. That was the official story anyway. The unofficial story was that he was *lohamim*. He'd been born in Paris to a Jewish family, and at the age of twenty, had applied to move to Israel. A Mossad case officer working in the immigrations department saw his potential, created a new identity for him, gave him the name Arslan Sinno, and used the *sayanim* – the Mossad's network of global sympathisers – to get him the job at Credit Suisse. The rest Sinno had done for himself.

He had become a pillar of the Lebanese establishment. And yet all through those years, he had actually been a Mossad agent.

Sam knew the password that granted instant access to Sinno's office. You just told his secretary you needed to examine account 11756 and you were shown straight in. No such account existed, of course. It was just a code.

Sinno was a tall man, now in his late fifties, immaculately dressed in a grey wool suit, and with heavy brown eyes that followed you around the room. He shook Sam by the hand, and offered him a seat. 'I thought you'd retired, Mr Woolfman,' he said. 'The last I heard, you were no longer . . .' He paused, choosing his words carefully. 'One of us.'

'I just changed jobs, that's all,' said Sam. 'From *kidon* to *sayanim*. My days as an assassin were over. Like most of us, I'm not getting any younger.'

'So you are . . .?'

'Ostensibly, a private investigator,' said Sam. 'People come to me with investigations, mainly because of my Mossad history. But I still report back to head office. This way, we get to find out who is interested in our operations . . . and I get to work on mysteries it would be too sensitive for the Mossad to work on by itself.'

Sam knew it was a lie. But he had to find a way of getting Sinno to talk to him. If he knew he was no longer reporting back to the Mossad, he would show him the door immediately. He was a man of fierce loyalty.

'And what do you want to know?'

'Three CIA men died on Flight 103, the plane that crashed ten days ago,' said Sam. 'They were working on freeing the American hostages in this city. I'm trying to figure out if they might be connected to the crash in some way.'

Sinno poured himself a glass of ice-cold water from the bottle on his desk. He took one sip. 'How much do you know about the Beirut operation of the CIA?'

'Almost nothing.'

'It is one of the most corrupt and inept of that organisation's bureaus,' said Sinno. 'The Americans have no idea what is happening in the Middle East, and they never will. And the reason for that? They have no intelligence operations worth the name here in Beirut. They are too busy running drugs.'

'Drugs?'

Sinno nodded. 'There is a man called Foley running the bureau here,' he continued. 'He had debts . . . bad debts. The station here has been dabbling in the drugs trade, which, as I'm sure you know, has become about the only profitable part of the Lebanese economy since the civil war started.'

A CIA station trading drugs? Was that possible? Sam thought to himself. It was only a few years since the world had learned about how the CIA was involved in the smuggling of illegal arms supplies to the Iranians, the sworn enemies of the United States. If they could do that . . . then why not trade in drugs as well?

'Are you sure?'

'Some of the money they make passes through this very bank.'

'Could that be linked to the bomb on Flight 103?'

Sinno shrugged. 'Anything is possible where the Beirut operation is concerned. But I haven't heard anything about it.'

'So how are they getting the drugs into the US?'

'Through the diplomatic bag. It's brilliant and simple, like all the best plots. The bag goes from here to Washington every day, and the drugs go with it.'

Sam thanked the man for his time, and scribbled down the number of his hotel, asking him to call him if he heard anything else. Next, he took a cab across town to talk to Bassem Jaber, who ran a trucking business based on the out-skirts of town. Jaber was another *lohamim*, a man with a carefully created identity that had allowed him to slot right into Palestinian society. Sam was still pondering the revelation that the Beirut bureau was shipping drugs back to America. Could that have something to do with the crash? He talked to Jaber for twenty minutes but it turned out he knew nothing. He wasn't aware of the drug smuggling, and he'd never heard of the three CIA agents who died on the plane.

It was late afternoon when Sam stopped by the office of Shadi Al-Zarif. Whereas many of the agents Sam knew of in Beirut were men planted in the city by the Mossad, Al-Zarif was a more mainstream contact. A man who had been turned by money. He ran A1 Express, one of the largest firms of motorcycle couriers in the city. A1 delivered documents for all the major banks, companies, and embassies, and was also the local agent for one of the big American courier companies. It delivered thousands of documents every day. Intelligence agencies were always keen to tap into courier firms. There were few better ways of keeping tabs on information than inspecting the contents of packages going into an embassy or government buildings, and, since his was the biggest, Al-Zarif's was the one they were all after. He simply sold himself to the highest bidder, and that happened to be the Mossad. In fact, Sam suspected he sold himself to several agencies at the same time. After all, the agencies didn't talk to one another. If you sold your information to the Mossad, why not sell it to Iran's VEVAK, or Egypt's GDSSI (General Directorate for State Security Investigations) as well?

Sam was kept waiting in an outside office for almost forty minutes before he managed to see Al-Zarif. He was a short, fat man, with heavily greased hair, and a thick gold medallion on his barrel-like chest. The office had fierce air conditioning, but there were still beads of sweat dripping from Al-Zarif's face.

'You want to know about the drug-running operation organised by the CIA,' said Al-Zarif, leaning conspiratorially across his crowded desk. 'Then I'll tell you something. It was about to be blown wide open.'

'Blown open . . . how?' asked Sam.

'The three guys who they sent over here to investigate the hostages. They started poking around in the city's under-world, talking to all kinds of people, finding out things that are better hidden away. And they found out about the drugs trade.'

'You sure about that?'

Al-Zarif nodded. 'I know the guy who told them,' he said. 'He was supposed to be giving them a lead on where the hostages might be, but once they got wind of the drug dealing they decided to start chasing that instead.'

'And then what happened to them?'

'They left Beirut.'

'To where?'

'I've no idea.'

Sam walked from the office. He was supposed to be meeting Orla back at the hotel at six and he didn't want to keep her waiting.

The CIA in Beirut was dealing in drugs, he reminded himself.

The three CIA men sent to the city – Prentiss, Valentin, and Hanold – found out about it.

Maybe they were about to blow the whole case open.

They quit the city.

And shortly afterwards, they died on Flight 103.

# FORTY-EIGHT

**Beirut, 29 November**

Sam could see Orla walking out of the hotel.

She was heading down the street, only a few yards, to the small grocery store on the corner.

He could see a man walking behind her.

A man with a gun in his hand.

Sam started running.

The man was closing down on Orla. The street was busy at this time of the evening, and so far she hadn't seen or heard anything suspicious. The man looked about twenty-five, an Arab, with a black beard, wearing a leather jacket and jeans. He was starting to push through the people, one of whom had spotted the gun and was backing away nervously. Along the street, Sam could see a black Ford moving alongside the man.

Sam knew exactly what he was doing.

He'd done it himself.

A street hit.

It was the simplest form of assassination there was, and, for precisely that reason, one of the most effective. There were no complex plans to go wrong. You walked up to your target in the street, pointed the gun, and made sure you blasted at least three bullets into their head. If there was time, you emptied the whole chamber. A car pulled alongside you, you jumped inside, and sped away. Amid the confusion and the panic, there was no chance of your being stopped, and the chances of anyone getting a good look at your face were minimal.

It was quick, effective, and deadly.

Sam could see that the man was now just ten yards behind Orla, while Sam was another ten yards behind him.

Five yards, that was what my training told me, thought Sam.

Get to within five yards of the victim, then start firing.

Any further back, and you could miss.

Any closer, and the target might start to run. And a running target is a lot harder to hit.

The chances are, his training was the same as mine.

Sam pushed himself harder, gaining on the man. He didn't want to shout a warning, not yet anyway, because even though Orla would dive for cover, the assassin would immediately start firing at her.

He could see him starting to raise his right arm. The one with the gun in the hand.

He was steadying himself for the shot.

Three yards separated him and Sam.

Sam hurled himself forwards. His right hand grabbed hold of the man, yanking him backwards. 'Dive,' he shouted towards Orla. 'Dive . . .'

At his side, Sam could hear a man shouting. A woman was screaming at her children to get away. Some cars were slowing down to see what was happening: behind them, other cars were starting to honk their disapproval.

The man's hand swung around. There was a handgun gripped tight into his fist – a Browning High Power Mark II, noted Sam as it smashed into the side of his face. He could feel its cold metal piercing the skin on his cheek, and a trickle of blood started to drip down the side of his face. Briefly, Sam could feel his balance loosening, and he rocked back on his heels. But he was still holding on to the man, clinging to his right hand like a limpet hanging on to a ship. His left hand balled up into a fist, then crashed hard into the man's stomach. He was strong, but so was Sam, and the force of bone colliding into muscle was intense. Sam's hand hurt like hell, but his target had all the air blown straight out of his chest. He was doubled up in pain, gasping for air. It was a brief moment of vulnerability, and Sam knew he had to make it pay. He smashed his right hand down hard into the back of the man's neck, whilst his knee crashed up into his chin. Between the force of the two blows, both coming from opposite directions, his nervous system was reeling. His head was dizzy, and his eyes were closing.

I could kill you right now, you bastard, he muttered to himself.

But I haven't finished with you yet.

To the left, there was a narrow alleyway. Sam yanked the man hard, and dragged him down it. He smashed him once, then twice up against the brick wall, so hard that the force of the impact loosened the mortar out of the brickwork. There was barely any consciousness left in him. From his pocket, Sam whipped out the Beretta, smashing it across the man's face, twice.

At his side, Orla had run down the alleyway.

She looked bewildered and afraid.

'Get behind me,' shouted Sam.

She was too frightened to respond. Sam grabbed hold of her, and yanked her backwards, so that she was shielded from the street.

Sam wedged the barrel of the gun tight into the man's throat. His eyes were barely open, but Sam could see that he was still conscious. 'Who the fuck sent you?' growled Sam.

The man was breathing heavily, and spitting goblets of blood from his mouth.

But he remained silent.

'Tell me who the fuck you work for, or I'll kill you right now,' barked Sam.

Nothing.

'You've got three seconds,' shouted Sam.

The man's eyes closed. A man closes his eyes, thought Sam, and he accepts his fate.

'One . . .'

'Maronite,' the man croaked.

'What?' barked Sam.

He loosened the gun a fraction from the man's throat.

*Maybe the bastard was going to talk.*

'Maronite . . .'

A shot.

The man's head slumped forwards. There was a splattering of blood smeared across the side of his head.

'Shit,' muttered Sam.

He let go. As he did so, the body slumped to the ground.

With the Beretta still in his hand, he looked towards the street. He could see a rifle being folded back inside the waiting Ford. The car pulled away from the kerb, and screeched into the traffic, honking wildly.

Sam grabbed hold of Orla's hand.

He started to run down the street. There were people shouting and screaming all around them but most of them were too terrified by the sound of gunfire to try and intervene. Somewhere in the distance, Sam could hear the roar of a police siren kicking into action. He kept running, arriving panting at the entrance to the hotel. Suddenly he paused, wiped the smear of blood from the side of his face, and recovered his breath. Inside he asked calmly for the key, took the envelope that had been left for him, and walked up to the room. As he closed the door, he glanced across at Orla.

'We've got thirty seconds to get washed, and get the fuck out of here,' he said.

'What?'

'Just do what I tell you,' barked Sam.

He splashed some water across his face, and stuffed his few belongings into his bag. He steered Orla towards the door, and out into the corridor. Sam checked right and left. There was nobody there. He walked towards the stairs, went down two flights, then walked through the kitchen into the back alleyway. A few steps led up to the street behind the hotel.

'Just keep walking,' he hissed to Orla. 'Don't run.'

They walked in silence for the next ten minutes. They headed due south from the hotel, towards the docks. So far as Sam could tell, no one was following them.

'What the hell was that all about?' asked Orla eventually.

Sam could hear the fear in her voice. He'd lost count of the number of times people tried to kill him when he was in the Mossad. That was one of the reasons he left: he figured that when you couldn't count them anymore, it was time to get out. But your first assassination attempt was like your first kiss. It stayed with you. And although Orla had had a tough life, he didn't reckon anyone had tried to kill her before.

He paused, looking straight at Orla. 'The man was about to kill you.'

'But someone shot him . . .'

Sam nodded. 'He was about to speak,' said Sam. 'I think that he was about to tell me something, so they shot him.'

'What did he say?'

'Maronite, that was the word he used,' said Sam. 'Maronite.'

# FORTY-NINE

**Beirut, 29 November**

Arslan Sinno showed them into the room.

After leaving the hotel, Sam had opened the envelope that had been waiting for him. Sinno had called, and when Sam found a phone box, he called him straight back. Sam told him an attempt had been made on their lives: he was one of the more senior Mossad agents in the city, and so far as he knew, Sam was still on the payroll. They needed a safe house until they could get out of Beirut. Sinno gave them an address, and told them he would meet them there at nine o'clock. They got straight in a cab.

The apartment was in one of the streets leading away from Ramlet al-Baida, the beachfront suburb of the city. It was one of a row of apartment blocks on the street. It was late by the time they arrived, and there were dark clouds hanging across the Mediterranean. The streets were mostly empty. Sinno met them in the foyer, and led them up to the second floor. He looked worried, judged Sam. You could see it written into his face.

*But not as worried as I am.*

It was a two-bedroomed apartment, maintained by the bank for the use of its clients, but also loaned out to the Mossad in emergencies. It was simply furnished, with a sofa, a television, a small kitchen area, and a fridge stocked with tins and dried milk and cereals. In the cupboards, there was a selection of casual clothes, in all the standard sizes, and in the bathroom there was a cabinet stocked with medical supplies and a first-aid kit. Inside a desk in the main room, there was a false passport you could stick your own picture into, a credit card, and $5,000 in cash. If you looked behind the hot-water tank in the cupboard in the hallway, Sinno explained, there was a false panel. Pull that away and you would find a stash of ammunition.

Everything a Mossad agent on the run might need.

Orla made three cups of instant coffee in the kitchen, stirred in three spoonfuls of sugar, and brought them through to the small sitting room. Sinno looked at his distastefully, but Sam took a long gulp. It tasted disgusting, but the mixture of caffeine and sugar was soon in his bloodstream, reviving his strength.

'He used the word Maronite,' said Sam, looking up at Sinno. 'That was the only word I could get out of him before they killed him.'

'The Maronites are the main Christian Church in the Middle East,' said Orla. 'They make up about a quarter of the population here, but there are an estimated fifteen million Maronites around the world.'

Sinno looked closely at Sam. 'Have you got some kind of quarrel with the Vatican?'

Sam nodded towards Orla. 'She does . . .'

'Because the Maronite Church takes its orders directly from Rome.'

'Then that's who tried to kill us,' said Sam.

'And that's not all,' said Sinno. He looked across at Sam. 'The reason why I called you was to give you one additional piece of information.'

'Which is?'

'The drug-running operation being run by the CIA in this city . . .'

'Yes?'

'The drugs are supplied by a man called Ahmed Shabaan.'

'The Falcon?'

'The same.'

Sam put down his coffee cup.

'Last I heard, he'd retired.'

'From terrorism? Maybe, maybe not. With the Falcon, nobody really knows. He certainly hasn't retired from business. He's shipping drugs all through the Middle East, acting as conduit from the poppy fields of Afghanistan to the markets in Europe and America.'

It didn't take Sam long to work out the implications. If the Falcon was the source of the CIA's drugs, could he also have had something to do with the bombing of Flight 103?

*With the Falcon, anything was possible.*

It was impossible for a man who'd once been in a Mossad assassination unit not to know about the Falcon. The terror leader had been on top of the Mossad's most-wanted list for three straight years. Sam's unit had been dispatched to Malta once to eliminate him. They'd had a tip-off he was staying in a small hotel in the village of Valletta, but by the time they arrived on the scene, he'd either already vanished, or the lead had been a false one. That was the closest they'd ever got to him. At the time, Sam had wondered if the Falcon had a mole within the Mossad. He always seemed to be one step ahead of them.

'A word of warning for you, Mr Woolfman,' said Sinno. 'Ahmed Shabaan is one of the deadliest asssassins in this part of the world. If he's after you, your life expectancy isn't going to be very long.'

'I know.'

'You should leave Beirut immediately.'

Sam stood up. 'Can you get me a new passport?'

'Yes, of course.'

'By tomorrow morning?'

Sinno nodded towards Orla. 'For the girl as well?'

Sam pulled the Beretta from his pocket, and checked the clip. It still had a full chamber of bullets. 'By tomorrow morning.'

'Consider it done,' said Sinno.

Sam nodded towards Orla.

'And if I'm not here, make sure she gets away somewhere safe.'

'Where are you going?' asked Orla.

Sam could hear the anxiety in her voice.

'Someone knew where we were staying,' he said. 'And they must have told the Maronite Church.'

He slipped the Beretta back into his belt.

'And that person must have been medallion man Al-Zarif.'

# FIFTY

**Beirut, 29 November**

Sam could see a light still shining in the office.

It was just after ten at night, but he knew Al–Zarif liked to work late. According to Sinno, who kept close tabs on all the Mossad informers in the city, he kept a mistress who lived in an apartment building close to the upmarket Safi Village development. He usually left the office about seven, ate dinner at her apartment, then returned to the office for another couple of hours in case his wife called him.

Or in case an assassin came around, thought Sam with a grim smile.

He stepped close to the building.

There was a row of courier bikes parked outside: they were mostly Kawasaki Z900s, a cheap but rugged low-maintenance bike, with a few Yamahas and Hondas as well. One counter was open, and Sam could see three bikers collecting parcels and returning to their vehicles. The office didn't shut until midnight, and it opened up again at four in the morning to collect the packages that arrived overnight at the airport, to work out the distribution routes around the city.

Nobody paid Sam any attention as he walked into the office.

People went in and out all the time.

He kicked the door shut with the back of his foot, and slipped the Beretta from his pocket. It was pointing straight at Al-Zarif. 'Say a single word, and you're a dead man,' Sam growled.

Al-Zarif's eyes were wild with fear. The sweat that normally covered his face was now dripping off him: Sam had seen men in the sauna who looked drier.

'What . . .'

Sam took another two paces forwards.

He was holding the gun straight in front of him, close enough for Al-Zarif to smell the grease inside its barrel.

'Someone knew where I was staying.'

'I don't know what you're talking about.'

Sam took another pace forward.

'I'm going to pull this trigger in three seconds,' he said quietly. 'Unless I start hearing something interesting enough to make me change your mind.'

Al-Zarif had thrown his hands up to shield his face. 'There's a contract out on you and . . . the women you with, a girl named Orla Sheehy.'

'From who?'

'The Church,' said Al-Zarif. His hands were shaking and his voice was cracking. 'The Maronite diocese is paying $10,000 for any information on your whereabouts.'

'And you told them . . .'

Al-Zarif remained silent.

What's he supposed to say, thought Sam to himself.

I just sold you to an assassin for $10,000.

'I'm going to make you a deal.'

He could see Al-Zarif starting to relax. He could see a glimmer of hope.

'I want you to pick up the phone right now, and tell your contact that I came to the office tonight, that you had a gun ready, and that you shot both me and Orla.'

'But—'

'Just do it.' Sam leaned in close to his face. 'Right now . . .'

Al-Zarif picked up the phone. The conversation was terse and brief. By the time he finished, he looked back at Sam. 'I've told them you are dead.'

Sam had understood enough of the Arabic to know he was telling the truth.

It might not fool the Vatican for long. They would make their own checks. And they would know soon enough that Orla's lawyers were still pressing them for the money.

But it might buy us a couple of days.

*And maybe that's all I need.*

Sam wedged the gun into the side of Al-Zarif's neck. He pushed it hard, so that the man could feel the steel of its barrel squeezing into the veins. With his left hand, he gripped his head, and twisted it around so that he was looking straight at him.

His eyes were bulging and his lips were quivering.

'I'm going to count to three again . . . and if I don't get what I want I'm going to kill you.'

He leaned in close to the man's face.

'Where did the three CIA men go?' snapped Sam.

'Who?'

'The three CIA guys who found out about Shabaan running drugs through the Beirut CIA station,' growled Sam. 'Where the hell did they go?'

'I don't . . .'

'Fine by me,' said Sam. 'I was hoping I'd have an excuse to kill you.'

'But—'

'One,' snapped Sam.

He paused for just a fraction of a second, jabbing the gun even harder into the veins in Al-Zarif's neck. 'Two . . .'

'To Cyprus,' spluttered Al-Zarif. 'They were flying back to America from there.'

Slowly Sam released his grip.

'Shame,' he said. 'I was looking forward to your funeral.'

He walked towards the door. 'But if anyone else tries to kill me or Orla in the next few days then I'm coming straight back here to kill you.'

# FIFTY-ONE

**Beirut, 30 November**

Sinno handed across the two passports.

Sam opened his first. The name was Salah Hemeid, and the passport was Egyptian. The photograph was perfect. As far as Sam could tell, so was the entire document. Beirut was one of the main centres of forgery and deception in the world, reflected Sam. If you couldn't get a decent fake passport here you couldn't get one anywhere.

Next, Orla checked hers.

Nehad Selaiha, it said. Also Egyptian. Aged twenty-three. And, so far as she could tell, the passport was also flawless.

'Good luck,' said Sinno.

'Thanks,' answered Sam.

They were meeting at the marina, to the west of the main docks. It was just after four in the morning, and the city was still dark. Along the marina, there was a row of expensive yachts, as well as some smaller sailing dinghies. Sinno had secured the services of a speedboat from one of his wealthy clients. From Beirut to Nicosia in Cyprus was a distance of just 131 nautical miles, or 151 standard miles, and the boat was capable of a steady seventy miles an hour on calm seas, meaning the journey should only take a little more than two hours.

Both Orla and Sam climbed aboard. The boat was a

Rizzardi 50 Open Topline, a luxurious vessel built by the Italian speedboat manufacturer Cantieri Navali Rizzardi at its yard in Sabaudia. Its twin diesel engines generated 733 horsepower, enough to power the boat across an ocean. A short-hop across the Mediterranean was no problem.

Sam slipped down into the cabin while the captain powered the boat out into the open sea. For the next two hours he completed his notes, thinking through the precise sequence of events that might have led up to the crash of Flight 103. As he talked it through with Orla, he felt certain he was getting closer to the solution. But there were still questions that needed answering.

The captain dropped them off at a small private marina twenty miles from Nicosia. They had new passports, but after the assassination attempt, Sam preferred to keep his trips through any official border posts to a minimum. From there, they found a taxi to take them into the city.

Basaran Duzgun ran a small real-estate office in the centre of town, brokering land transactions. It was a business that required a well-cultivated network to make it prosper, and Duzgun was a man who knew just about everything that happened in the city. On the side, he helped the Mossad out with information. To most of his friends, he was Greek Cypriot of many generations. In fact, his mother had been Armenian, and like most Armenian refugees, was actually Jewish. Duzgun preferred living and working in Cyprus. He had no desire to ever move to Israel. But he had heard his mother's stories about how the mob sometimes turned on the Jews, and how they needed their own homeland, a place of refuge when no one else would take them. And it made sense to him. So he helped the Mossad when he could.

Sometimes he got paid for the information, and sometimes he didn't. It didn't matter greatly to Duzgun. He was an agent of conviction.

Sam and Orla met him in a small café, 500 yards from his office. Seven years ago, Sam's unit had been dropped into the country to assassinate a Palestinian terrorist leader who had been planning to explode a ship loaded with chemical explosives at Haifa docks. Since then, he'd had no contact with the man. It was a principle of the Mossad's *sayanim* network that you never used a member unless you needed to. They were there for emergencies, not everyday favours.

But to me, thought Sam, this is an emergency.

Duzgun shook Sam's hand, and ordered himself a coffee. He was a tall, distinguished man, approaching fifty, in a well-cut suit, and an immaculate white shirt. He glanced across at Orla and smiled. 'You should try and see some of the sights this time, Sam,' he said.

'I haven't enough time.'

'What is it you need to know?'

Before meeting with Duzgun, Sam had called Carter Jenas in New York. Sam had a simple question for him. He wanted him to check the airline's records, and find out where three of the passengers on Flight 103 had booked their tickets. The names of the passengers: Jim Prentiss, Scott Valentin, and Ben Hanold.

Jenas had told him to call back in thirty minutes. He'd have the information for him by then.

Just before he'd sat down in the café, Sam had slipped across to another phone booth, fed in a small mountain of coins, and put another call through to New York. When he got through to Jenas, he had the answer. The tickets were booked at the Skettos Travel Agency in Nicosia. They were booked on the morning of the crash, and paid for on the spot.

Sam looked across to Duzgun.

'I need to know if you've heard of the Skettos Travel Agency.'

Duzgun nodded, stirring two sugars into his coffee.

'It's run by a Greek Cypriot called Grigorios Petrakis,' he said. 'A good guy, if a little too fond of a glass of wine at lunchtime. There are plenty of travel agents in Cyprus, but Petrakis looks after his clients, so he gets by. And, of course, he's a front . . .'

'Who for?'

'The CIA.'

Sam nodded. He knew the CIA maintained a network of friendly travel agents. The Mossad did the same thing, and, so he imagined, did the KGB, or at least what was left of the Russian intelligence agency now the Soviet Union had collapsed. Maybe the British and the French did as well if they could afford it. There was no better way of keeping tabs on people moving around the world than having a network of travel agents.

'Will he talk to me?'

'Petrakis? No way.'

'I need to know whether the CIA knew three of the men who were booked on to a flight.'

'Then you'll have to pressurise him.'

'What's his weak spot?'

Sam could see Duzgun thinking for a moment. When he was an agent, he'd learned that every man had some form of weakness you could exploit: a mistress, a gambling debt, a family he loved more than himself. Find it, and you could find a way to make him co-operate with you.

'Same as most men.'

Sam smiled. 'What's that?'

'He's afraid of getting shot in the head.'

Sam paid for the coffees, and started to walk. It was a stroll of ten minutes through the narrow, shaded streets of Nicosia, and then along the Kanlidere River from the café to the offices of the Skettos Agency. It was a compact office, with a cheese shop on one side of it, and a wine merchant on the other. He told Orla to wait for him in a restaurant.

This he needed to do alone.

He could see a man sitting at one desk, who he assumed to be Petrakis. At the other desk, there was a woman in her forties typing. An elderly couple was perusing some flight brochures with Petrakis and they didn't seem to be in any hurry. Sam walked next door, and browsed though the racks of wine, and waited. Eventually the owner asked him if he wanted to buy something. Sam told him no, and went to check out the cheese instead.

After ten minutes, he saw the elderly couple depart.

Sam slipped inside the front door, shutting it firmly behind him.

He could see Petrakis glancing up at him.

'We need to talk in private,' he said.

He was looking straight at Petrakis as he spoke.

'We can help you with any booking you like right here,' said Petrakis.

From the tone of his voice, it was clear that had not yet decided whether he was irritated or confused.

'In private,' hissed Sam.

'I—'

'About the agency,' said Sam.

Petrakis fell silent.

He looked across at the secretary, and barked something in Greek. Flustered, she looked across at Sam, then collected her jacket and walked out. Sam didn't speak any Greek, but he figured she'd just been told to take an early lunch.

Petrakis looked back at Sam. 'So . . .'

Already Sam had sat down at the desk, looking straight at Petrakis. He pulled the Beretta from his pocket, and slammed it down hard on the desk. One reason he'd wanted to travel to Nicosia by private boat was because he wanted a gun with him, and you couldn't take those through

289

customs. It wasn't pointing at Petrakis, but there was no mistaking its menace.

'We can play this hard or we can play this soft,' he said. 'It's your choice.'

'Who the fuck are you?'

'It doesn't matter who I am.'

Petrakis sat back in his chair. 'So what do you want to know?'

'You booked three men on to Flight 103, right?'

'The plane that crashed?'

'Right . . .'

Petrakis looked suspicious.

'Their names were Jim Prentiss, Scott Valentin, and Ben Hanold.'

There was a flicker of recognition in Petrakis' eyes. He remembered them well enough, thought Sam. It wasn't every day that a small agency like this got three transatlantic bookings.

'Okay, I remember,' said Petrakis guardedly. 'A terrible tragedy.'

'Did you tell the agency about the bookings?'

Sam had folded the gun into his lap as he posed the question. It was invisible from the window, but it was pointing straight at Petrakis' belly.

'What agency?'

'The CIA.'

'I'm a travel agent,' said Petrakis. 'The only people I deal with are airlines, hotels, car rental agencies . . .'

'Like I said, we can play this hard or soft,' said Sam. 'You can answer my questions honestly, or I can shoot you once in the belly. It won't be a fatal wound, but it will be enough to persuade you to start talking before I put the second bullet in your head.'

It wasn't often you saw the colour drain out of a man's face, reflected Sam. But you could see it now. Petrakis' swarthy, tanned skin was turning slowly white. He wasn't a brave man. He was just a travel agent who liked to make some money on the side, and didn't see why he shouldn't make it from the CIA. He certainly hadn't reckoned on taking a bullet. And, now he was faced with that prospect, he clearly didn't like it.

He was trembling, and there was sweat pouring off his face.

'Just tell me . . .'

'I phoned the agency right after I made the booking,' said Petrakis.

'Which bureau?'

'I phoned the Athens office,' said Petrakis. 'That's the deal. They pay me a monthly retainer, and I call them every time I get a booking that seems in any way out of the ordinary. Each time I call, I get a small bonus, added on to the monthly payment.'

Sam folded his gun into his pocket, and stood up. 'You never saw me, understood?'

Petrakis nodded.

Sam walked out of the office. Behind him, he could see Petrakis putting up the 'Closed' sign, and heading towards the café across the street. He could probably use a stiff drink, he thought to himself.

He stepped into a phone booth, and piled another heap of change into the machine. He could always reverse the charges, but if you did that, then a record of the call would be logged. It was eleven o'clock here in Nicosia, which meant it was still only four in the morning in New York. Jenas wouldn't be getting much sleep, decided Sam. But that was his problem.

Right now, sleep was probably the least of his worries.

'Carter,' said Sam as soon as the phone was answered.

'Yes,' answered a groggy-sounding voice at the other end of the line.

'Can you be in Frankfurt tomorrow morning?'

'I guess,' said Jenas.

'As soon as you land, go straight to the Steigenberger Airport Hotel,' said Sam. 'Ask for Mr Salah Hemeid.'

# FIFTY-TWO

**Frankfurt, 1 December**

The Steigenberger Airport Hotel was a big, V-shaped concrete building. It was located just 900 metres from the airport terminal building, although the rooms had been soundproofed with such Germanic precision you could imagine you were in peaceful countryside, and not right underneath one of the busiest flight paths in Europe.

Sam and Orla had arrived late last night. They took a flight from Cyprus to Athens, then another flight to Rome, before catching the last Lufthansa flight of the day up to Frankfurt. They could have flown direct, but Sam was determined to create a trail that was as confusing as possible.

The Vatican had been trying to kill them.

And if the Falcon had any idea how close they were to solving the mystery of Flight 103, he'd be trying to kill them as well.

Each time they passed through security, their passports were accepted without question. Sinno's forgeries were good, as you would expect from one of the Mossad's most reliable agents. It was almost midnight by the time they checked into the hotel. They grabbed some much-needed sleep. Sam already had an idea he was facing a long day. Quite possibly the longest day of his life.

Jenas arrived just after breakfast.

He'd taken an overnight flight from New York direct

into Frankfurt. One of the advantages of working in the airline industry, he explained later. You could always get a flight at the last minute: the airlines always made seats available for each other's high-ranking staff if they needed them in an emergency.

'So what's the big rush?' he said, sitting down next to Sam and Orla, and pouring himself a coffee.

'What we have so far is explosive,' explained Sam.

He started to explain.

Jenas sat in rapt attention as Sam ran through the details of what he had discovered.

The CIA station in Beirut was secretly smuggling drugs back to the United States. It was putting them in the diplomatic bag. The drugs were supplied by a man called Ahmed Shabaan, also known as the Falcon, and one of the most feared terrorists in the Middle East.

Three CIA agents were sent to Beirut to work on freeing the American hostages held there. They discovered the details of the drugs trading. They were heading back to Washington.

'The CIA knew they were coming home because they booked their tickets through a travel agency that also acted as a front for them,' said Sam.

Jenas looked worried.

He might have expected to be told that one of the Middle East terror groups had bombed his company's plane.

He might have expected to be told that it was the IRA.

Or maybe a lone madman.

Those were all explanations he could have dealt with.

But the CIA?

That, he wasn't expecting.

'You're talking about drugs being on board the plane, Mr Woolfman.'

'Sam.'

'Okay, Sam,' said Jenas irritably. 'Still, cocaine and heroin

294

don't cause a 747 to fall out of the sky. Not unless they happen to be handing them out on the flight deck.'

'But the Falcon had access to that diplomatic bag,' said Sam. 'All he had to do was replace the consignment of drugs one night with a bomb. And it would go right through the system without being checked.'

'Why would he do that?'

'The Iranians paid him.'

Jenas was looking at Sam intently now.

'The Falcon used to be one of the most feared terror operators in the whole of the Middle East,' said Sam. 'He was the Mossad's most-wanted terrorist for several years in a row, but we could never catch up with him.'

'So what happened to him?'

'He quit, or so everyone thought. He turned himself into one of the Middle East's drug lords, a link man between the Afghan poppy crop and the West. But I'm certain he's still available for terrorism, so long as you pay him enough money.'

'And the Iranians?'

'The A300 that was shot down by the Americans at the start of November,' said Sam. 'I reckon, the Iranian's were determined to retaliate. It's all there in the Koran, the same as in the Bible. An eye for an eye . . . all that stuff. So they wanted to take down a plane.'

He paused, looking straight at Jenas.

'An American plane.'

'And they chose ours?'

'They hired the Falcon to do it, because he's the best,' said Sam. 'Bringing down an airliner is not easy, as you know. If I wanted to do it, the Falcon is the man I'd go to as well.'

Sam drained the last of his coffee. 'And the CIA knew about it.'

'They *knew*?'

'Of course,' said Sam. 'Just take a look at how it all pieces together. They knew their bag was being used by the Beirut bureau to smuggle drugs. They also knew their three agents were coming home to blow the whole scandal wide open. That was going to be a catastrophe for the agency. Heads were going to roll right at the highest level. They couldn't let it happen. So they knew there was a bomb on the plane, and they also knew Prentiss, Valentin, and Hanold were on the flight. So they let it blow . . . problem solved.'

'What makes you think that?'

'They sent out a warning to embassy staff around the world,' said Sam. 'They were told not to get on Flight 103. Dozens of them cancelled at the last minute, your own records already show that. Why would they be doing that if there wasn't any threat to the plane? Next, two independent witnesses saw an American Black Hawk helicopter drop down on the scene of the crash minutes after the plane came down. They could have only done that if the chopper was already scrambled and up in the air. They must have known it was coming down. And they must have been looking for something specific.'

'Like what?'

'Any papers their three agents could have been carrying with them. They had to make sure they didn't survive the crash.'

'What we have there is conjecture,' said Jenas. 'Interesting conjecture, but conjecture all the same. We can't go around accusing the CIA of allowing an American 747 to be blown out of the sky with the loss of 270 lives. Not without proof. We'll be crucified.'

'But we can get proof,' said Sam.

'How?'

'Right here in Frankfurt,' interrupted Orla. 'We just need your authority.'

296

'My authority?'

Orla nodded.

'We need to interrogate the baggage handlers,' she said.

# FIFTY-THREE

**Frankfurt 1 December**

The interrogation room was underneath the main customs
hall, through which anyone getting off a plane at Frankfurt
airport had to pass.

It was down two flights of stairs, the third doorway off a
narrow corridor. In total there were eight rooms down here.
If your papers weren't in order, and you were on any of the
wanted lists maintained by a European Union government,
this was where the German Federal Border Guard – the
Bundesgrenzschutz – brought you for questioning.

The room had plain white walls, and measured twenty
feet by thirty. There was a small metal table, and two chairs,
but apart from that the room was completely empty.

Jenas had struck a deal with the airport security staff. They
knew which airline he worked for, and they knew what had
happened to Flight 103. Frankfurt's officials were desperate
that none of the blame should attach to them. The last thing
they needed was any kind of evidence that it was negligence
in their security procedures that had allowed the bomb to be
put on board the aircraft. So Jenas told them he needed to
put all the baggage handlers through a simple polygraph test
to try and eliminate the possibility that the bomb was loaded
in Frankfurt.

They agreed readily.

Anything that would pin the blame on London rather

298

than Frankfurt suited them just fine. And Jenas assured them that was what they were trying to prove.

It wasn't true, of course.

But it secured their co-operation.

Which suits me just fine, decided Sam.

He had decided right after he got through with talking to Petrakis that the CIA must have known that their three agents were travelling back to Washington on Flight 103. After all, he'd told the Athens bureau, and that information would have made its way back to Langley. They might also have known about the diplomatic bag being used to ferry drugs back to the United States. If they did, then the baggage handler would probably be part of the conspiracy. They could interview the handlers at Heathrow – and if they needed to, they would – but there were far fewer of them at Frankfurt because it was a much smaller airport.

This was the place to start – and if they found what he thought they might find he'd be a step closer to wrapping this case up.

While Jenas was fixing the interviews, Orla had arranged the polygraph kit.

The lie-detecting system was supplied by a local Frankfurt company called IDT Electronic Systems AG. A polygraph works on fairly simple principles. A series of tiny electronic measuring devices constantly monitors a person's blood pressure, pulse, respiration, and skin conductivity while the person is asked and responds to a series of questions. The device measures their physiological response during the interview, concentrating on the nervous system. The theory is that lying is stressful, and even if that stress might be hidden from view, it will still be picked up by changes in blood pressure or pulse or some other internal symptom. The system is not infallible. There are accomplished liars who can get through a polygraph test with their untruth remaining buried within them. But in Sam's judgement, they were very rare.

The results of the polygraph test, he felt certain, would give them precisely the evidence they needed.

There were forty baggage handlers on duty at Frankfurt airport on the night of 19 November, when Flight 103 set off on its fateful journey. Frankfurt was one of the most modern and mechanised airports in the world, and the baggage system was no exception. Even though the airport could handle up to forty flights an hour, and up to 8,000 passengers, carrying as many as 12,000 bags, it didn't take a vast crew of men to handle them all. The check-in desk put a bar-coded tag on to each bag, and then it was steered by a central computer towards the plane it was meant to be travelling on. It was the same with transfer flights. If a bag was checked right through to a final destination, the bar code would register that with the central computer, and the bag would be steered to its connecting flight. Nobody had to check it again before it completed its journey. Naturally the system wasn't completely perfect: even in Germany it went wrong sometimes. Bags would fall off the conveyor belt, and had to be picked up and put on the right plane. Sometimes a bar code would get obscured, and the computer couldn't read it: one of the staff would then have to intervene.

But usually it worked just fine.

Except on the 19th. Something must have happened that night.

Sam felt certain of it.

They brought the baggage handlers in one by one. The men had been told that it was just routine questioning as part of the investigation into the crash. They let Orla start the interrogation. Of the three of them, she had by far the friendliest face. She started with an easy test question: Which country won the last World Cup? Among polygraph testers, that was known as the 'control question'. The machine would measure the physiological reaction when it was answered, and that would give a benchmark against which to judge the rest of the answers.

Most of the baggage handlers were Turks. Germany has a vast army of poorly paid Turkish 'guest workers', and since handling baggage in the underbelly of the airport was neither very well paid nor very high-status work, most of the applicants were Turks. Young German men could find better jobs. If they couldn't, then they preferred to stay on welfare. Most of them were helpful and attentive, noted Sam. But they were also nervous. The Turks were often picked on by the local German police, and that had made them justifiably suspicious of any form of authority.

Allowing ten minutes for each man, it took slightly more than six hours to interview the entire shift. The questioning focussed on the bags that were put on Flight 103, and where they all came from. The majority of the passengers getting on to the plane were boarding at Frankfurt, and checking their bags in at the airport. Thirty passengers had arrived on connecting flights, and their bags had been transferred within the airport. They included Prentiss, Valentin, and Hanold who'd arrived on the incoming flight from Cyprus, although the records showed that they'd only brought hand luggage with them and so didn't have any bags to be transferred. Sam was interested, but didn't want to track down their luggage. Whatever else happened that evening, it was unlikely the three CIA men planted the bomb on the plane.

'So what do we have?' said Jenas after they had finished the interviews.

'A lot of Turks who were just doing their jobs,' said Orla.

'And three Americans,' said Sam.

Of the forty men they had just interviewed, thirty of them had been Turks. Another seven were Germans. Three of those were students who were working on the night shift

301

because it helped them to pay their way through college, while the other four struck Sam as the kind of misfits you'd find in any job that required very unsociable hours.

There were also three American citizens: Dave Chandler, Ken Streeter, and Ron Rodrigo.

'So the question is, why would someone come all the way from the United States to Frankfurt, go to all the hassle of getting a work permit, just so they can get themselves a lousy job like being a night shift baggage handler at Frankfurt airport?'

Jenas shrugged.

'I reckon they were placed here by the CIA,' said Sam.

'You sure?'

'Think about it,' said Sam. 'The diplomatic bag from the Beirut office gets put on the Lufthansa flight every evening, and is brought here to Frankfurt. Then it's transferred on to Flight 103, which takes it on to Washington via London. I reckon the CIA would want to make pretty damned sure that nobody was tampering with the bag along the way. How are they going to do that? By having their own people in place to watch it.'

Jenas nodded. He picked up the phone, and placed a call with the airport's head of security, a retired major with the Bundeswehr, the German armed forces, called Edgard Zwirn. They needed Dave Chandler brought back in for questioning, he told him.

Right now.

Chandler was from Wisconsin originally, but had lived in Germany for three years now, and was fluent in the language. He was a tall, thin man of thirty, with brown hair and a beard. He was dressed in the blue overalls all the baggage handlers wore. 'We need to know about the diplomatic bags,' said Sam, as soon as he had been brought back into the interrogation room, sat down, and hooked up to the polygraph machine.

'What bags?'

'Every evening US Embassy diplomatic bags on their way back to America come through this airport,' said Sam. 'Are you familiar with them?'

Chandler shook his head.

Sam glanced towards Orla, who was looking down at the polygraph results.

She shook her head, and mouthed a single, silent word. *No.*

He's lying, thought Sam.

'Who do you work for, Mr Chandler?'

'Frankfurt airport.'

*He's lying again.*

'Why did you come to live in this country?'

'I like bratwurst.'

*Another lie.*

Sam paused, looking straight into the man's eyes. 'You're not a very good liar, Mr Chandler,' he said. 'Now you can start co-operating with me, or I can go to the press and reveal that David Chandler is obstructing an investigation into how nearly three hundred people lost their lives on Flight 103.'

He remained mute.

'You need that kind of shit?' interrupted Jenas.

Again, he said nothing.

'And right after the press get through with you,' persisted Sam, 'I'm going to contact each of the lawyers for each of the families of each of the three hundred dead people and I'm going to suggest they sue you for obstructing the investigation.'

'So you'll spend the rest of your life in court,' said Jenas. 'And probably be bankrupted as well.'

'Unless you decide to start telling us the truth.'

The expression on Chandler's face suddenly changed. 'On what conditions?'

'Total anonymity,' said Sam. 'Anything you tell us today doesn't go beyond these four walls. We just want to find out what happened, that's all.'

Chandler nodded.

He glanced at each person in turn. And then he started to speak.

'Okay, I'm on the payroll of the CIA,' he said. 'Frankfurt airport pays me a salary as a baggage handler, but then I get a salary on top that is paid out of Washington. The job is to check the diplomatic bag gets on to the right flight, and to make sure that nobody tampers with it.'

Sam glanced at Orla.

He could see from the look she gave him that the polygraph results were positive.

*He's telling the truth this time.*

'So what happened on the night of the 19th?' said Sam.

The mute, blank stare on Chandler's face returned.

'I said, what happened?' snapped Sam.

Chandler glanced back up at him, his expression a mixture of anger and fear.

'The bag is more like a crate when you get used to it,' he said. 'It came off the Lufthansa flight from Beirut, and down into the loading bay. Usually the bags for connecting flights go on to a conveyor belt, they get scanned by the computer, then they get steered automatically towards their final destination. But the computers don't always scan perfectly. You know how it is. You fly to Athens, and your bag catches the flight to Stockholm. It happens all the time. Of course we don't want it happening to the diplomatic bag. So what happens is this. I lift the bag up off the belt from the Lufthansa flight when that comes in, then I carry it about fifteen yards, and make sure it gets on to the belt that will take it to Flight 103.'

'And you look in the bag?'

'Christ, no,' snapped Chandler. 'I wouldn't ever look inside.'

There was a pause.

Sam glanced towards Orla, and she nodded curtly back. He is telling the truth, she was saying.

But there was something else.

*Something he hasn't told us yet.*

'And . . .' he said, leaning forward.

Again, silence.

'What happened on the night of the 19th?'

'The bag was heavier than usual,' said Chandler. 'Part of our job is just to report on anything unusual. And on the 19th, that crate weighed significantly more than usual.'

'How much more?'

'Twenty, maybe thirty pounds,' said Chandler.

'Did that happen often?'

Chandler shook his head.

'Christ no,' he replied. 'The bag always weighed pretty much the same. It's just papers and stuff inside . . .'

'So what did you do?'

'I put the bag down, and I went to call our handler in the Bonn bureau,' said Chandler. 'There's always a duty officer present, and if anything suspicious happens relating to the diplomatic bag, we're meant to call them. So I get this guy on the phone, and I say, "The bag is a lot heavier than usual . . ."'

'And what did he say?' asked Sam.

'This was the weird thing,' said Chandler, glancing up at Sam. 'He just said: "We know. Let it go."'

# FIFTY-FOUR

**Frankfurt, 1 December**

Sam stood up, and started unhooking the wires that connected Chandler to the polygraph machine. 'Thank you for your co-operation, Mr Chandler,' he said formally. 'You can go now.'

He turned to look at Orla and Jenas.

'They knew,' he said simply, his voice drained of all emotion. 'The CIA knew that there was a bomb on the plane, and they let it take off.'

'Sure sounds that way . . .'

'If only we could prove it,' said Sam, grinding his fists together.

'We can.'

Sam paused.

He was looking straight at Jenas.

'We can?'

'Sure.'

Jenas stood up. There was a half-smile on his lips, but little sign of amusement. 'We tape all the calls by the baggage handlers,' he said. 'The tapes have already been shipped back to New York as part of the investigation, but they will be right there. If Chandler had the conversation he says he had, then it will all be on the tapes.'

'Then we've got them,' said Sam. 'The CIA deliberately allowed Flight 103 to be blown up even though they could have prevented it because they wanted to get rid of Prentiss, Valentin, and Hanold. The drug running out of Beirut is going to continue. The hostages are going to rot in their cells. The CIA doesn't care about anything except for covering up its own crimes.'

'So who are we going to tell?' asked Orla.

'Jim Geldens, the chairman of the airline,' said Jenas. 'Let him go public with this, then they won't be able to cover it up.'

'They'll try,' warned Sam.

'But we'll have enough information to blow them away,' said Jenas.

Orla had already stood up from her polygraph machine. 'Then we'd better get straight back to New York,' she said. 'There's a Lufthansa flight that leaves at 0500, if they've got seats.'

'Hell, we'll ride in the cockpit if we have to,' said Jenas. 'This can't wait.'

# FIFTY-FIVE

**New York, 2 December**

The Lincoln was driving down 7th Avenue, on its way into the centre of Manhattan from the airport.

The Lufthansa flight had landed at JFK at seven this morning. Jenas had already called ahead to his office, and told them to have a car waiting for them. 'And tell the chairman, I'll be in his office at eight sharp,' he told him. 'And I'll be able to tell him what really happened to Flight 103.'

All three of them were sitting in the back seat of the spacious limousine. Lufthansa had upgraded them to first class for the flight from Frankfurt, which was only half full anyway. Along the way, Sam and Jenas had sketched out the first draft of a complete dossier showing exactly what happened to Flight 103.

So long as Jenas could get hold of that tape, the case would be complete.

Even the CIA wasn't going to be able to wriggle off this hook.

Sam was contemplating their reaction, when the bullet smashed into the side of the Lincoln, hitting the machine with the force of a sledgehammer.

The car rocked.

Sam looked down. Orla hadn't realised what had happened yet. The New York streets were full of people shouting and vehicles backfiring, and, as anyone who has witnessed it up close will tell you, gunfire isn't necessarily that loud. But Sam knew what was happening.

There was a tear in the skin of the Lincoln where the bullet had ripped through the metalwork.

'Get down,' he shouted.

At least the bullet hadn't hit her.

'I'll take the wheel,' shouted Sam.

He could hear another round of gunfire peppering the car.

The bullets were clattering into the thick bodywork of the car like pellets of hail.

Sam tossed himself over the front seat, pushing the terrified driver out of the way.

Looking to the right, he could see two men standing on the corner, laying down round after round with what looked from a distance like fully automated machine guns. All around them, people were screaming and running for cover.

Both men had covered their faces with masks.

It was impossible to get a clear look at either of them.

Sam pushed his foot down hard on the accelerator.

The Lincoln Town Car was a 1991 model, powered by the top of the range Windsor five-litre engine. It wasn't the smoothest engine in the world, but it had plenty of kick on it. The car roared and jumped forwards. There was a mass of screaming people all around them. Sam looked to see where the assailants were. Both men were still standing on the side of the street, spraying the car with bullets. They were to Sam's left. He turned the wheel frantically to the right: there was a turning right next to them, and if they could get down that street they had a chance of escaping. Like all American luxury cars, the Lincoln was automatic, which meant you couldn't throw yourself down into a low gear to try and turn faster. Instead, Sam jerked hard on the handbrake, throwing the steering wheel left at the same time. The car started to swerve viciously into the corner. Sam could see the road opening up ahead of them. They had turned into West 34th Street, just past the Penn station subway stop. Sam released the handbrake he'd used for turning and kicked hard on the accelerator. The car roared, then accelerated. Within seconds, they had travelled a half-mile down West 34th, and turned down 11th Avenue in the direction of the Lincoln tunnel.

'Pull up,' shouted Jenas.

Sam slammed his foot on the brakes.

The Lincoln shuddered to a halt, its wheels screeching against the tarmac. They had pulled up close to the junction of 11th Avenue and West 46th Street. It was a grimy, mostly industrial area, dominated by the roaring traffic of the nearby Lincoln Tunnel. Jenas shouted at the driver to move on in the Lincoln, while they took their chances on foot. Sam grabbed hold of Orla's hand. As the car drew away he saw its frame had been ripped apart: two back windows had been smashed, the boot had been ripped to shreds of torn metal, and there was smoke rising from the bonnet.

'Run,' shouted Jenas. 'Get the fuck out of here.'

Sam followed him. He was pushing Orla forward as they ran down up towards the junction with 10th Avenue. Fifty yards short of that, Jenas slipped into an alleyway, beckoning Sam and Orla to follow him.

On one side of the alley, there was a boarded up Italian restaurant. Jenas stopped running, waiting for Sam and Orla to catch up with him. 'I used to be a cop around here,' he said. 'This place will be safe enough for a few hours.'

He removed one of the boards, and opened the broken window behind it. Pushing the window ajar, Jenas helped Orla inside. Sam followed her. It was dark inside, the only illumination coming from the morning sunlight streaming through the broken window. The window had led into the kitchen. It was clean, but it was clearly several years since it had last been used. The work surfaces were all bare, and, inside the pizza oven, there was a pile of half-burnt charcoal.

Jenas led the way through to the main restaurant. All the windows were boarded up, leaving the room shrouded in a pale, half-light. There were a dozen tables grouped near the centre of the restaurant, each one covered in a thin film of dust. A couple still had candles stuck into wine bottles in baskets on them, the wax peeling off at the edges. Jenas pulled a lighter from his pocket, and lit one of the candles. The flame flickered upwards, illuminating his serious expression.

'This place shut about five years ago,' said Jenas. 'The local mafia use it sometimes if they need to hide someone for a couple of days, and that means nobody comes near the place. Not unless they want to start a war with the Italians anyway.'

Sam pulled out a chair and sat down.

What they'd discovered was so explosive you couldn't expect it to be revealed without a struggle.

But he hadn't expected a hit this quickly.

'Who the hell was that?' he asked.

He glanced at both Jenas and Orla.

But no one knew the answer.

'I reckon it was the CIA,' said Jenas.

'Or Shabaan,' said Sam.

'Maybe they are working together,' said Orla.

He looked at her. Sam hadn't considered that possibility yet.

*But maybe she was right.*

'What we know for certain is we're about to drop the CIA into one of the greatest scandals it has ever been involved in,' said Jenas.

'The CIA could have found out very easily from the

Lufthansa flight records that we were landing at JFK this morning,' said Sam.

'And Chandler might have told them he'd revealed his conversation with us . . .'

'We should have stopped him,' said Orla.

'We couldn't, we don't have any powers to detain an American citizen living in Germany,' said Jenas.

Sam could see the flash of anger crossing Orla's face. 'So the CIA know that we are in America. And they are trying to kill us . . .'

'We need to get this story out in the open,' said Sam.

'Meaning . . .?' asked Orla.

'If we can get a press conference organised for this afternoon, and get this whole conspiracy blown wide open, then we have a chance. The CIA are trying to kill us because they are desperate to cover up their role in the downing of Flight 103. But once it's public, we're untouchable.'

'You're right,' said Orla. 'If anything happens to us, they'll be in even deeper trouble. Everyone will assume it was them.'

'You stay here,' said Jenas. 'You be safe. I'll return soon with the chairman.'

# FIFTY-SIX

**New York, 2 December**

Jim Geldens was a tall man, with greying skin, tanned hair, and dark green eyes that focussed hard on anyone he was talking to.

He climbed cautiously into the room, through the same broken window that Orla and Sam had climbed through earlier in the day. Jenas followed closely behind him, his expression serious and concerned. Geldens walked through the kitchens, and out into the main body of the restaurant, flicking some dust off the shoulders of his pinstriped suit as he did so.

Sam had heard of Jim Geldens.

A veteran fighter pilot, who'd fought with distinction in the Korean War, he'd become a civil pilot, then switched to management, and had risen to the top of the airline five years ago.

Unlike most corporate executives, he probably wasn't afraid to pick a fight with his own government, judged Sam.

'Not the kind of place I'm used to holding meetings,' he said, glancing across at Sam.

'Lives are at stake,' snapped Sam.

'This is the only safe place we can talk,' said Orla. 'Step outside and we risk being killed . . . by your government.'

'So I hear,' said Geldens.

His expression was grim, determined.

'Jenas here says you have quite a story to tell, Mr Woolfman.'

Sam started at the beginning. He described how he'd followed the trail that led him from Lockerbie, to Tel Aviv, into Beirut itself and finally to Frankfurt. The clincher had been the testimony they had bullied out of Chandler.

'The CIA may not have put the bomb on the plane,' said Sam, 'but they knew it was there, and they had the opportunity to take it off. They didn't because they wanted to be absolutely certain that Prentiss, Valentin, and Hanold died on that plane.'

'We need to be completely certain that Chandler made that call the way he said he made it,' said Geldens. 'They are going to beat the hell out of us once this goes public.'

'We are,' said Jenas.

From his briefcase, he took out a portable Toshiba cassette player, putting it down on one of the tables.

He pressed play.

The voice was overlaid with a layer of static. But you could hear the words quite crisply.

'It's Dave here,' the voice was saying.

Sam recognised it at once. It was Chandler speaking.

'The bag is a lot heavier than usual . . .'

'We know,' replied a gruff voice. 'Let it go . . .'

Geldens nodded.

'So you see—' said Sam.

'I know,' interrupted Geldens. 'They blew the plane up . . .'

He took the dossier from the table.

'I'm going to present this at a press conference this afternoon,' he said. He looked up at Sam. 'Well done,' he said crisply.

'We'll arrange for the payment to be transferred to your account,' said Jenas.

'The United Dominions Bank,' said Orla.

Jenas smiled. 'Never heard of that one.'

'It's based in Nassau,' said Sam. 'Small bank. But I've grown to trust it over the years.'

'As you like,' said Jenas. 'You need some help getting out of here?'

'Does your airline fly to Mexico?' said Orla.

'Sure,' said Geldens. 'There's a three o'clock departure.'

'With connections down to Cancun?'

Geldens smiled. 'One of our most popular routes.'

'Can you get us a pair of seats?'

'It's done,' said Geldens. 'You might even get an upgrade.'

Sam put his arm around Orla's waist. They climbed out through the small window and down into the alleyway beyond. 'I think we've earned a rest,' she said.

# FIFTY-SEVEN

**New York, 2 December**

JFK was busy this afternoon, noted Sam.

In the days immediately after Flight 103 came down, airports around the world had emptied. But it was amazing how quickly people moved on.

He sipped on his coffee. He was sitting in the departure lounge. They'd already checked in, and the flight for Mexico City was due to depart in another hour.

Orla had walked across to the clothes shops, planning to get a swimsuit, a couple of new dresses, and some shoes. They were touching down in Mexico City later this afternoon, then flying on to Cancun. At the travel desk in the airport, he'd booked them a double room at a five-star hotel overlooking the seafront. They needed at least a few days to recuperate. Maybe a week. Maybe even more.

And after that?

They'd see.

Right in front of him, a TV screen was tuned to CNN.

'Breaking News' flashed up across the screen.

'Extraordinary developments today in the story of Flight 103,' said the newsreader. 'The chairman of the airline has alleged that the CIA knew of the bomb on board the airlines and did nothing to prevent it. According to Jim Geldens, the agency was determined to cover up an alleged drug-smuggling scandal in its Beirut bureau, and wanted the plane to come down to assassinate three of its agents who were returning to the United States to expose the agency.'

Sam glanced around the coffee shop.

People were standing around the television screen.

A few looked angry. Some were bewildered. 'How the hell could they do that?' said one man.

Good question, thought Sam to himself.

For a brief moment, Sam found himself thinking about the nearly 300 people who'd been standing around in the departure lounges in Frankfurt and London waiting to board Flight 103. None of them knew they would be dead in just a few hours.

'We're going over live to our reporter outside the CIA headquarters in Langley,' continued the newscaster. 'What's the latest you have for us, Kathleen?'

An attractive young blonde in a black suit was standing outside the agency's HQ. It was a grey, overcast day, and there were at least a dozen television reporters lined up in a row outside the building.

'The agency is making absolutely no comment on the allegations from the airline's chairman as of this hour,' said the reporter. Everyone in the coffee bar was following her words intently, noticed Sam. 'A spokesman for the agency says they will investigate the allegations fully in due course, but they can't say anything yet.'

'And what's the mood over there like, Kathleen?'

'Angry and confused,' said the reporter. 'Off the record, many people can't believe the agency would deliberately kill two hundred and seventy innocent people, most of them Americans. But if it is true, the finger of suspicion is being pointed at Bill Horton. He's the operation director of the agency, and the man who runs its Middle East desk.'

Sam could feel a man bumping into him.

About forty, wearing jeans and a leather jacket.

Already his coffee had spilled out over the floor.

There was a bulge inside the pocket of the man's jacket.

Sam felt sure he recognised the shape.

A gun.

He jabbed his left elbow hard up into the man's chin, smashing hard into the bone. While he was temporarily dizzy, Sam's right hand smashed into the back of his neck, clamping down on his neck. His left hand then grabbed the man's right arm, twisting it behind his neck, so that he was effectively disabled.

'Hey, what the fuck?' shouted the man.

Sam could see the bulge in the man's pocket. He felt inside.

It was a tin of cigars, and a lighter.

'Shit,' he muttered under his breath.

*But I can't be too careful. They'll be coming for us again.*

'I'm sorry,' he said, letting the man go.

'Christ, it was only a cup of coffee, you asshole,' snapped the man.

Around them, people were backing away nervously from the confrontation.

At his side, Sam could feel Orla leading him away. The man was still shaking his head, and a security guard was walking briskly towards the coffee shop to see what the commotion was all about.

Sam stared up at the screen. They were now showing live footage of Geldens delivering his accusations at the press conference. 'We've finished with all that,' said Orla, steering Sam towards their gate. 'Our flight is about to leave.'

'You're right,' said Sam.

'But one thing is still troubling me.'

Sam looked up at the departures list.

Their flight was now boarding.

'What document did the Vatican have stored away that Father Trapini was so worried about?'

'I was bluffing.'

'I know,' said Orla thoughtfully. 'But there's a secret there . . . I feel certain of it.'

They had been flying for two hours now, halfway into the five and a half hour journey, and Sam was starting to feel drowsy. Only half of the A300's seats were filled today, and there was plenty of space to move around. They had taken two seats close to the wing, right up by the window, and there was no one sitting next to them.

Orla was looking out of the window. The plane was over Florida, cruising through the clear blue sky, before tacking slightly to the west, and completing its journey over the crystal waters of the Gulf towards Mexico City. The air was crisp and clean, with no sign of clouds, and no hint of turbulence. You could see for miles in every direction.

'It's almost Christmas,' said Orla suddenly.

Sam took a moment to admire her. For the two hours they had been in the air now, she had seemed, for the first time since he'd met her, to start to relax. She wasn't proving herself all the time. She wasn't trying to show how much she knew, how quick she was, or how tough she could be. She was just being herself. Quite possibly, for the first time in her life.

'I don't think I've ever spent Christmas with a family,' she said. 'One day, I'd like to do that.'

'What about . . . before your parents died.'

Orla shrugged. 'I was small,' she said. 'I don't remember anything. I guess maybe I blanked it out.'

'You will one day.'

'What about you?' she said. 'Will you be going back to...'

She paused, glancing away from him, looking towards the window.

'Your wife and children.'

She had never mentioned them before, noticed Sam. And even now, she did so reluctantly. They'd been thrown together by the investigation, and they'd pulled through. But maybe that was all that was between them, an investigation. Maybe it was like one of the office romances: get outside of the workplace, and it all fell apart. In truth, neither of us yet know, reflected Sam. We're about to find out.

'I'll need to see the kids,' said Sam. 'As for Elena? I'm not sure she wants to see me right now.'

'She must be crazy.'

Sam shook his head. 'It's wasn't easy for her,' he said. 'She thought she was marrying Sam Woolfman, but it turned out she was shacked up with the Mossad. And frankly, that's a difficult organisation to love.'

'I'm sure I could manage it,' she said.

She rested her head on his shoulder and closed her eyes. Sam could hear the steady throb of the plane's two General Electric CF6-80 engines, and feel the warmth of Orla's breath on his neck. He kissed her gently on the forehead, and pushed her next to the window, making sure she was lying comfortably. He closed his own eyes, and tried to sleep. But it was impossible. I can't seem to relax on planes anymore, he decided. And it's not hard to figure out why that is.